"*Wasn't it obviou [...] I don't fit in.*"

"What's fitting in?"

"Being to the manor born, for one thing. Suffering from a two-fer complex doesn't cut it in your crowd."

"What the hell's a two-fer complex?"

"Reading menus from right to left. Always looking for bargains. Trying to stretch your pocketbook by getting two things for the price of one."

To Courtney's surprise, Jeff threw back his head and laughed. "Oh, Court, the wealthy aren't immune to that malady. When it comes right down to it, everybody loves a bargain. The trick is to know when you've found a genuine one."

"That leaves me out. I can't tell real diamonds from paste, sable from fake fur—"

"That stuff's boring, not to mention insignificant. Whether we do or don't wear designer suits is superficial. The only thing that matters is how well we suit each other. And have no doubt about it, Ms. Hughes, you suit me just fine. To be specific . . . you fit me like a glove."

A fiery blush stole over Courtney's face. . . .

Dear Reader,

Welcome to the Silhouette **Special Edition** experience! With your search for consistently satisfying reading in mind, every month the authors and editors of Silhouette **Special Edition** aim to offer you a stimulating blend of deep emotions and high romance.

The name Silhouette **Special Edition** and the distinctive arch on the cover represent a commitment—a commitment to bring you six sensitive, substantial novels each month. In the pages of a Silhouette **Special Edition**, compelling true-to-life characters face riveting emotional issues—and come out winners. All the authors in the series strive for depth, vividness and warmth in writing these stories of living and loving in today's world.

The result, we hope, is romance you can believe in. Deeply emotional, richly romantic, infinitely rewarding—that's the Silhouette **Special Edition** experience. Come share it with us—six times a month! With this month's distinguished roster of gifted contemporary writers—Bay Matthews, Karen Keast, Barbara Faith, Madelyn Dohrn, Dawn Flindt and Andrea Edwards—you won't want to miss a single volume.

Best wishes,

Leslie Kazanjian,
Senior Editor

MADELYN DOHRN
Two for the Price of One

Silhouette Special Edition

Published by Silhouette Books New York

America's Publisher of Contemporary Romance

For Joyce Thies and Janet Bieber,
a.k.a. Janet Joyce,
the best mentors any writer could ever hope to have.
Thanks for your friendship and support.
You brought new meaning to the expression
"two for the price of one."

SILHOUETTE BOOKS
300 East 42nd St., New York, N.Y. 10017

ISBN: 0-373-09616-X

First Silhouette Books printing August 1990

Printed in the U.S.A.

MADELYN DOHRN

lives in a small Ohio town with her professor husband and family. After years of teaching college English, she decided to try her hand at writing a romance and soon found herself captivated by the task. When she's not in front of her word processor, she likes to travel, read, entertain friends and keep fit with dance-aerobics.

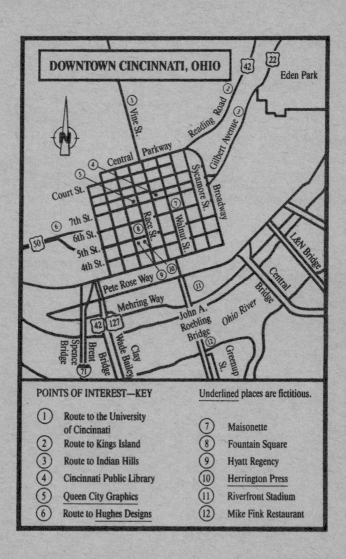

DOWNTOWN CINCINNATI, OHIO

Eden Park

Vine St.
Reading Road
Gilbert Avenue
Central Parkway
Court St.
Sycamore St.
Broadway
7th St.
6th St.
5th St.
4th St.
Race St.
Walnut St.
Pete Rose Way
Mehring Way
John A. Roebling Bridge
Ohio River
L&N Bridge
Central Bridge
Spence Bridge
Brent Bridge
Clay Wade Bailey Bridge
Greenup St.

POINTS OF INTEREST—KEY

Underlined places are fictitious.

1. Route to the University of Cincinnati
2. Route to Kings Island
3. Route to Indian Hills
4. Cincinnati Public Library
5. Queen City Graphics
6. Route to Hughes Designs
7. Maisonette
8. Fountain Square
9. Hyatt Regency
10. Herrington Press
11. Riverfront Stadium
12. Mike Fink Restaurant

Chapter One

"Blast!" Courtney Hughes slammed down her office phone and spared it a brief, menacing glare. Then she snatched up the newspaper lying beside her desk and hurriedly flipped through it. "Double blast!" she repeated after examining the staff box at the top of the editorial page.

"Must have been a dynamite call."

Courtney's head shot up. "Bill! Where did you come from?"

Her visitor uncrossed his arms and pushed away from the door frame where he'd propped his lanky form. "Same place you did—Queen City Graphics. That is, until you jumped ship a few months ago and sailed off on your own. How's it going? Problems?"

"Nothing major," she said with the flip of a hand. "Only a simple lawsuit."

"You're joking, of course."

"Afraid not."

"Leave it to you to make graphic art a hazardous profession." Bill walked into the room and sat down beside her. "I dropped by to see if you'd like to go to lunch, but I take it you've just lost your appetite."

Courtney darted him a wry smile. "You've got that right. But," she added, reaching over to pat his arm, "it doesn't mean I'm not glad to see you. If ever I needed a friend, it's now."

"And who better to fill the bill than ol' Bill himself?"

Courtney groaned. "My pal, the punster. But an accurate observation, nonetheless."

When she and Bill had met ten years ago at the University of Cincinnati, both had been struggling freshmen and financially strapped. Aside from a mutual interest in art, their desperate economic plight had drawn them together.

At first, Bill had wanted to be more than friends, but Courtney had gently discouraged his romantic advances. Because he didn't press her, they were able to remain good companions and cement a friendship that had lasted well beyond graduation.

Remembering, Courtney assured him, "You couldn't have picked a more opportune moment to stop by."

"Are you going to tell me what's wrong? Or do I have to sit here and watch you fume while I slowly starve to death?"

Courtney chuckled. "And I thought I was hiding my feelings so well!" She got to her feet and tugged him out of the chair. "Come on, let's get you a pastrami on rye. I haven't forgotten what it's like to listen to a growling stomach. Not a pleasant sound—whether the stomach's yours or mine."

The small corner deli was crowded with noisy patrons. At first glance, Courtney would have sworn that half the office force in Cincinnati had squeezed inside for lunch, but fortunately a number of patrons were waiting for carryout orders. Before long she and Bill were able to grab a small table.

Between sips of a large soft drink, which was all the lunch Courtney felt able to handle, she explained her problem. "It seems that I've stepped on the toes of Herrington Press."

Bill swallowed a huge bite of his sandwich, then whistled. "The giant of Cincinnati publishing! Good grief, Court, how did you manage to do that?"

"My logo offends them."

"Your interlocking *H* and *D* for Hughes Designs? That's been your special signature since college days. I don't understand."

"It seems it's not as unique as I thought. I was trying to check the Herrington trademark in the *Reporter* just before you materialized on my doorstep, but it's not in the staff box. They must only carry it on those expensive books they publish. But from the description their lawyer gave me, it's darn close to mine. I've been warned to 'cease and desist.'"

"Can't say I've ever seen it, either. What's it look like, anyway?"

"Let me show you." She fished a pencil from her bag and scribbled on a paper napkin. "This is theirs. And, as you know," she said, as she finished the last stroke, "this is mine. See? Their *P* and my *D* are similar."

Bill wrinkled his brow and considered the drawing. "Yeah, but not exact duplicates."

"Nonetheless, too close for comfort. Mr. J. E. Herrington's comfort in particular. He doesn't want anyone thinking my little business is a branch of his."

"I'd say it's his loss. You're damned good, Court. If I hadn't gotten used to three square meals a day, I'd have been tempted to go in with you. But I'm not as daring as you are."

"Keep complimenting me like that, and I'll forgive you for deciding to stay with Queen City Graphics."

He grinned. "When Hughes Designs is well established, and you can afford an assistant, I'll reconsider."

"Thanks a bunch."

Bill swiped a trace of mustard from his lips. "Why didn't you find out about this when you had your logo registered?"

"I have to confess I haven't gotten around to that little detail yet."

He looked surprised. "Why not?"

"Lots of reasons. Time, money. Anyhow, since trademarks don't *have* to be registered, I temporarily shelved it."

"I can relate to that. Meanwhile, what are you going to do about this lawsuit thing?"

"There won't be any legal action if I immediately withdraw my logo. But first I intend to check out theirs with my own two eyes. I'm not relying on that lawyer's description, though if he's as accurate as he sounded, I think they have me." Courtney sighed. "Trouble is, that symbol feels like a part of me. Hughes Designs has been my dream for as long as I can remember. What's more, I've had my sign painted and my stationery and business cards printed. All that stuff I'd put off ordering until I'd gotten a little ahead. Now every bit of it will have to be scrapped."

"What a waste!"

"To be honest, it's not a major loss. No doubt J. E. Herrington would consider it pocket change. But it's enough to hurt. Besides, trashing reams of stationery and a brand new sign may do permanent damage to my psyche. And just when things were finally looking up! It makes me so darn mad."

"Is it only the money that irks you? Or are you riled because Herrington Press is throwing its weight around?"

Courtney dipped her head slightly. "You know me pretty well, don't you? I guess it's a little of both." She wadded her paper napkin and tossed it on the table. "Frankly, I don't see why a small business like mine should bother an outfit like Herrington Press."

His eyes slanted toward Courtney's hastily sketched comparison. "Neither do I. But you know how big companies are. Their trademark is registered, so *they* have the legal foot to stand on."

"Which puts me in a no-win situation. If I don't comply and retract my logo, I'll be slapped with a lawsuit. If I do back down, I'll lose double what I've already spent since I'll have to replace everything I'm forced to dump." She swirled the ice in her drink and scowled. "Maybe I shouldn't have taken out that half-page ad in the *Cincinnati Daily*."

"You took out a half-page ad in the *Reporter*'s biggest rival?"

"It wasn't meant as a slight. Their rates are cheaper."

"Damn, Court! No wonder you caught Herrington's attention. I'm sure he keeps careful tabs on the competition."

She raked a hand through her golden blond hair. "The more I think about it, the madder I get. I'd like to give Mr. High-and-Mighty Herrington a piece of my mind."

Bill's mouth lifted in an off-center grin. "Something tells me you're going to. I already pity the man."

"Hey, whose side are you on?"

"Years of faithful friendship, and still she asks." He slapped a flattened palm over his heart. "I'm wounded."

Courtney laughed. "You're wonderful, Bill, even if you do make outrageous puns and tend to get melo-dramatic. I appreciate your letting me rant and rave. And spoil your lunch. I hope I haven't ruined your digestion, too."

"Not a chance."

Courtney's expression sobered. "Thanks for always being there for me. Have I told you lately how much I appreciate your friendship? You're the closest thing to family—" She broke off, realizing that she was embar-rassing him by her uncharacteristic show of sentiment.

"No need to get all mushy over a little moral sup-port. You'll notice I didn't offer to punch Herrington out for you."

"But you would if I asked."

"Yeah, I guess I would at that." His eyes softened. "You . . . you . . . mean a lot to me, Court."

"Now who's getting mushy? And over a workaholic who loses her temper at the drop of a hat and shies away from anything domestic. How could you?"

"I guess there's no accounting for taste," he said with forced lightness. "But back to Herrington. Maybe it's not such a bad idea to meet with him. Who knows? He may turn out to be the sympathetic sort and give you a break." Bill blew out a gusty sigh. "On the other hand, I wouldn't count on it. Just be careful, Court. You could get hurt."

"Who me?"

"Guys like Herrington eat small fry like you and me alive."

"Let him try!" she huffed.

"I don't like the sound of that. Seriously, Court, promise me you'll make a real effort to keep your cool."

"Scout's honor. I'll behave like a proper lady. But I can't let this thing go without confronting Herrington in person. What kind of man would sic his lawyers on me the way he did? Without so much as a courtesy call?"

"A smart one." Bill picked up the tab and pushed back his chair. "Obviously, your reputation has preceded you," he quipped.

Courtney's chin soared in mock offense. "Just for that nasty crack, you can spring for my cola."

"Honesty is so costly."

Grinning, Courtney pulled several packets of sugar from a glass container on their table and tucked them in her skirt pocket.

Bill's eyebrows rose. "Up to your old tricks?"

"You know my motto. Never leave a restaurant empty-handed. I don't take anything I'm not entitled to. You ordered coffee and didn't use any sugar, so I'm simply helping myself to yours."

"That's what I love about you, Court. You're so ethical."

"Hey, it's not like I'm pilfering the flatware."

"Still, isn't it time you broke that little habit? You're no longer half-starving."

"True, but if J. E. Herrington has his way, I may be standing in a soup line again."

Herrington Press occupied an imposing old building in Cincinnati's downtown district. The vintage 1920's structure housed the daily newspaper, founded by the great-grandfather of its current head, Jefferson E. Herrington, III, as well as a smaller book publishing business, which the family operated more as a cultural contribution than as a profitable venture. Specializing in limited editions, this wing of the firm was dedicated to producing leather-bound classics, printed on high-quality paper and illustrated with the finest engravings. Recently, they'd commemorated the city's bicentennial with a moderately priced illustrated history. Courtney had purchased a copy for herself, as much for the artwork as for the commentary. It was that book that had confirmed the remarkable similarity between her logo and the Herrington trademark.

Now she stood squinting toward the top of the stately building, wondering which windows fronted Herrington's private office. Probably the ones that provided an unimpeded view of Cincinnati's time-honored landmark—Fountain Square. She looked down the narrow city street, a concrete canyon flanked by skyscrapers, to where the Tyler Davidson Fountain sparkled in the spring sunshine. When she'd worked for Queen City Graphics, she'd often carried her lunch to the plaza and enjoyed a summer picnic at the base of the fountain. Today's warm April sunshine and the water cascading from the Bavarian-made statuary reminded Courtney of how much she missed those pleasant breaks from the daily grind.

A quick check of her watch confirmed that she was a tad early for her appointment. Good, she thought. She didn't want to get off on the wrong foot by arriving even a few seconds late. Squaring her shoulders, she approached the ornate wooden doors that guarded Herrington Press. As she reached for the brass knob, wind whipped at her short hair, lifting and tossing it into a disordered mass around her face. She was glad she had time to stop off in the ladies' room to give her appearance a final check. She was going to need all the confidence she could muster for this meeting.

Courtney ran a hand over the top of her head. At least this new layered cut lent her a more mature, professional look than the shoulder-length pageboy she'd favored throughout her teens and early twenties. Nor did the style rob her of femininity. In fact, wispy bangs added a softness that was lacking when her hair was longer and she hadn't bothered to do more than bend under the blond ends.

In the rest room Courtney pulled a brush through her haphazard waves, tucked in her blouse and smoothed the skirt of her mint-green suit. Though the fabric wasn't expensive, she liked the fit. She hoped it made her appear chic.

Even if it didn't, she couldn't complain. She'd shopped for, selected and purchased it with her own money. She still couldn't believe that she finally owned a wardrobe that wasn't put together with hand-me-downs or Salvation Army rejects. Lord knows, she'd had her fill of wearing other people's clothes.

Not that she was above borrowing when necessary. Her silk scarf was on loan from Mary Mitchell, who occupied the apartment above hers. Courtney felt it did wonders to dress up the outfit, making it look, at least to her eyes, far more costly than it was.

Once more she glanced at her watch and nearly panicked when she saw the time. Had she dallied that long? Or was she subconsciously attempting to postpone what was bound to be an unpleasant confrontation? No matter, it wouldn't do to keep the president of Herrington Press waiting.

Courtney hurried toward an elevator and pressed the button for the fourteenth floor. A minute later she was standing in a reception room that fairly shouted old money. She took in the walnut paneling, leather upholstery and original oils. Already she felt out of her element, but she didn't dare betray her nervousness. In a calm voice, she announced herself to a stylish blonde whose nameplate identified her as Gladys Feldkamp.

"I'm afraid Mr. Herrington's in an editorial meeting. It's just getting under way, so you may have a long wait."

Courtney's spine stiffened as tension gave way to anger. Who did the man think he was? "But I have an appointment," she protested.

"I know, and Mr. Herrington said to tell you he's sorry for the delay. Something came up that demanded his immediate attention. I tried to reach you, but no one answered at your office."

"That's because I'd already left. To get downtown takes me a good forty-five or fifty minutes—what with the traffic and finding a place to park."

Ms. Feldkamp's smile was diplomatic. "I'm sure it does. Could I bring you some coffee or a magazine?"

With an effort, Courtney held onto her temper. "That's kind of you, but I won't be able to wait. I have a client to see later this afternoon. Since I don't have an assistant," she added meaningfully, "I had to close my agency to come into town, and I need to get back as soon as possible."

"I understand. Would you like to schedule another appointment?"

And go through all this grooming—not to mention the sweaty palms—again? Courtney agonized silently. *Thanks, but no thanks!*

"It's difficult for me to leave my business," she said aloud. Though Courtney realized that the receptionist was not to blame for her boss's rudeness, she balked at the idea of setting up another meeting. She was primed for this one. Despite the brave front she'd put up for Bill, it had taken all her nerve to come here.

Maybe, she considered, as she stood tapping her foot, Herrington had a valid reason for putting her off. Then again, maybe he didn't. Maybe his "emergency" was only an excuse to get rid of her. Maybe he hoped she would tire of hanging around and decide to leave. Maybe he was subtly but deliberately canceling on her.

Her foot beat a faster tattoo against the marble floor. She bet he wasn't in a meeting at all!

It wouldn't surprise her. She'd been shunted aside before by bigger and more powerful people. People who were forever telling her what to do, where to go.

Growing up in a string of foster homes, Courtney had become used to being shoved around—physically as well as emotionally. When she was a child, she'd been forced to hold all the resentment and anger inside. But as soon as she was on her own, she'd felt free to release the tight rein she'd long kept on her temper. Sometimes it erupted with the force of Mount Saint Helens. She could feel another such explosion coming on.

Bill's advice to keep her cool flitted through her mind, but Courtney paid it no heed. The more she thought about Herrington's arrogant dismissal, the angrier she got. She could feel her blood pressure rising by the minute.

Courtney wasn't about to reschedule any more than she was going to sit around twiddling her thumbs until J. E. Herrington decided to spare her a minute. As far as she was concerned, their showdown would take place now or never!

Realizing Ms. Feldkamp was looking at her expectantly, Courtney returned her polite smile. "Could you tell me where Mr. Herrington's meeting is taking place?"

The woman indicated the office on her left. "In there. You'll be able to see him the minute it's over."

"Thank you. You've been most helpful." Pivoting on a heel, Courtney made a beeline for the door.

Gladys Feldkamp jumped out of her seat. "But you can't go in now."

"Can't I?" She twisted the knob. "Watch me."

Courtney shouldered through the door with Ms. Feldkamp right on her heels. "Mr. Herrington, I'm sorry," the receptionist said, stepping around Courtney to apologize. "She refused to wait."

A tall man rose from his place at the head of a polished mahogany table. "It's all right, Gladys. Ms. Hughes, I presume."

"Correct," Courtney answered tersely. "And I presume you are Mr. J. E. Herrington?" Good grief, was *this* prime masculine specimen the president of Herrington Press? She'd envisioned an aesthetic-looking, prematurely balding man, not a gorgeous hunk who looked like a candidate for the latest Chippendales' calendar!

"Yes, I'm Herrington. Under the circumstances, however, it would be a mockery to say I'm pleased to meet you."

She lifted her chin at what she hoped was a defiant angle. "No need to stand on formalities, Mr. Herrington. I believe we had an appointment. To discuss a matter of concern to us both."

Noting the raised brows and amused expressions of the men and women around the long table, Courtney wished the floor would open up and swallow her. She hoped her reddened cheeks would be mistaken for anger. Come what may, she had to stand her ground. Having boldly taken the offensive, she refused to give J. E. Herrington the satisfaction of watching her retreat.

Herrington cleared his throat, then hastened to introduce Courtney. Well acquainted with office gossip, he wanted to squelch any rumors that might arise from her storming the boardroom. "Ladies and gentlemen—" his gaze swept the table before returning to Courtney "—may I present Ms. Courtney Hughes of Hughes Designs. Ms. Hughes, my editorial staff. In case you haven't heard," he told the interested group around the table, "Hughes Designs is using a logo that could easily be confused with ours. Though our lawyers notified her to withdraw it, Ms. Hughes insisted upon discussing the matter. Unfortunately, this meeting took precedence."

He was a model of control, which for some reason set Courtney on edge. Either Jefferson Herrington was a bona fide stuffed shirt, or he was a match waiting to be struck. When he addressed her again, she had to make a conscious effort to keep from balling her fists.

"Didn't Ms. Feldkamp call and explain that I couldn't see you until later?"

"She tried, but she missed me. By that time I was on my way here."

"Then, would you mind waiting? We shouldn't be more than an hour. Meanwhile, Ms. Feldkamp can make you comfortable with some refreshments and magazines."

"She already offered. But I can't wait."

"Then perhaps you'd like to leave and come back another day."

Since the suggestion was more a command than a request, Courtney pulled herself erect. "That wouldn't be convenient, either. You're not the only one pressed for time, Mr. Herrington. I had to close my agency to keep this appointment, so it's not only work time I'm losing. You could be costing me clients as well."

He shifted his weight and clamped a hand on his waist, the unconscious gesture parting his suit coat and pulling his shirt tight across his chest. "I see. I wasn't aware you ran a one-person operation. Or that your services were in such demand." His voice was even, but a muscle twitched in his jaw. He strode around the table and, taking Courtney's elbow, nodded to his editors. "Please carry on while we discuss this in private."

Herding her inside his office, Jeff motioned to a plush chair. As soon as she was seated, he propped a hip on the side of his desk and fixed her with deep-set hazel eyes. "I'm not in the habit of being interrupted in the middle of a business meeting."

"And I'm not in the habit of being addressed in that tone."

"Lady, this is my office, and I'll address you any way I like. You're the one who's been extraordinarily rude, but I'm willing to overlook that for now." Ignoring her unladylike grunt, he went on. "Frankly, I don't see that we have anything to discuss. Didn't our lawyers advise you that we have prior claim to the logo you're using?"

"Mr. Eldridge wasn't that considerate. What he said was that I'd be *sued* if I didn't immediately withdraw it."

Taken aback, Jeff straightened. "He threatened you with a lawsuit?"

"In a word, yes."

Jeff mouthed a short, pungent word and slumped onto a chair. "I'm sorry if Stewart got a little high-handed. He has a way of antagonizing people. Courtroom tactics, I guess. Believe me, he comes off gruffer than he intends."

"You can't imagine how reassuring that is," she said sarcastically. "Especially when I got the distinct impression that if I didn't run right out and rip down my sign or hold a public burning of my business cards, he'd pay me a visit and personally break both my arms."

To her surprise, Jefferson E. Herrington, III, threw back his head and laughed uproariously. "If you ask me, he's the one who might have ended up with broken bones."

Despite herself, Courtney grinned. For the first time since she'd crossed the threshold of Herrington Press, she let herself relax. Not much, but enough to joke, "He might have at that. Look, all I want is to reach some sort of compromise. I'm kind of attached to my logo. And I have—for me anyhow—lots of money invested in it." Absently she fingered the locket at her throat. "It seems a shame to pitch reams of quality letterheads and business cards, plus pay for a new sign. Couldn't I keep my logo—at least on a trial basis? I promise not to misrepresent my agency as a part of Herrington Press. I'll even run a disclaimer in all my ads. Granted, my design is close to yours, but it wasn't intentional. Nor is it an exact duplicate."

Jeff leaned forward and braced his arms on his thighs. "If it were up to me, maybe we could work something out. But my father has a voice in this—a rather strong voice, I might add—and he's quite protective of the company name. He doesn't want anyone linking Hughes Designs with Herrington Press." At Courtney's injured expression, Jeff held up a palm. "Now don't get your dander up again. We're not passing judgment on your work. We're merely trying to protect our reputation. If you were in a different city, it wouldn't matter so much. But Herrington Press is practically a Cincinnati tradition. And you have to admit that our publishing house has a legal right to its trademark."

"I'm not disputing that. I'd only hoped to buy some time...and keep my budget from developing a giant hole."

"I appreciate your position, Ms. Hughes, but consider this—isn't it smarter, especially since you're just starting out, to get established with a logo no one is going to challenge? You want people to identify your work by it. Changing horses in midstream will only defeat your purpose."

Why she found herself backing down, Courtney didn't know. But there was something about J. E. Herrington, III, that made her trust him. Though she'd come to their meeting certain that he was going to play Goliath to her David, she'd been dead wrong. In fact, he'd been far kinder than she probably deserved.

Courtney sighed. All along she knew she'd been grasping at straws, but it wasn't in her nature to capitulate without a fight. Well, she'd given it her best shot. Maybe it was time to throw in the towel. "You're right, of course, but compared to Herrington Press, my business is so insignificant. I guess I was hoping I wouldn't have to change my logo."

"Sorry to disappoint you, but I'm sure you can appreciate our objections." He rose, signaling that the interview was over. "I really do have to get back to my meeting."

"I was just going."

Her words were light, but the slight droop of her shoulders gave her away. Without thinking, he suggested, "Tell you what. Why don't you drop off a portfolio of your work. Maybe if Dad sees some of your designs, he'll agree to meet you halfway." Jeff knew he was putting off the inevitable. Once his father set a course, he rarely retreated. But for some reason Jeff wanted to let her down easy. "I'll speak to him, but I can't make any promises."

Courtney brightened. "Fair enough."

He started toward the door. "I'll let you know the final outcome."

"In other words, don't call us—we'll call you." Jeff flashed her a warm smile, and Courtney's heart gave a strange little kick.

"Very perceptive, Ms. Hughes."

"I wasn't being critical. You've been most considerate. Are you always this nice to people who barge in on you uninvited?"

"Good public relations."

"Gee, and I could have sworn it was my winning personality."

Laughing, he opened the door. "No comment."

She blushed, and Jeff found the color in her cheeks enormously appealing. When was the last time he'd seen a woman blush?

"For what it's worth, I apologize for disrupting your meeting. I...that is, I—I didn't believe you really were...I thought you were giving me the runaround. I was a bit startled to see all those people in there."

"No harm done."

"Thanks for saying so." She hesitated. "One more question. Is it okay if I continue to use my logo? Until you get the final word from your father."

"Why not? Meanwhile, I'll make sure Stewart doesn't fling you in jail. But try to keep a low profile."

"You've got a deal."

He took her hand in his and was struck by its delicacy. "Not yet, but we'll work on it."

After Courtney's departure, Jeff wasn't in any hurry to return to the boardroom. He closed his office door and slumped down on the chair she'd vacated. It still held her body warmth, an observation he found curiously unsettling.

He dropped his head back. Courtney Hughes intrigued him. Why, he wasn't sure. She was poles apart from the sophisticated women he usually found attractive. Yet something about her tugged at him. And it wasn't just sensual, though she was easy enough on the eyes. He had to admire her for not being a pushover. It had required courage as well as a brazen disregard for manners to burst in on him the way she had.

But for all her brashness, his heart went out to her. Though she'd been dressed in the latest fashion, she was obviously pinched for money. How Amelia's tongue would have wagged over her off-the-rack clothes! What was it his would-be fiancée had once sniffed? That polyester had never touched her skin? Courtney Hughes's blouse hadn't had a natural fiber in it. The same could be said for her suit. It fit her trim figure to perfection and accented her intelligent green eyes, but it had come straight out of a discount store. No wonder she was concerned about losing money on that logo. She must be struggling to keep her fledgling business alive.

Well, he would see what he could do with his father, but the man was a hard nut to crack. Herrington Press was his life. Sometimes Jeff felt his father would rather lose his son than his business. For the most part, he'd been an absentee parent, devoting every ounce of energy to the *Reporter*, Cincinnati's top-circulating newspaper. Though the book publishing was almost a sideline, J. E. the Second also took fierce pride in the quality of the volumes it printed.

But Jeff bore him no ill will. Perhaps his values were misplaced, but his father meant well. He'd wanted to keep the business solid for his only son. As soon as Jeff had graduated from Harvard, he'd been groomed to take over the company.

A little over a year ago, the elder Herrington, satisfied that Jeff was ready to carry on the family tradition, had relinquished the presidency to become chairman of the board. Though he retained a controlling interest in Herrington Press and spent a few hours each morning in his office, he was virtually retired. All that remained to make his life complete was for his son to marry Amelia and give him an heir. Better yet, several heirs.

Frowning, Jeff pushed to his feet. Whenever he thought about Amelia Meyer, he felt a vague sense of unease. For too long now he'd delayed breaking completely with her, probably because he knew it would be awkward. For both of them and their families.

Of late, though, she'd been making more and more domestic noises. His fault, he supposed, for straddling the fence so long. They'd never become too intimate. Not for her lack of trying. But ever since he'd lost Vicky, Jeff hadn't known *what* he wanted, and so he'd tried not to encourage Amelia too much.

Though at times he rationalized that she would make the perfect corporate wife, the ideal socialite mother, the spark simply wasn't there. The truth was, Amelia bored him. He hadn't realized exactly how much until he'd run into Courtney Hughes.

He knew she wasn't his type, that in her own way she wouldn't suit him any better than Amelia did, but Jeff suspected he'd never once be tempted to describe Courtney as boring. Brash, certainly. Audacious, definitely, and more than a little saucy. But not boring.

Before rejoining the others, he stopped by Gladys's desk. "Courtney Hughes will be dropping off some material for me in a day or so. Would you see that I get it right away?"

"Yes, sir. And again, I'm sorry for letting her slip past me, but she had the door open before I could get out of my chair."

Jeff grinned. "She does seem to have a tendency to come on like gangbusters, doesn't she?"

As he entered the boardroom, he realized that he hadn't felt quite so exhilarated in years.

Chapter Two

Courtney rang the bell to Mary Mitchell's apartment and wondered if her friend could hear it over the childish voices whining on the opposite side of the door.

"Mine," Julie squealed.

"No, mine," Jenny countered.

Little feet stamped, and the wailing rose in volume.

Courtney smiled to herself, picturing the tug-of-war going on inside. She had no trouble distinguishing Julie's voice from Jenny's, just as she had no difficulty knowing which name belonged to which identical twin. She was also familiar with how their squabble would be resolved. Any moment now their mother would intervene, and the three-year-olds would dissolve into tears. The two would wind up consoling each other, then go off to play together peacefully. Until the next crisis.

Courtney would never forget that day a little over a year ago when the threesome had moved into the apartment right above hers. One corner of her mouth turned up in a wry grin. Their presence had been somewhat difficult to miss, so she'd baked a dozen muffins, climbed the stairs and welcomed her new neighbors. As it turned out, she was the only tenant who had.

And so her friendship with the recently divorced Mary and her energetic daughters had begun. Sometimes she would accompany them to the grocery store or the park or the zoo. Mary was always grateful for the adult company and the extra pair of hands. At other times, Courtney volunteered to baby-sit. Not simply as a favor to Mary but because she liked to. She adored the "Mitchell moppets," as she was fond of calling them, and before long considered their mother her best friend. Their willingness to "adopt" Courtney into their close-knit family had given her a rare chance to live the childhood she'd been denied.

"That does it!" came the commanding sound of Mary's voice breaking into the din. "As of right now, this book belongs to neither of you. Until you settle down and behave yourselves, it goes on *my* shelf."

Cries of protest accompanied the announcement, and Courtney jabbed the bell again. She kept her finger pressed on the buzzer until she heard Mary's steps hurrying toward the hall.

"Lord, am I glad to see you!" her friend exclaimed when she'd flung open the door.

"That's a better welcome than I got at Herrington Press."

Mary motioned her inside. "I can't say I'm surprised."

"Aunt Court! Aunt Court!" Instantly the twins ceased their whimpering to scamper across the floor.

Like miniature cannonballs, they hurled themselves straight into Courtney's stomach.

She gave a mock grunt at the impact, then stooped down to wrap an arm about each tiny body. "You two sound happier than you did a little while ago."

"You heard?" Mary moaned. "I'm sorry, Court. I hope you weren't trying to work. They've been full of it all day. I expect an eviction notice from Mr. Schnidhorst any second."

Courtney hiked a shoulder. "I don't think their scrapping carried as far down as the first floor. Anyway, they weren't bothering me in the least." She gave Julie and Jenny kisses on top of their curly black heads. "Where's the harm in a healthy disagreement between siblings?"

"Easy for you to say. You're not their mother."

"What did you bring us?" Julie asked, breaking away from Courtney's embrace and tugging on the strap of her bag.

"Show us," Jenny begged. She, too, pulled away and began jumping up and down. Julie followed suit, adding unsynchronized hand clapping to the commotion.

"Girls," Mary admonished, "mind your manners. Courtney can't bring you something every time she visits us."

"Yes, she can," Julie countered.

Jenny's lower lip came out in an offended pout. "She always does."

Smiling, Courtney began to rummage through her purse. The girls were satisfied with so little. A mint. A nearly exhausted tube of hand lotion. A piece of junk mail. Courtney always found something of little or no value to delight them. It had become a game that she enjoyed as much as the twins did.

Making a serious production of investigating the contents of her bag, Courtney said, "Let's see what I can find. Maybe...aha! What have we here?" Like a magician, she slowly pulled out Mary's scarf, then viewed it with faked dismay. "Oops, this isn't your size. I do believe it belongs to your mommy. With my thanks for the loan." She smiled at Mary, laid the square of silk on the coffee table, then eyed the impatient three-year-olds. "Shall I give my bag another try?"

"Yes, yes," they cried in unison.

Courtney once more pretended to be performing a magic trick. Her green eyes widened dramatically as she produced two narrow, satin ribbons. Dangling each from an index finger, she asked, "Now who wants to wear the red first and who the blue?"

Chubby hands reached out to claim their prizes, and Courtney tied the bright bows in place. Finished, she stood up and surveyed the girls. "My, but you look pretty. Why don't you run into your room and take a peek in the mirror."

Mary sank onto the couch. "That'll keep them occupied for all of two minutes. Then Jenny'll want the blue and Julie won't agree to switch."

Courtney snapped her fingers. "I knew I should have bought them both the same color."

"Nonsense. If they get duplicates of everything, how are they going to learn to share? With a little patience, I figure they'll get the hang of it by their twentieth birthdays. Meanwhile—" she patted the place beside her "—sit down and talk fast. What happened at Herrington Press?"

"Nothing much. Unless you consider making a fool of myself news."

"Tell me about it," Mary said.

Courtney launched into a description of her afternoon meeting. "In the end," she concluded, "I found myself almost conceding defeat. Jefferson Herrington's a real charmer. He's not an easy man to hate."

"Apparently. How can you hate a man with thick dark hair, broad shoulders, hazel eyes, sensuous lips?"

"I don't remember mentioning the word *sensuous*. All I said was he had kind of full lips."

"In my book, *full* translates to *sensuous*. He sounds like a dream. Didn't you wonder what he'd be like to kiss? Didn't you long for a teeny-weeny nibble?"

"Certainly not! I was too nervous, then too mad to think about necking with the man."

"Well, if *you're* not interested, introduce me."

Courtney sniffed. "Stop panting, Mary. I could swear he had an unavailable sign hung around his neck. He didn't come on strong, or try to impress me with his position, or anything like that. Except for one angry sentence, he handled himself with calm and patience. He was . . . nice. I couldn't help liking him."

"Sounds promising. What did Bill have to say?"

Courtney's expression was droll. "He wasn't interested in a physical description."

"No, silly, I mean about the outcome of your meeting."

"Bill was Bill. He clucked like a mother hen over my temper, claimed I was lucky to emerge from the confrontation with no visible scars, warned me not to get my hopes up and reminded me his shoulder was always available if I needed it. He really is a sweetheart."

"Uh-oh," Mary said, nearly bolting from her seat.

"What's the matter?"

"Haven't you noticed? It's too quiet in there."

Both women sprang up and raced toward the back of the apartment where they found Julie and Jenny in front of Mary's low vanity. Lipstick was smeared over their faces, some of it in the vicinity of their mouths, nail polish was dribbled across the glass top of the table, and the air positively reeked of their mother's most expensive perfume.

Mary's fists flew to her hips. "How many times do I have to tell you two my makeup is off limits?"

"Pretty, Aunt Court?" Julie asked, revealing fingers smeared with red lacquer.

"Dandy, love." Looking at Mary, she apologized, "Sorry. My innocent compliment seems to have opened Pandora's Box."

"More like my cosmetic kit. Don't blame yourself. I should have suspected the worst when my horoscope read, 'You have a surprise in store today.'"

Courtney captured four little hands in her two and towed the girls toward the adjoining bathroom. "Come along, you glamour pusses, and let me clean you up while your mommy deals with this mess. Then we're going down to my apartment for a pizza supper."

"Mommy, too?" Jenny wanted to know.

"I think she may decide to pass this time. We'll just make it a trio, okay?"

"What's a trio?" Julie asked.

"The same as three," Courtney supplied. "You, Jenny and me. One, two, three."

Jenny looked puzzled. "I'm three already."

Courtney freed a hand to wipe a smudge of lipstick from one small nose. "I'm talking about three people, not three years, love. If Mommy didn't have to stay here to... work, she'd make four."

"Bless you, Court. Has anyone ever told you you're an angel?"

"Not in my memory. But feel free to flatter me as much as you like."

Mary began to pick up overturned bottles and recap tubes. "You're a natural mother, you know that?"

Courtney shrugged. "Thanks, but that's one tag I'm never going to claim."

Before Mary could pursue the cryptic remark, Courtney hustled Julie and Jenny through the bath-room door and turned on the tub faucets.

Courtney got to the phone on the third ring. "Hughes Designs," she trilled.

"Jeff Herrington here."

Courtney almost dropped the receiver. She'd expected to hear from Ms. Feldkamp about her portfolio, but instead the president of Herrington Press himself was on the other end of the line.

"I was wondering if we could meet," he said. "Per-haps over dinner."

"Dinner?" Courtney repeated, astonished at how glad she was to hear his mellow baritone.

"You do eat, don't you?"

"Of course, I—"

"We'll combine business with pleasure. That way you can't accuse me of wasting your time or losing you cus-tomers."

Laced with humor, the gibe amused rather than of-fended her. "How thoughtful. When?"

"Are you free Saturday night?" At her affirmative reply, he suggested, "I'll pick you up about eight. By the way, your portfolio was impressive."

"But—"

He chuckled. "The news isn't all bad. We'll discuss it Saturday."

"In the meantime, I may die of curiosity."

"I don't think so. That's an affliction that mainly strikes cats."

Her mouth twitched with amusement. "I can be quite feline when I choose."

"No kidding? You're forgetting that I've seen your impersonation of a lioness."

"I guess I don't come across very kittenish, do I? Aren't you afraid I might embarrass you again?"

"As I recall, I wasn't the one with a red face. Besides, I'm willing to take my chances. What's your address?"

Courtney gave him a street and number on the west side of town.

"Until Saturday, Ms. Hughes."

Even before she'd put down the receiver, she heard a dismissive click. "Goodbye to you, too," she said, cradling the phone.

Courtney didn't need to be told that she'd lost their logo war—she'd expected as much—but Jeff's voice had sounded friendly. Did he have a compromise in mind? If not, why was he inviting her out?

To soften the blow, you dummy. To ply you with wine and caviar and who knows what, so you'll be grateful for his generosity and not cause a stink.

After that little scene she'd created in his office— what he'd pointedly referred to as her lioness act—she could hardly blame him. He probably wanted to be sure he had her off his back. Then, too, Jefferson E. Herrington, III—had he really identified himself as plain Jeff?—was the soul of diplomacy. He'd intimated that public relations was important to Herrington Press. In all probability, one of his ancestors invented the art.

Well, there wasn't much she could do if he turned her down about the logo. In the two weeks since they'd met, business had been brisk at Hughes Designs, and retaining her trademark no longer seemed top priority. Not that she wouldn't regret losing the money that changing it would entail. But she'd already come up with an alternative logo, and, as Jefferson—rather Jeff—had said, the sooner she started using it, the better. If Herrington Press was willing to spring for dinner to soothe her ruffled feelings, why should she object? She'd played by the rules and withdrawn the last half-page ad that was due to run in the *Daily* at the end of the month. She deserved to get something out of this fiasco, and a good meal was better than a flat no.

But, lordy, where would he take her? And what should she wear? It was already Wednesday, and she was two days behind schedule on her biggest job to date. She didn't have time to go shopping, even if she could afford to. But she had nothing appropriate for a five-star restaurant, and something told her that she and Jeff would be dining in style. He could, after all, write it off as a business expense. Besides, she certainly couldn't picture J. E. Herrington, III—or even plain Jeff Herrington—seated in a chili parlor or fast-food establishment or, for that matter, in any of the moderate-priced cafés *she* frequented!

Courtney sighed. She would talk to Mary. Her friend would think of something. Too bad Mary Mitchell was inches taller than her own five feet four. The woman had a gift for fashion and owned some spectacular outfits. Not that her wardrobe was filled with designer clothes, but it surpassed what Courtney owned.

The office phone rang again, and Courtney no longer had time to worry about what she would wear to a fancy restaurant.

Courtney's buzzer sounded at precisely eight o'clock the following Saturday, just as she was slipping into a pair of strappy heels that Mary had picked up for her at a shoe outlet. They were a nearly perfect match for the color of her turquoise dress, a loosely belted linen that her friend had insisted upon altering to fit her. "If he asks, you can tell him it's from the Mitchell collection," she'd intoned snootily, and Courtney had wanted to hug her. Mary's large dangling earrings added exactly the right finishing touch.

Courtney gave herself a last-minute mirror check, feeling almost elegant.

At the door, she fluffed her hair, took a deep breath and twisted the knob. The sight of Jeff in a perfectly tailored lightweight gray suit and pale blue dress shirt sucked all the air from her lungs. He was even better looking than she remembered. For a minute she just stared.

"Hi," he greeted.

"Hi," she returned in a slightly throaty voice.

Jeff smiled, his gaze raking over her. "You look lovely tonight."

"Thanks," she stammered. "So do you."

He laughed. "May I come in?"

"Oh, sorry." She stepped aside and let him enter, aware that her heart was pounding ridiculously out of control.

"These are for you."

Courtney's fingers trembled as she accepted the long box and worked off the lid. Beneath a blanket of green tissue paper were a dozen long-stemmed red roses.

"How beautiful! Thank you," she said, amazed that she had the breath to speak. No man had ever given her flowers before, and though she knew they were nothing but a peace offering, the gesture touched her. Tears threatened behind her lids, and before Jeff could see them, she turned away. "I'd better put these in some water."

While she was out of the room, Jeff took a seat on her faded sofa. The decor of Courtney's small apartment was makeshift and even though it was almost obsessively neat, she'd somehow managed to create a homey effect. A few magazines were carefully arranged on the round white coffee table that in another lifetime had served as a spool for telephone wire. A few plants, a small overstuffed chair, a couple of colorful, plump pillows and a drop-leaf table completed the furnishings.

By the time Jeff had finished his survey, Courtney returned with the flowers. They looked woefully out of place in her chipped glass pitcher, she thought, but it was the best she could do. She placed them in the center of her table, stood back, studied the bouquet, rearranged a bloom and, at last satisfied, swung around to face him.

"Thank you again." To cover her awkwardness, she snatched up the evening bag she'd borrowed from Mary. "Where are we going, Mr. Herrington?"

"Jeff. Mr. Herrington's my father."

"Very well. Where are we going, Jeff?"

"La Maisonette."

Courtney had never expected to set foot in the nationally acclaimed restaurant, famous for its fine French cuisine, but she had often fantasized about what it would be like to eat there. With feigned nonchalance, she chimed, "Excellent choice."

"You've dined at La Maisonette, then?"

She cut him a sage smile. "Frequently—in my imagination."

Amused at her sense of humor, he winked knowingly. "In that case, you can order for me."

"Only if the entrées have numbers. My French is a tad rusty."

They were both laughing as he escorted her out the door.

Courtney might have been intimidated by the quiet elegance of La Maisonette had she not spent the first two years after she'd been orphaned with an English professor and his family. Along with introducing her to cultural events, the Grangers had taught her the finer points of table manners: when to use a fork, when a spoon, and which cutlery to pick up first. Though she'd had little occasion to put her knowledge to the test after she'd left the Granger household for a second foster home, then another and another, she'd never forgotten the lessons. This evening they would stand her in good stead.

They drove to Sixth Street in Jeff's silver Mercedes. On the way he engaged her in small talk, and Courtney was amazed at the range of subjects they covered—everything from the Reds' chances for a pennant this season to the latest political events. Courtney was glad she made a habit of watching the nightly news on TV and of reading a weekly world affairs magazine. She had no trouble holding up her end of the conversation.

She noticed, however, that Jeff carefully avoided any mention of the topic uppermost in her mind: why he'd wanted to see her again. By the time they'd parked and been seated at the restaurant, she was consumed with curiosity.

"Well," she ventured after the waiter had brought their drinks, "enough of this chitchat. How about telling me what this meeting's all about?"

"Later. I don't like to discuss business on an empty stomach."

"Are we going to discuss business?" Courtney asked, thinking that Jeff Herrington hadn't the faintest notion of how it felt to have an empty stomach. There were times in college when she'd attended receptions for the sole purpose of lining her pockets with finger sandwiches and cookies. It was the only way she could assure herself of food for her next meal. Pushing back the memory, she pressed, "I was under the impression—"

"Later," he repeated. "I have your portfolio in the car. Speaking of which, where did you learn to draw like that?"

Courtney took a sip of her white wine. She remembered that she'd included several Cincinnati sketches as well as advertising materials in the packet she'd left at Herrington Press. "I'm not sure. As far back as I can remember, I liked to scribble and paint. Then my senior year in high school, I won an art scholarship to the University of Cincinnati. At U.C., I enrolled in a co-op program, and not only earned money for my education but also gained invaluable experience in graphic design."

"I take it that neither of your parents is in the field."

Courtney fingered the stem of her wineglass. "Is that a sneaky way to find out about my background?"

Jeff was baffled by her sudden defensiveness. "I won't deny that I'd like to know more about you, but if you think I'm prying, you can always refuse to answer."

Her eyes rose to his. "Forgive me. That was rude. But given the source, not unexpected. Right?"

"The point is, I really don't know you very well."

"I'm not much for talking about myself."

"In other words, you prefer to remain mysterious."

"It's not that. I simply don't have a family history. Not like you, anyhow."

"What do you mean? Everybody has a family."

"But yours is different. You have all this tradition. Jefferson E. Herrington the Third. It sounds so...so..."

"Stuffy?" he supplied.

"I wasn't going to say that," she objected, disarmed by his lopsided smile. "Even so, you can probably trace your genealogy back to the Mayflower. As for me, well, I not only come from humbler stock, but I never knew my grandparents, so I can tell you next to nothing about them. Or even about my parents. They both died when I was small."

"Both?"

She nodded, and Jeff detected a fleeting look of raw pain in her eyes. Instinctively, he reached out and covered her hand. "I'm sorry."

His touch was gentle, compassionate. He squeezed her fingers lightly, then retreated. The gesture was comforting rather than sexual, but Courtney's skin tingled from the warmth of his touch. She suddenly felt glad to be with him and found herself opening up as she had to few others.

"You know, so am I," she admitted. "After all these years, I'm still sorry I never really got to know my parents. Daddy was a pharmacist, Mom was—what's the fancy title for a housewife? A domestic engineer?"

"Good for her. I'm sure you appreciated having her at home."

"I don't have a lot of memories. Just a few. Of homemade chicken noodle soup and good-night kisses. Of Daddy reading me the comics or a bedtime story. Little things like that."

"Those things aren't little," Jeff said.

Something—regret? hurt?—flashed in his eyes and was gone before Courtney could decide. "You're right. They're everything to a child."

"What happened to your parents?"

"When I was six, Daddy died of a rare blood disease. The following year Mom was killed in an auto accident."

Jeff's eyes were full of compassion. Though he, too, had suffered a wrenching loss in his own life, he'd been an adult when Vicky had died and far better able to cope than a defenseless child. "I can't imagine ... That must have been really tough for you. Any brothers or sisters?"

"No. I was an only child of only children."

"That's too bad. A sibling might have given you some comfort. A little support."

"As it turned out, it was probably for the best. My closest relatives were a couple of great-aunts, but neither of them felt particularly maternal."

"You lived with them?"

"No." She took another taste of her wine. "You certainly ask a lot of personal questions. I'd say it's your turn to answer a few."

Jeff picked up his Burgundy. He wasn't satisfied to let her story drop, but he knew he would have to wait. She'd told him all she would for the present. Swallowing a sip, he set down his glass and invited, "Fire away."

"I know something about your family, but not a lot about you. Are you married, engaged, involved?"

Jeff almost choked. "You certainly are direct. Is this a proposal?"

Courtney reddened. "Don't flatter yourself. I'm just trying to cover a lot of ground in one question."

Jeff smiled. When had he enjoyed a woman's company more? "To answer your questions, no, no, and not exactly."

"Who's the 'not exactly'?"

"A woman I've been seeing. Her name's Amelia. Our parents are friends. Lately I've come to realize that's all we are to each other, too." He regarded her with steadfast eyes. "How about you? Mind answering the same three questions?"

"No."

"No, you would mind, or—"

"No to all three."

Jeff wasn't certain why he felt relieved, but he did. "Now that we have that out of the way, maybe we can enjoy our meal." As if on cue, the waiter appeared with their appetizers.

During their leisurely dinner, they returned to casual topics and discovered that they shared a real passion for baseball and jazz.

"I'm also partial to carnivals," Courtney admitted. "The first foster family I lived with took me to several every summer. They gave me as much spending money as they gave to their own kids, and I always made a beeline for the fish pond. There you were guaranteed a prize. My only regret is that I never won a toy animal at one of those booths where you try to knock down bottles with a tennis ball. My aim was always a mile off. Maybe that's why I became fascinated with baseball. It not only takes skill but more brains than most people realize for one player to throw out another. And the pitchers—such speed and accuracy boggles the mind.''

She looked up to see Jeff studying her. "What's the matter? Did I use the wrong fork or something?"

"Not at all. Your manners are impeccable."

"Then why are you staring?"

"I just noticed your green eyes have little gray flecks that dance when you're happy. At least, I think you're happy."

"Stuffed is more accurate," Courtney said, trying to ignore the little skitter of pleasure that coursed through her. "Dinner was fantastic. Even if I couldn't pronounce a single dish."

"I'm glad you enjoyed it. Ready for some shop talk?"

"Could we order coffee first?" she asked hopefully.

"You bet."

After Courtney had laced the dark brew with cream, Jeff asked, "Which do you want first—the good news or the bad?"

"I think I already know the bad news. Is dessert the good news?"

Jeff chuckled and lifted his cup. "Where did you get that sense of humor?"

"Not too clever, is it?"

"On the contrary. I think it's refreshing. And, given the traumas of your childhood, remarkable."

Courtney decided that she was right about Jeff's being diplomatic. She would have to watch herself. She could get used to his brand of charm. Not that she need have any worries on that score. Their paths weren't likely to cross after he took her home this evening, and they once more went their separate ways.

Blotting her lips, she acknowledged, "It's called survival. When you're bounced from foster home to foster home, seeing the comic side of life comes in handy."

Jeff sobered. "I imagine it does." He wanted to know more, but felt that he'd probed enough for one night. He wouldn't risk pushing; she might resent him for it later. That he was considering seeing her again came as a small shock. He knew he wasn't thinking in terms of a strictly business relationship, but that's what she was waiting to hear about.

Returning his cup to its saucer, he began, "Since you've surmised the bad news, I might as well confess I couldn't dissuade Dad. He insists you change your logo."

"I guessed as much. As a matter of fact, I already have a new design in mind. I checked, and my sign painter agreed to make the necessary change on my present shingle, so I can save money there. The stationery, business cards, et cetera, will have to go. Some I'll use for scratch. The rest I can always donate to the Boy Scout paper drive."

"That much, huh?"

Courtney lifted her shoulders. "So I exaggerate. But there's enough."

"I'm sorry. It's hard to part with something important to you. Obviously you were attached to that logo."

"I've made harder adjustments in my life."

Because the remark was a simple statement of fact—without a trace of self-pity—Jeff experienced a sharp tug on his heartstrings. With an effort, he managed to keep his voice level. "Maybe what I have to suggest will make the pill a less bitter one to swallow. I'm sure you've heard about the kind of books we publish at Herrington Press." At her nod, he continued, "Right now we're working on a history of printing in Cincinnati, and frankly we could use a good illustrator. Would you be interested?"

Courtney couldn't have been more stunned. Was he offering her the job? Or merely inviting her to apply for it? She would jump at the chance to do a Herrington book, but she didn't want to appear overeager. Deciding it was wise to hedge, she said, "It depends. Are we talking deadlines? Because I currently have all the work I can handle. Anything extra would have to be squeezed in nights and weekends. I don't mind long hours, but I can't promise to produce on schedule."

"No rush. History isn't going to change. I think you'll enjoy the work. The book will be a special limited edition, a collector's item. Each drawing is to be carefully reproduced, and you'll have the final okay on the artwork." He paused, wondering why she was hesitating. "The job's yours if you want it."

"Why me? You could have your pick of artists."

"Let's just say I like your style. I found your work . . . exciting. Detailed but spirited."

"That's very flattering, but how can I be sure you're not offering me this merely to ease your guilty conscience? Or worse yet, as a charitable gesture."

"I'll admit I feel bad about the loss you'll sustain because of your logo, but you can be damned sure I wouldn't give you the commission if I didn't consider your work first-rate."

She studied him for a long moment. "I don't know. I want to believe you, but it sounds too good to be true. There's got to be a hitch."

"Trust me. I promise you won't be held to a time-table. You'll be paid per drawing, and you can name your price. We'll set a fair range, but I'm aware some sketches may be more involved than others. We can work out the details later and sign a formal contract."

Courtney didn't know why she was dragging her heels. But she wasn't sure she wanted to work this closely with Jeff Herrington. She was already more attracted to him than was good for her, and she was afraid he wouldn't be an easy man to keep at arm's length. Yet he was offering her a chance to make her work and her name better known. And when the job was finished, she was certain to have a fatter bank account.

But at what cost? The price of a broken heart?

From beneath hooded lids, Jeff observed her while she finished her coffee and tried to make up her mind. He could almost hear the mental wheels whirling in her head. He hoped she would say yes. He wanted to see more of Courtney Hughes, much more, though, God knows, nothing was ever going to come of it. Despite a few similar interests, their backgrounds were too diverse. Still, he found himself contemplating how much else they might have in common.

Why did she hold such fascination for him? He wouldn't call her beautiful, but she had depth, character. Like the golden locket she kept toying with, her face was heart-shaped. Though she was blessed with high, patrician cheekbones, her small nose bordered on pixieish and her mouth was a bit too wide. But the imperfections somehow proved arresting. Her short, wavy hair reminded him of the color of wheat. It framed her face charmingly, and Jeff had an irrational urge to muss it up and watch it drift back into place. By far, her eyes were her best features. Big and green with just a hint of gray, they reflected her many moods.

Jeff recalled the imperious flash of her eyes that day she'd barged into his office. But they could also mist with gratitude as they had a few hours before when she'd uncovered the roses. Or sparkle with happiness when she recalled a fond memory. Or project a wounded vulnerability when she discussed her past.

"No strings?" she asked, breaking into his reverie.

"You have my word."

Courtney smiled. "When do I begin?"

"I'll ask our lawyer to draw up the contract and mail you a copy, so you can look it over before you sign." He signaled to the waiter for their check. "Why don't we celebrate? I know a great little place where they play jazz until dawn."

"Afraid not. Tomorrow after church I have to go back to the office to finish a job. Then I promised to baby-sit for my upstairs neighbor. Believe me, for that alone I need my rest."

Courtney spoke the truth. Never had she felt more in need of sleep. Perhaps it was the trouble over the logo, she wasn't sure, but something had triggered the recurring nightmares she'd struggled against since childhood.

Jeff stood and pulled out her chair. "You like kids?"

"Love them. Especially Jenny and Julie. They have me wrapped around every one of their twenty little fingers. Unfortunately, they know it."

"I'd like to meet them sometime. Maybe they'll let me in on their secret."

"Their secret?"

"How they wrap you around their fingers."

She picked up his hand and examined it. "Wouldn't do you any good. Yours are all too big. I'd never make it halfway around."

His smile grew wider. "Wanna bet?"

Chapter Three

Unconsciously, Courtney chewed on a thumbnail while she scrutinized the political poster spread out before her. For the past hour, she'd been arranging and rearranging slogan and photo, but she still wasn't satisfied with the results.

As if in challenge, Nat Hamilton's handsome face smiled up at her. Despite his movie-star good looks, Nat managed to reflect the perfect combination of concern and commitment. His penetrating eyes and confident expression promised voters that what he might lack in experience and insight, he would more than make up for with energy.

Courtney heaved an exasperated sigh. What could the problem be? Her eyes narrowed thoughtfully, and then out of the blue it hit her. It wasn't the arrangement of lettering and picture that was causing her trouble, but the print style she'd chosen. It simply wasn't striking enough to complement Nat's charisma.

Why hadn't she realized that before? What would her favorite art professor say? Dr. Vito was the one who'd recommended her to Nat, a young lawyer, who this fall would be making his initial bid for a seat on city council. So far Hamilton had been pleased with her work. She hadn't hit a single snag with the brochures and other campaign literature. Thinking it would be her easiest assignment, she'd saved the poster for last.

Courtney shook her head. How could she have missed something as obvious as the lettering? Was it because looking at Nat reminded her of a certain printing company president she'd recently met? Was Jeff the reason her vision was clouded, her senses muddled?

Both men were heart-meltingly attractive as well as bright and personable. But there the resemblance ended. Not only had Nat made rather than inherited his fortune, but he was a married man with two point five children—his wife was expecting an addition to the family in a few months—while Jefferson Herrington, III, was a wealthy playboy without a care in the world.

After the initial shock over her discovery that the president of Herrington Press was young, handsome and sexy, Courtney had made a point of finding out about him. She had checked through back issues of both the *Reporter* and the *Daily* and learned that rarely a week passed that Jeff didn't make the society pages. Since it was a section of the paper she never consulted, she'd missed the careful tracking of his social life.

It should come as no surprise, then, that he was a man who could flirt with remarkable sincerity one minute and appear totally unconcerned about a woman the next.

Over a week had passed since Courtney had last seen Jeff, and she still burned from his parting shot. Maybe he was irked that she'd turned down his offer of capping off their evening at a jazz bar. At any rate, when she'd asked him how soon he would like to see some preliminary sketches, he'd left their next meeting up to her. "Whenever," he'd said. "I've got plenty of irons in the fire, so don't push yourself. Call when you have something to show me."

Instead of being pleased that he was sticking to his resolve not to pressure her, Courtney found Jeff's nonchalance mildly annoying. What did he mean by "plenty of irons in the fire"? Was that a reference to his work, or a sly way of letting her know about the many women in his life? As if she gave a fig!

Because he was in no hurry to see either her or her sketches, Courtney had been determined to complete the commission in record time. As soon as the courier from Herrington's had delivered a packet of faded brown photographs from which she was to work, she'd begun the first series of drawings. But getting up an hour early each morning to tackle the project was, she admitted, taking its toll. If she weren't so tired or so irked by Jeff Herrington's conflicting signals, she wouldn't have been stumped by the campaign poster.

Frowning at the direction her thoughts were taking, Courtney again contemplated the layout. Now that she knew how to correct the problem, she'd better get on with it.

But moments later—and much to her dismay—she found that a more flamboyant type style still didn't solve her dilemma. Courtney propped her elbows on the table and peered long and hard at Nat's photo. Was she so exhausted that her eyes were playing tricks on her, or was there actually a hint of weakness about the man's mouth that not even his highly touted professional photographer could disguise?

Deciding it surely must be the former, she set aside the layout. She would tackle it again first thing in the morning. Right now she had more pressing work to complete. Like next week's ads for a local grocery chain.

Then maybe she could close shop and go home. A chilled glass of chablis and a bubble bath sounded terribly inviting. After a long, hard day, those were the only rewards she permitted herself. As a child, Courtney learned to shun luxury—or any hint of soft living for that matter. The lesson had worked to her advantage. If she'd succumbed to self-indulgence, she would never have had enough money to get Hughes Designs off the ground.

She stretched her arms in a high V, then reached for the partially finished grocery layout. It was nearly seven o'clock. Another hour, and she would have the ad ready to drop off on her way to work in the morning.

Shortly before eight, she was putting on the final touches when her phone rang.

"Don't you ever go home?"

Courtney thought she recognized the voice on the other end of the line, but she could be mistaken. Perhaps her ears as well as her eyes were deceiving her. Wary, she tossed back, "Who wants to know?"

"Jeff Herrington."

"Oh!" Could the edge of annoyance in his tone be attributed to the fact she hadn't instantly identified him?

"I've been trying to reach your apartment since a little after six. I dialed your office as a last resort. Are you aware of what time it is?"

The question smacked more of accusation than idle curiosity. "Sorry if I don't keep bankers' hours."

He suddenly laughed, and Courtney was startled by the warmth of the sound. "I guess you meant it when you said you were busy."

"Don't tell me you've changed your mind about putting the new book on the back burner," she said, curious why he'd waited until after the close of the business day to inquire about the illustrations. But then Jefferson Herrington, III, was probably used to having people jump whenever he got the least bit antsy.

Courtney was privately congratulating herself for having almost finished the sketches for chapter one when Jeff threw her a curve. "I wasn't calling about business," he remarked "—but something more . . . relaxing. There's a baseball game at Riverfront this evening. I happen to have a spare ticket."

"Tonight?" Courtney asked in a tone sharp with resentment at the eleventh-hour invitation.

"Bad timing, I know. And I apologize for calling so late, but I remembered you were a Reds fan, and I hated to see this ticket go begging. What do you say?"

"More to the point, what would what's-her-name say?"

"Amelia," he supplied. "She hates baseball. Besides, we're no longer dating."

That bit of information sent Courtney's heart racing. Though pride dictated she give him a flat no, she was tempted. It was rare that she treated herself to a Reds game. Few of her friends—Bill especially shunned anything remotely athletic—shared her enthusiasm for baseball, and half the fun of attending was having someone else along to help shout encouragement to the batter or hurl insults at the umpire. On top of that, she hadn't had an evening out since Jeff had treated her to dinner at La Maisonette.

But even if she could humble herself, she was hardly dressed for the ballpark. Her prim little blouse and skirt were appropriate office attire, but not what she would choose to wear to Riverfront. Nor were her new high heels meant to be worn at a stadium. "I don't think so," she said at last, softening the rejection more than she'd intended.

As if reading her thoughts, Jeff urged, "Don't worry about changing. Come as you are. If you haven't eaten, we can grab a couple of hot dogs at the game. I can be at your agency in half an hour. We may miss the first two innings, but seven out of nine isn't bad."

Courtney had to smile. Though Jeff Herrington could be aloof when it pleased him, he could also make a woman believe that he wanted—needed might be more accurate—her company. What the heck? she silently decided. If she refused, she would only be denying her own pleasure. And Jeff might get the impression that she was stalling under the mistaken notion that his invitation constituted a real date instead of a friendly gesture to a fellow baseball fan. If Bill had phoned at the last minute to ask her to an art opening, she would accept, wouldn't she?

Telling herself that the promise of junk food as well as an exciting game was too much for any mortal to resist, Courtney quipped, "How can I argue with logic like that? Throw in a beer and some popcorn, and you're on."

* * *

"You didn't really just *happen* to come by this ticket today, did you?" Courtney asked around a bite of her hot dog. "Own up. I bet the Herrington family has had sitters' rights to this box ever since the Reds moved from old Crosley Field."

Jeff smiled. "What tipped you off?"

She ignored the glint of humor in his eyes. "I'm almost afraid to raise my voice in this section."

He rested his arm over the back of her seat and took a long swallow of his beer. "Don't be. I plan to have a good time, which means jumping up and yelling on occasion. Feel free to join in.

"Tell me something," she said, her eyes on the batter. "Why did you wait so long to ask me? Some woman stand you up?"

"Such a suspicious nature you have. No, nothing like that."

She swung her gaze to his and missed the strike. "Why then?"

"I was afraid you'd say no," Jeff answered honestly. Though his mind had conjured up one flimsy excuse after another to confer with her, then casually bring up the game, he'd held off dialing her number all week. After Courtney had cut short their one dinner together, he feared she would turn him down. Even if she hadn't actually slammed the social door in his face, she'd left him with the idea that she preferred to keep their relationship professional.

Ordinarily he would have agreed that it wasn't wise to mix business with pleasure. But for some crazy reason, he couldn't get Courtney Hughes out of his mind. Ever since she'd forced her way into his office, fairly breathing fire, he'd labored to convince himself that the tug he was feeling—the tug that went beyond mere physical attraction—was nothing more than sympathy coupled with the appeal of the unfamiliar. One more evening together, he'd at last concluded, would be enough to confirm his suspicions and clear his mind.

Jeff waited for her reaction to his admission, but Courtney appeared not to have heard him. Cincinnati was down by one, with runners on first and third, and her concentration was riveted on the field. Once again he was struck by her contrast to the women he ordinarily dated.

Courtney was so . . . so vibrant, so natural. She wore little makeup, but she didn't need to resort to such artifice to make her face glow. Though she sat very still, her palms clutching the armrests, her eyes shone with a child's excitement. When she turned her head, he detected those intriguing shards of silver in their green depths. Her cheeks were flushed with color, and he could see the effort she exerted to hold herself in check. Far from Amelia's undisguised boredom at sports events, Courtney was totally engrossed in the action unfolding on the artificial turf below.

But despite her obvious joy in the game, she didn't appear totally comfortable. She would be more at home, he thought, if they weren't in the pricey blue seats. High up in the red section, she would probably be hunched forward, pounding her fists and screaming support with the rest of the crowd.

Courtney's unease had a surprising effect on Jeff, exposing a protective instinct buried deep within him. It was all he could do not to lift his hand to her cheek and brush a stray curl back into place.

"What made you think I would?" she commented when the manager of the rival team jogged out to confer with his pitcher.

The question seemed to come straight from left field, jolting Jeff out of his musings. "Would what?" he asked, having forgotten his original query.

"Turn you down."

He shrugged. "A hunch."

She gave him a long, measuring look. He was wearing a knit shirt and jeans, both of which molded his body as well as the baseball uniforms outlined the contours of the players on the diamond. But more attractively, she determined, since Jeff's muscles weren't overly developed like those of professional athletes. In casual clothes, he appeared younger, almost boyish, but no less commanding than he had in the perfectly tailored suits she'd previously seen him in. She found the laugh lines that radiated from the corners of his eyes enormously appealing. Suddenly realizing that her look had strayed to his sensually shaped lips, she jerked her attention back to the game. "You're not at all what I expected."

"Oh, yeah? What did you expect?"

She gave him another sidelong glance, this time coupled with a mischievous grin before once more returning her gaze to the pitcher's mound. "You don't want to know."

Jeff's protest was swallowed by the smack of wood against leather, followed by an earsplitting roar from the crowd. Along with nearly 40,000 other fans, Jeff and Courtney sprang to their feet.

"A home run!" she cheered. Without thinking, she wrapped her arms around Jeff's neck and gave him a spontaneous hug.

Before he could react, she pulled away. It happened so quickly that Jeff questioned whether she was conscious of her action.

Or of the effect it had on him.

"Great game!" Courtney exclaimed as they filed out of the stadium.

"It's always a great game when the home team wins. Would you like to stop somewhere? To celebrate."

"You're really into celebrations, aren't you?"

"I beg your pardon?"

"That's what you asked when I agreed to do your book. I believe your exact words were 'Why don't we celebrate?' "

"I'm flattered you remembered."

"I never forget an invitation to party," she remarked jokingly.

Jeff located an opening in the crowd and with his hands loosely banding her waist, he guided her through. "That makes two of us."

She eyed him over her shoulder. "If the gossip columns are half true, you're a real party animal, aren't you?"

"Don't tell me you believe everything you read in the papers?" he asked tongue-in-cheek.

"In this case, I think they have you pegged. But I guess you come by it naturally." Jeff, she'd discovered, wasn't the only Herrington who made the society pages with regularity. His parents were also frequently mentioned or pictured. Looking up at him, she remarked, "When you were a kid, the parties at your house must have been something else."

"Right," he replied, controlling the sardonic edge that threatened to creep into his voice. Little did

Courtney know they were far from the carefree occasions she obviously imagined. He recalled how even birthdays in the Herrington mansion were choreographed events. His father often capitalized on these celebrations by combining them with business. Jeff's guests were usually the children of those with whom his father had dealings. Consequently, the parties were planned to entertain the parents as much as their sons and daughters.

He wouldn't have known what a real kids' party was like had it not been for Frank Schmidt, his grade-school buddy. By Herrington standards, the Schmidts may have come from the wrong side of the tracks, but nobody could have been more genuine or warmhearted. And they sure had a knack for making a kid happy.

Maybe that's why he wasn't big on formal social gatherings now. He much preferred the company of a few close friends to large parties where the talk was mostly superficial and inane. Still, as a businessman he had to concede that a certain amount of socializing was necessary.

As the crowd began to disperse, Jeff no longer had an excuse for keeping his hands at Courtney's waist. Reluctantly dropping them, he took his place beside her, matching his steps with hers. "What do you think? The night's still young. Shall we go somewhere and toast the Big Red Machine?"

Courtney was in an expansive mood. She hadn't felt so relaxed in months. Maybe years. Impulsively, she linked her arm with his. "How about to Skyline? I could do with a big bowl of Cincinnati chili."

Amused, Jeff allowed, "Good idea." He'd been thinking more in terms of an intimate little club, but a chili parlor would be more her style. To be honest, he

rarely indulged in a night cap, anyhow. And Courtney's spirits were certainly giving him a big enough
high. To chase the wayward thoughts from his mind, he
joked, "I can see the way to your heart is definitely
through your stomach."

"That's supposed to be the woman's line."

He laughed. "Let's not get technical."

Jeff took her hand as they crossed Second Street and
headed toward the garage where he'd parked his car.
The warmth of his fingers wound lightly about hers
stirred something deep within Courtney, and she fought
back a desire to give his hand a squeeze. Instead, she
looked away toward the shimmer of the stadium lights
on the dark waters of the Ohio River.

Jeff noticed the direction of her gaze. "Beautiful,
isn't it?"

"Always. I especially like the view from Columbia
Parkway. At night the Ohio reminds me of a golden
chain studded with diamonds."

"The Queen City's jewels," he reflected, picking up
on the image and noting her pleased smile. "I love it,
too."

"I sometimes think it would be fun to live for a while
on the river. Just drift along in a boat and take life
easy."

"Your fascination with the Ohio comes through in
your art."

She glanced at him quizzically. "How do you know
that?"

"Your portfolio. It contained two marvelous watercolors set along the banks."

"I guess you could say I'm something of a river rat."

"Me, too. We'll have to go water-skiing sometime
and have dinner on one of the boats. Maybe at Mike

Fink's,'' he said, mentioning a floating restaurant docked at the bottom of Greenup Street on the Kentucky side.

"I've heard about it," Courtney replied, a bit disoriented from the offhand way Jeff brought up another date. Surely he wasn't serious. Aside from enjoying baseball, jazz and the Ohio River, she couldn't imagine that she interested the urbane Mr. Herrington. But then, he probably hadn't gone out with many women who jumped up and down and shouted over a base hit or clutched him in a bear hug when the Reds got a home run. To Courtney's chagrin, the more the evening wore on, the more uninhibited her behavior had been. She was hardly the femme fatale type he was accustomed to escorting, she reminded herself.

Jeff stopped at the nearest Skyline restaurant, one of a number scattered throughout the city. "I suppose you like your chili five-ways," he remarked, scooting into the booth beside hers.

"You suppose right. I want the works—meat sauce, beans, spaghetti, cheese, onions. And lots of those little oyster crackers they serve with it."

"Why doesn't that surprise me? Make it two bowls of five-way," he told the brunette, who'd set glasses of iced water before them.

"You want anything to drink?" she asked.

Jeff's smile was off-center. "I'm sure we do."

"A large cola," Courtney requested.

"Double it," Jeff informed the waitress who scribbled down their order and scooped up the menus before leaving.

"I used to wait tables," Courtney said as she watched the woman hand the cook their order. Inwardly, she chided herself, *Way to go, Courtney. What a fascinating conversationalist you are.*

"No kidding? Where?"

"In a German restaurant. It ranks right up there with my co-op job." Remembering, Courtney grew wistful. When she'd been hired at The Sausage House, she'd felt she had died and gone to heaven. Working part-time at the restaurant had enabled her to save a little money against emergencies. More importantly, it had made possible at least one nutritionally balanced meal a day. Before that, she sometimes had to skimp on food to buy books and art supplies. Hardly realizing what she was saying, she added, "I ate dinner every night."

"That's customary, isn't it?"

"I mean the food was free," she spouted and immediately wished she could take back the words. By thinking aloud, she'd revealed far more about her past than she'd intended. Anyhow, discussing the state of her stomach—or her bank account—could only bore Jeff.

For his part, Jeff wanted to explore her last remark, but he didn't have a chance since their waitress reappeared with their order. He was amazed at how tasty the chili was and said so. "You know I've lived here all my life, and this is my first bowl of Cincinnati chili."

"Then you led a deprived childhood."

"Poor little rich boy, right?"

"You said it, I didn't," Courtney taunted impishly, but something about his tone gave her pause. Maybe growing up to be president of Herrington Press wasn't all it was cracked up to be.

Jeff took another taste of the spicy concoction. "Hmm, this stuff could become addictive."

"Weird as it might seem, I believe cinnamon gives it that distinctive flavor. Makes a great midnight snack, doesn't it?"

"You bet," he agreed, savoring another spoonful.

"I'd like to see you again," Jeff ventured as they climbed the steps of her apartment building.

Courtney turned toward her door. "I'm sure you will. The first drawings are nearly finished. As soon as they're ready, I'll bring them by your office."

"That's not what I meant, and you know it." He stayed her hand as she was about to insert her key in the lock. When she twisted around to face him, he released her wrist and braced his hands against the door, effectively hemming her in.

"Do you think that's a good idea?"

"I'm not sure," he answered honestly. "I only know I'd like to get to know you better, Courtney. And not just professionally."

"I see." She experienced a flicker of anxiety. "What if the feeling's not mutual?"

"Then I won't push."

"Good, because otherwise I'd have to cancel our contract." She looked him in the eye. "I don't go to bed to get jobs."

He returned her direct gaze. "I didn't think you did. And I don't force women to get what I want."

Courtney believed him. Despite an aura of quiet authority, Jeff Herrington wasn't the type to take advantage. Hadn't he gone to bat for her with his father? Hadn't he treated her with more consideration than she felt she deserved? Yet she persisted in reading something sexual into his kindness. And his interest. Was that because she secretly wanted him to desire her? Or because her years of struggle and survival had warped her more than she realized?

All at once she was ashamed of herself for being so suspicious. "I'm sorry if I seem unappreciative. It's just . . . I don't like to be crowded."

"Who's crowding?" He pushed away from the door and presented her with flattened palms.

She smiled at the gesture. When her eyes rose to meet his, their gaze collided and held. For several seconds, neither moved. Then without touching her, he lowered his arms and bent his head to cover her mouth with his.

His lips were soft and undemanding, brushing hers with the lightness of a butterfly's wing, but in no time Courtney's senses were swimming. Mary was right. Jeff's mouth was incredibly sensuous. His kiss was warm, gentle and unbearably sweet. All the more arousing for its restraint. She'd never experienced anything like it. Wanting more, she wound her arms about his neck to pull him nearer.

With that encouragement, Jeff pressed one hand against her back while he brought the other to her cheek. She smelled of soap and lavender, and it occurred to him that the combination was more intoxicating than the delicate scent of an expensive perfume.

All evening he'd been dying for a taste of her. With the tip of his tongue, he traced the shape of her lips. He wanted to coax her mouth open and slip inside for a deeper sample, but he didn't dare. She'd said she didn't like to be crowded. He would have to back off if he stood any chance with her at all.

Forcing himself to withdraw, Jeff slid his hands to her waist and stepped away.

It took a moment before Courtney registered what had happened. Her eyes drifted open. Dazed, she peered up at him.

"I've wanted to kiss you ever since you stormed into my office," he confessed.

"You did? Why?" she asked with that candor he found so refreshing.

"I'm not sure. Maybe together we can find out."

"I'm not your type, you know."

"How about letting me be the judge of that? May I call you again? For dinner?"

She couldn't prevent her lips from curving into a smile. "You just said the magic word."

"What's that?"

"Dinner."

He grinned and skimmed a finger over the tip of her nose. "I'll be in touch."

Courtney watched him as he turned and disappeared down the steps.

Several days later, Courtney curled one leg under her and settled back on the Mitchell living room sofa. "What do you think, Mary? Was it a mistake to agree to go out with Jeff again?"

"Don't be ridiculous," Mary scolded, dropping down beside her. Though she spoke to her friend, her eyes were on Julie and Jenny, who were serving tea to two rag dolls at a child-sized table. "Of course, if you've developed a terminal case of cold feet, I'll be glad to fill in for you. I know he's gorgeous. And from all indications, I'd say he seems like a decent sort. I can't understand why you ever hesitated."

"That's just the point. Nobody's *that* perfect. He's got to have an angle."

"Has Jeff given you any reason to believe that?"

"No, but—"

"But what? Maybe he simply enjoys your company."

"Sure. And it snows at the equator. I can't think of a single reason why he'd want to date me. I mean, we're such opposites. We might as well belong to two different galaxies."

"Maybe he's fascinated by the difference."

"Sur-re," Courtney said, this time stretching out the word to give it a caustic edge.

Mary's brows rose. "You're attracted to him, aren't you?" When Courtney refused to answer, Mary went on, "Don't sell yourself short, my friend. You're a pretty terrific woman. It's no wonder Jeff asks you out."

"All I can figure is that he's after a quick fling in the sack."

"You haven't heard a word I've said, have you?" Mary complained. "And you haven't answered my question. You're attracted to the man, aren't you?"

"As I told you before, Jeff's hard not to like. But so's Bill, and I'm not interested in getting involved with him."

"The chemistry isn't there for you and Bill. If it is for you and Jeff, I say go for it." Mary leaned over and laid a hand on Courtney's arm. "Life's dealt you some crushing blows, Court, and I suspect that no matter how much you've achieved, you haven't completely recovered from them. Don't think I'm trying to minimize the loss of your parents. I'm not. I've seen how rough Paul's and my divorce has been on the twins, and they get to see their father every other weekend. But just because you've gone through even worse experiences, don't always expect the rug to be pulled out from under you. You're twenty-eight years old. It's time you enjoyed life a little. That's my advice.'' She jabbed a finger at Courtney's chest. "And don't forget you asked for it."

"Maybe you're right."

"I know I am. Lighten up. Play it by ear. Speaking of which, is that water I hear?'' Abruptly, she jumped up and headed for the kitchen, Courtney right behind her.

Julie and Jenny were standing on chairs at the sink, up to their armpits in suds.

"We're washing our tea dishes, Mommy,'' Julie proudly announced.

"So I see,'' Mary returned, eyeing the miniature Niagara pouring down her wooden cabinets and forming a large pool on the linoleum.

"Then we'll give our dollies a bath.'' Jenny threw a dimpled smile over her shoulder.

"Aren't kids wonderful?'' Mary observed, heading for the sink and cutting off the water.

Courtney started toward the utility closet. "I'll get a mop for the floor."

"No,'' Mary protested. "I'll deal with this. To twist an old saying of my mother's, you can wait until you have children of your own."

"Right,'' Courtney mumbled.

Though she wasn't unhappy to leave the messy kitchen to Mary, her friend's flippant remark filled Courtney with a deep sadness. She would never hold a baby of her own in her arms, let alone know the pleasures or trials of motherhood.

Years before, she'd made her decision. Or rather fate had made it for her. No matter how much she was tempted, no thing, no person would ever change her mind.

Chapter Four

On Friday Courtney agreed to watch the twins while Mary enjoyed an evening out with a man she'd met at work. She had toyed with the idea of keeping the night free, thinking Jeff might call, but when Thursday came and went with no word from him, she'd told Mary, whose regular teenage sitter had come down with a case of the flu, not to worry. She would take over.

The three had gone to Courtney's apartment since Julie and Jenny liked to kneel on chairs at her drawing table and scribble in their coloring books. Courtney was only too happy to indulge the twins. She could work beside them and get a head start on next week's ads.

"Can we have pizza for supper?" Julie asked, propping her chin on a small fist and turning hopeful eyes on Courtney.

"I already ordered it, lamb. You hungry?"

"Can we sleep here tonight?" Jenny broke in.

"That's the plan."

"On the couch? By the TV?" Julie wheedled.

"No way. Right over there in my bed," Courtney said, pointing out that the small sofa wouldn't accommodate two.

Just then the doorbell chimed, and both girls slid off their seats and squealed, "The pizza! The pizza!"

"Not so loud," Courtney admonished. "You'll scare away the delivery boy."

"Shh," Julie and Jenny whispered as they trailed in tandem behind their honorary aunt.

After grabbing her wallet on the way to the door and pulling out a bill, Courtney unbolted the door. To her amazement, she came face-to-face with Jeff.

"Thanks," he said, eyeing the money. "But I wasn't expecting a tip."

"Jeff, what are you doing here?"

Julie came forward and stared at Jeff's empty hands. "Where's our pizza?"

"Did he eat it?" Jenny asked, poking an accusing finger at their caller.

Jeff glanced from one to the other. "Tell me there really are two of them. Or am I looking into a mirror?" He extended a hand and touched first Jenny's shoulder, then Julie's. "Nope. They're both real."

The girls giggled, and Courtney stepped aside to usher him in. "These are the Mitchell twins. Julie and Jenny, meet Mr. Herrington."

Jeff squatted down to shake each small hand. "Call me Jeff, if you like. I'm happy to meet you. Courtney told me how much she enjoys your visits."

"Do you know where our pizza is?" Julie asked, unimpressed by the compliment.

"I'm afraid not. Is one on the way?"

"It'll be here soon, girls. Meanwhile, you could help by getting out some napkins. You know where I keep them on the kitchen counter. Don't try to reach the plates. I'll put them on the table later."

"Is he staying?" Jenny asked.

"We'll see." Courtney turned to Jeff. "Would you like to?"

"I'd be honored. Will you have enough?"

"The nice thing about pizza is you can always make it go around. If you're still hungry afterward, we can walk down to Graeter's for ice cream."

At the mention of dessert, Julie and Jenny chorused, "Ice cream! Ice cream!"

"Pizza first," she said, bending down to talk to the pair. "Now, how many napkins do we need? Let's count. She took Julie's hand in hers and one by one raised four fingers, assigning each a name. "Jenny, it's your job to get out one napkin for each finger Julie's holding up. Got that, ladies?"

Two dark heads nodded in unison.

The lesson complete, Courtney sent the children off on their mission.

"Aren't they a little young to keep that straight?" Jeff wondered aloud.

"I don't expect them to. It's just a way of expanding on the one-for-me, one-for-you concept. They'll probably have the whole box scattered over the table, but so what? We'll need the extras before the meal's over."

"How did you learn so much about kids?"

"I did a lot of baby-sitting in college. Not only was it a fun way to earn extra money but—" she waggled her brows with comic effect "—I was always invited to raid the refrigerator."

He laughed, and the sound sent a prickle of aware-
ness up her spine. Tilting her head, she looked inquir-
ingly up at him. "Tell me, what brings you here?"

"I thought I'd drop off these old photos on my way
home."

"I see." She accepted the brown envelope that he
pulled from an inside coat pocket. "I didn't realize you
lived out this way." She knew that the Herringtons re-
sided in Indian Hills, one of Cincinnati's most elite ad-
dresses, and on the opposite side of town from hers.
She'd supposed Jeff had his own home there as well.

"I don't," he acknowledged, then had to improvise,
"but I had another errand to run in your neighborhood." He was spared further embellishment by the
arrival of the delivery boy.

Jeff was impressed by how well Courtney handled
Julie and Jenny. The energetic duo demanded a lot of
attention, but she didn't seem to mind in the least. She
wiped up their spills without making them feel clumsy
or foolish, listened attentively to their childish obser-
vations and flashed them an engaging grin when, at the
conclusion of the meal, they wiped their tiny mouths,
leaving more tomato sauce on their cheeks than on their
napkins.

Similarly, Courtney marveled at Jeff's own patience. He appeared unperturbed by the twins' fre-
quent questions and seemed to enjoy the trek to the ice
cream parlor as much as they did. The way they'd taken
to him, he could have passed for the Pied Piper.

"What'll it be?" he asked when they were seated at a
round, marble-topped table.

"St'awberry," Julie piped up.

"*Straw*berry," Jenny corrected in smug imitation of
her mother.

"Courtney, how about you?" Jeff asked.

"Vanilla chocolate chip. I can't resist those chunks of homemade candy they put in it."

With the tip of her tongue, she licked her lips, and for a moment Jeff's gaze was frozen on her mouth. Why had he ever thought it too wide to be attractive?

"What are you having?" Courtney asked him as a waitress appeared at their table.

Jeff's eyes flew up. "The same."

"The same as whom—the girls or me?"

"You," he replied, but he wasn't thinking about her preference in ice cream at all.

Back at the apartment, Courtney bathed the twins before tucking them in. Jeff surprised her by volunteering to read them a bedtime story.

"Only one book each," Courtney warned, effectively squelching any battle that might otherwise ensue. If limitations weren't understood at the outset, Jeff could grow hoarse before Julie and Jenny would ever close their eyes.

He kicked off his loafers and settled himself between them. Even though he was engulfed by two little dynamos, each vying for his attention, Courtney experienced a strange fluttery sensation at the sight of Jeff on her bed. Her mind conjured up a picture of him in a similar pose with his own children. He obviously liked kids and would make a super parent. She doubted, though, that he would enjoy fatherhood for long. He wasn't the type. Deep down, he was too much of a swinger.

Swallowing hard, Courtney made an excuse to leave the room, but his resonant voice followed her all the way to the kitchen. She could hear him imitating Donald Duck's quack or Minnie Mouse's squeak as he read through two stories about Disneyland.

When he'd finished, his audience begged for another tale, but Jeff held firm. "Courtney said one book each, and I think we ought to stick to the original agreement, don't you? We have to save some stories for another time."

"Will you come back and read to us again?" Julie asked.

"I'd like that," Jeff said. "But you have to feed me first. Is it a deal?"

"Yeah," Jenny promised. "Maybe Aunt Court will cook. She makes good spaghetti."

He kissed each curly crown. "You finagle me an invitation, and I'll be back."

From the living room Courtney heard the entire exchange. She noticed that Jeff made no definite promises to the girls, and for that she was glad. She would hate for them to be disappointed. Surely this evening was a fluke. He couldn't be *that* entertained by the children. Maybe he'd only lingered because he was bored or had nothing better to do.

Courtney crossed to the window and peered out at the darkening sky. In time, she would bore him, too. Hadn't Mary unwittingly confirmed her suspicions, saying that Jeff's interest had been sparked because she was unlike the usual company he kept? It had to be curiosity that motivated him because she wasn't in Jefferson E. Herrington's class at all. Not by any stretch of the imagination. Circumstances had brought them together, and circumstances would eventually part them.

"I think they're finally down."

Courtney whirled around at the sound of Jeff's voice.

"Sorry if I startled you."

"Just woolgathering," she admitted. "Would you like some coffee? I made a fresh pot."

"You read my mind."

Cups in hand, they settled onto the living room couch. Jeff had a way of looking at her that made Courtney feel he was hanging onto her every word. As a result, she'd often found herself disclosing details about her past that she rarely discussed. This evening was no exception. Maybe it was the relaxed atmosphere. Maybe the muted lighting of her one living room lamp. Maybe his easy way with the twins. Courtney didn't know. But for some reason her guard was down.

"Tell me about your foster parents," Jeff urged, and before Courtney knew it, she was talking about the Grangers, who, aside from her own parents, had given her the only real home life she'd known.

"They were a wonderful family of four. I think I already mentioned how they took me to carnivals. Mom and Dad Granger treated me like one of their own. When Betsy and Todd got roller skates, so did I. When they went to camp, I was allowed to tag along. Like a real little sister. Thanks to the Grangers, I learned proper manners and something about the fine arts. Dad Granger was in the English Department at U.C., and Mom taught elementary art in the public schools. She's the one who discovered I could draw."

"Do you still see them?"

"Not as often as I'd like, but we keep in touch. They were going to adopt me, but Mom got multiple sclerosis, and Dad was overwhelmed with medical expenses. He couldn't believe the diagnosis—or refused to accept it—so they went all over the country seeking miracle cures. They wound up in Arizona where, I suppose, his money ran out.'' Courtney's expression grew pensive. "I was with them for just two years, but they're more like family to me than the few relatives I have left. In fact, not long ago Betsy invited me to be a bridesmaid at her wedding, but I wasn't able to make the trip."

"They must be special people. For you to still call them Mom and Dad."

"They are," Courtney confirmed. "Very special." She didn't add that she always addressed each new set of foster parents that way. Childishly, she'd cherished the vain hope that she would be adopted. But only the Grangers had come close to making her dream a reality. If fate hadn't intervened and visited upon Mom Granger so debilitating a disease, Courtney's life might have been far different.

Strange. She hadn't even told Mary that story, yet after a few brief meetings, Jeff had coaxed some of her most private memories from her.

He, in turn, talked about the Schmidts. Frank had been his classmate in grade school. At the time, Frank's father worked for another Indian Hills family, and the Schmidts lived in a converted carriage house on the estate. Originally, Jeff's parents hadn't realized that their only child was visiting a blue-collar family when he went to play with Frank after school. By the time they discovered the truth, it was too late. He and Frank had formed a fast friendship that not even Jeff's being sent to an eastern boarding school had ended.

"Frank's dad, Al, became like a second father to me," Jeff admitted. "He now has his own garage and operates a marina on the river. That's where I keep my motorboat over the winter."

"What happened to Frank?"

"He's a big-shot lawyer in Chicago. We still see each other when he gets back to Cincy on visits. By the way, Al will be giving my boat its annual tune-up next week, and I'll be going down there to try it out. Want to come along? We can also have that dinner I promised you."

"If you don't mind," Courtney said without the slightest hesitation.

Despite their intimate conversation, when she saw him to the door, Jeff's parting kiss was chaste. His lips, barely touching hers, made her ache for more.

And that, Courtney reflected after she'd closed the door behind her, was scary. Every time things were going well, she could count on trouble ahead. Wasn't that the story of her life? First, she'd lost her parents, then the Grangers. When she was accepted into college and believed she was at last on her way to a better life, her scholarship and co-op jobs hadn't even begun to cover her expenses. Though welcome, sporadic baby-sitting did little more than pay for incidentals. Before that stint at the Sausage House had come along, she'd almost given up her hope of a degree. Some free-lancing, in addition to her work at Queen City Graphics, had helped her build up a loyal clientele and start her own firm. But she'd been in business for herself barely six months before the logo fiasco.

So went the story of her life. At least one down for every up.

Courtney had come to expect the worst when things were going the best. That's what disturbed her now. She hadn't felt this happy since her early years with her parents or her brief interlude with the Grangers. Being with Jeff was beginning to feel so right that she just knew it couldn't last. If she had any sense, she wouldn't see him again—except in a purely professional capacity.

And yet, in the corner of her mind, she could hear Mary's advice to "lighten up." Maybe her friend had a point. Why spoil life with aimless worry? Why not enjoy it while she could?

Courtney wouldn't have had to set her alarm. The twins jarred her awake, bounding into the living room at seven in the morning to turn on the cartoons.

Wearily, she threw back the sheet and dragged herself off the sofa. Though it was Saturday, she would have to put in a full day at the agency. If she stayed home to work, as she was tempted to do, she'd risk being coaxed away from her drawing table by the Mitchells.

Sleepy-eyed, she made her way to the kitchen and stuck a filter into her automatic coffee maker. By then, the girls had sprinkled more cereal on the table than into their bowls and were reaching for the pitcher. Courtney interrupted and poured a generous amount of milk over each helping of granola. After she'd made sure they had juice and toast, she sipped her coffee and answered their nonstop interrogation about Jeff. "Yes" she was doing some work for him. "No" she wasn't planning to marry him. And "maybe" he would read them another story someday. Both seemed smitten with the man, and Courtney could hardly blame them. They missed their father, and last night Jeff had good-naturedly filled that role in their lives.

Once breakfast was over, Courtney escorted the girls upstairs, where she shared a cup of tea with Mary and listened to a brief description of her friend's evening. But she didn't stay long.

Back at her apartment, she picked up the newspaper lying on her doorstep. With a sigh, she slumped into her favorite chair, ready for a few moments of quiet before she left for Hughes Designs. As usual, she turned first to the comics, a daily ritual she clung to in memory of her father. Even after she could make out many of the words herself, Courtney had continued to start each morning perched on his lap while together they followed the antics in their favorite strips. Much as Jeff had last night when he'd read to Julie and Jenny, her father would change his voice to impersonate the various characters. The recollection never failed to bring a tightness to Courtney's throat, a tightness that only a good chuckle over the funnies could dispel.

She was thumbing through the rest of the paper when her hands suddenly stilled. "Oh, no," she groaned and hastily whipped back the page. "This can't be."

For a few seconds, Courtney latched on to the pretense that her eyes had duped her. But they hadn't. There in large, heavy letters was an advertisement carrying the old logo for Hughes Designs. Courtney was certain she'd canceled the ad immediately after her second meeting with Jeff. It was the last of four she'd budgeted to run this spring. When she'd phoned to withdraw it, she'd promised to send in a substitute—one in which she could introduce her new logo—but she'd gotten too busy with other publicity jobs to worry about her own. Whomever she'd talked to at the *Cincinnati Daily* must have failed to pull the old ad. Or had run it when she neglected to send in a new one.

Whatever had gone wrong, the blunder was going to stir up a fresh batch of trouble. So what else was new? she thought dismally. Hadn't she been expecting a bomb to drop? Things were running too smoothly. At least, she consoled herself, if she needed a lawyer, she knew one to call. She doubted she could afford Nat Hamilton's fees, but possibly he could recommend somebody in her price range.

Though surely it wouldn't come to that. Jeff might be angry, but he wasn't vindictive.

Still, she'd given him her word. What was he going to think? Especially after he'd gone out on a limb, rewarding her with that commission, which not only promised to wipe out her losses but also turn her a tidy profit. Moreover, he'd taken her to dinner and, remembering her enthusiasm for baseball, treated her to a Reds game. Then last night he'd surprised her by obligingly playing daddy to the Mitchell twins. To top it off, though he made no secret that he might want more from her than illustrations for a book, he hadn't pressured or pushed. In fact, on the two occasions when he'd kissed her, he hadn't demanded as much as she'd been willing to give.

Fleetingly, Courtney harbored the vain hope that Jeff might not see the ad, but she knew she was only deluding herself. If he didn't personally spot the logo, somebody else at the *Reporter* was bound to. No matter how she looked at it, she had some tall talking to do.

But first, she intended to find out why the *Daily* had failed to kill the ad. Some unsuspecting soul was due for a dressing-down. At least, Courtney comforted herself as she dialed the paper, giving the culprit a piece of her mind would be some comfort, however small, for landing her in hot water.

Jeff was glad Al Schmidt was readying his motorboat for the coming summer. The pleasant evening with Courtney and those adorable little girls, plus the thought of a long day on the river, was making him un-characteristically lethargic this morning. Usually he was up and at the office by seven-thirty instead of lazing in bed fantasizing about a woman with green eyes and a winning way with children.

If his father had taught him one thing, it was how to work. Hard. Sure, while he was growing up, both his parents had encouraged him to enjoy himself, but that was mainly to keep him occupied while they followed their own agendas. Their tolerance ceased once he'd gone to work. His father had made it clear that he expected his son's total commitment to Herrington Press. Night and day.

"Always take advantage of social occasions," the elder Herrington had counseled. "When people are in a jovial mood, that's the time to conduct business. Never let opportunity pass you by."

The Herrington philosophy had stuck, and over the years, Jeff had become such a workaholic that he'd forgotten how to relax.

That is, until Courtney Hughes had made her uncer-emonious entrance into his life. Jeff stacked his hands beneath his head. Just recalling their first encounter brought an automatic smile to his lips, though when she crashed his editorial meeting, he hadn't been all that amused. For a few hairy moments, she'd had him hanging onto his temper by a thread. But her audacity, her strength, had plucked a responsive chord, and he'd had no trouble handling her with the same tact he would have accorded any other intruder.

Or being far more attracted than he'd counted on.

Jeff rubbed his eyes with the knuckles of his index fingers. He'd spent a sleepless seven hours thinking about Courtney. Keeping his distance from her was one of the most difficult tasks he'd ever set for himself. Last night he'd had to stuff his hands in his pockets to keep from hauling her into his arms and giving her a proper kiss. He wasn't certain how much longer he could hold out. Whether she demanded space or not, he yearned to draw her close. Very close.

Aside from her spunk, what was there about her he found so fascinating? Though Courtney was more than passably pretty, she would never turn heads like Amelia. Except maybe when she was excited or angry. Then her green eyes were shot through with those tiny silver flecks, and her pixieish face took on an animation that was difficult to resist.

The truth was that the stunning and coolly sophisticated Amelia failed to raise his temperature one degree while Courtney with her just better-than-average looks and scrappy personality exerted an undeniable pull on his senses.

Furthermore, she was an entertaining conversationalist. She had a quick wit and a keen sense of humor. During the few times they'd spent together, he'd laughed more than he had in the past six months. She'd rekindled the fun-loving side of him that had died with Vicky. Which was ironic, considering what a hard life Courtney had led. No wonder meeting her had sparked his final break with Amelia. An entire evening in Amelia's company paled in comparison to five minutes spent with Courtney.

Reluctantly, Jeff tossed aside the sheet and padded naked toward the bathroom. But not even the pelting spray of the shower could wash Courtney from his mind. She had so many traits he valued. For one thing, she was a survivor. Someone who'd overcome adversity without feeling sorry for herself. Someone who, against all odds, was determined to succeed, to make something of her life. On top of that, she was great with kids and gave of herself to her friends.

As a matter of fact, Courtney reminded him a lot of the Schmidts.

What was it Al had once told him? "There are people who are beautiful, and then there are beautiful people." Courtney, he decided, qualified on both counts.

As he toweled off, Jeff suddenly wanted to talk to her again. He wondered if she was up and decided that with the twins she had to be. He returned to his bedroom and reached for the phone, but it rang before he could lift the receiver.

"Jeff, this is Gregory Whitehead."

"Yeah, Greg. What's up?" he asked, certain his leisurely morning was about to come to an abrupt end. Gregory Whitehead was his managing editor, and he wouldn't be calling him at home unless he had an urgent problem.

"Have you seen the *Daily* this morning?"

"Not yet. Why?"

"You'll know when you take a gander at the ads. Particularly the half-pager on 21-A."

Courtney called the *Cincinnati Daily* and was put on hold for what seemed hours, but in reality amounted to a matter of minutes. Soon, a woman who identified herself as Carol Miller, head of advertising, came on the line. "How can I help you?" she asked.

"It may be a bit late for that," Courtney countered. Though unable to keep the anger out of her voice, she lodged her complaint with what she considered remarkable restraint.

Ms. Miller asked her to hold again while she personally checked their records. Courtney drummed her nails against the formica of the kitchen counter and listened with growing impatience to background music meant to entertain her while she waited. By the time Ms. Miller returned, she was ready to explode, but she held onto her temper, even when the woman explained that her ad had never been canceled.

"Do you remember who took it?"

Courtney searched her mind. "A Harry or Hank or something like that."

"Probably Hal."

"Yes, that's right. Hal. Ask him. I'm sure he'll remember."

"I'm afraid he left us a few weeks ago for a job in New York. Hal had a lot of loose ends to tie up," Ms. Miller explained. "And he had his own system of organization. I imagine one of our new employees picked up your ad by mistake. I'm sorry, but it's understandable, given several recent changes of personnel in our department. And since you were simply advertising your business and not offering a special sale, no harm's done."

Courtney started to object, but bit her tongue. The damage was far greater than Ms. Miller might suspect, but she had no desire to compound it by making trouble for someone else. No doubt the zealous employee who'd run her ad was only trying to prove himself to his superiors. Of all people, she knew what that was like. Hadn't she spent her entire childhood trying to ingratiate herself with others?

"Let me assure you," Ms. Miller said, misinterpreting Courtney's aborted protest, "there'll be no charge. The ad's on us."

Some consolation, Courtney thought. She was still left with a monumental problem—one that money couldn't fix. Nevertheless, she politely thanked the woman and replaced the receiver.

With a sinking heart, she pondered how to alert Jeff to the ad. In the end, she decided that the best policy was to take the initiative. To go to him rather than let him come to her.

An hour and a half later, Courtney arrived at Herrington Press, battling a heavy feeling in the pit of her stomach. Cheerful show tunes filling her car and a resounding internal pep talk had done little to bolster her spirits.

Gladys Feldkamp looked up as Courtney opened the door to the executive suite.

"Ms. Feldkamp," she said with surprise. "I didn't expect to see you here on a Saturday morning."

"I work half a day and take the time off on Thursday afternoon." She smiled broadly. "Mr. Herrington's expecting you."

"He is? I don't have an appointment."

Ms. Feldkamp's broad smile faded to a discreet curve of her lips. The subtle look implied she was well aware her boss had taken more than a business interest in the woman before her. "I know. I assumed...that is, he said he wanted to see you if you came by." She pushed the intercom button. "I'll let him know you're here."

No sooner had she announced Courtney than Jeff's terse voice filled the small room. "Show her in."

When Courtney opened his office door, Jeff was standing behind his desk, both hands molded to his hips. His face wore an angry scowl and a night's growth of beard. He must, Courtney vaguely deduced, have left home without shaving. The stubble darkening his cheeks and chin seemed at odds with his neat business suit.

"How could you—?"

"How did you—?"

Their voices collided, and each instantly fell silent.

"You first," Jeff invited.

"I can explain," Courtney began, coming toward him with more assurance than she felt.

"This had better be good." His steely tone was intimidating. "I just got a call from my father, and he's livid. But, then, he doesn't take kindly to deception. Nor do I. He's already alerted Stewart Eldridge to instigate legal action."

The words served as a challenge. Unaware that Jeff was still smarting from his father's severe tongue-lashing for letting a woman hoodwink him, Courtney advanced farther into the room. Propping her knuckles on his wide desk, she looked him directly in the eye. "I don't see why you bother with lawyers. You really don't need them. Not when you're so good at trying and condemning a person all by yourself!"

"What did you expect? We had an agreement. You promised to drop the Herrington logo—"

"*My* logo." She thumped her fist against her chest for emphasis. "It merely happened to resemble your trademark."

Jeff went on as if she hadn't interrupted. "Yet I pick up the paper this morning and see it scrawled across your half-page ad. What am I supposed to think?"

"Try this." Her eyes narrowed with righteous indignation. "Maybe there's been some mistake. Maybe Courtney's not to blame."

At her words Jeff's shoulders relaxed a fraction. "What kind of mistake?" He motioned her to take the seat next to his desk.

"I'd rather stand."

"Suit yourself." He settled onto his chair and folded his arms on the gleaming surface of his desk. "I'm listening."

"How refreshing! Well, get this, *Mr.* Jefferson E. Herrington, the Third, because I'm only going to say it once. I cancelled that ad, but the *Daily* slipped up. True, I promised them a substitute, and I'm partly at fault for not sending it right away, but I didn't think there was any hurry. I called and pulled the original, and I considered the matter settled."

"Did you? Then how lucky for you they went with it anyway when you failed to replace it. Might as well coast along on the Herrington trademark as long as possible. Right? Especially when you had a ready-made excuse drummed up."

"What?" Courtney gasped. "You think I'm lying?"

Her protest went unacknowledged. "What's the matter? Get greedy for more business, Courtney? Seems to me you have more than you can handle now. Especially if you can't find a few minutes to dash off an ad for your own agency."

She braced her palms on the desk and bent forward. "That's low, Herrington. Low."

"Lower than giving your word and not honoring it?"

She went pale at the accusation, and Jeff involuntarily winced. He didn't much like himself for pushing her in a corner, but Courtney had hurt him. His father's disparaging remarks about his judgment didn't wound nearly as much as her betrayal. He'd bent over backward to help her—not simply because he was en-

amored but because he believed in her. He'd thought
she was a woman of substance. Somebody with backbone and character. And for thanks she'd played him
for a fool.

Courtney recovered quickly. Though Jeff was determined to believe the worst of her, she refused to break
down in front of him. Not before she set the record
straight.

Stiffening her spine, she flared, "Have it your way.
Think what you want. Take me to court. That's what
you're spoiling to do. I assure you, it won't be the first
time I've been slapped down—for no fault of my own.
But make no mistake. I'm not the guilty party here."
That said, she whirled about and bolted for the door.

Just before she spun away, Jeff caught the glint of
tears. More eloquently than words those shimmering
green eyes told him all he needed to know. She was
speaking the truth. And more. Whether she was aware
of it or not, she'd just confessed something painful
about her past.

Suddenly he felt ashamed of himself for not trusting
her. Why hadn't he considered that she would have had
nothing to gain by deceit? It would have been stupid for
her to use the logo when she wasn't hurting for clients.
And if Courtney was anything, she wasn't stupid.

Before she could reach the knob, he caught her
shoulders and roughly turned her toward him. "Not so
fast."

A lone tear had escaped her eyes and was trailing
down her cheek. Angry that he'd seen it, angry that
she'd let him get to her, she lashed out, "Let me go."

"Oh, damn, Courtney. Don't cry, babe." He brought
his thumb to her cheek and brushed away the drop of

moisture. "Look, I'm sorry. I was wrong. Okay? But I thought you'd double-crossed me."

"Get your hands off me!"

He let his arms fall to his sides, but took a step forward.

"Don't touch me!" she protested. Alarmed by the determined look in his eyes, Courtney retreated and felt her back hit the door.

"I won't lay a hand on you. I promise."

"Good," she said. "Now if you'll excuse me—"

Jeff came closer. "Just remember. I didn't say anything about my mouth."

This time when his lips met hers, they weren't gentle.

Chapter Five

Courtney brought her palms to Jeff's chest in an automatic gesture of resistance, but she was powerless against the confident assault of his mouth. His lips rolled and rocked over hers with an urgency that demanded rather than invited participation. But, true to his word, he didn't touch her. His hands remained flush against the door, his body a fraction of an inch from hers—not quite making contact but close enough to trap her.

Not that he needed to.

Never before had Courtney been aware of the power of a man's mouth. In a matter of seconds, Jeff robbed her of breath. And her reason. If she were capable of coherent thought, she might have resented the devastating onslaught, but just as she'd been too startled to evade him, she rapidly discovered she had no desire to. The nip of his teeth, the rough texture of his tongue, the abrasiveness of his whiskered cheeks, the warmth of his breath mingling with hers, the fierce pounding of his heart beneath her fingertips—each sensation excited Courtney beyond her wildest imaginings. It was as if she had waited a lifetime for this moment.

And Jeff still hadn't laid a hand on her! Only their lips were fused.

When his tongue plundered and filled the depths of her mouth, her knees weakened and threatened to give way. To keep from falling, she clutched a handful of his shirt for support.

At her response Jeff pressed one hand between her shoulders, the other to the small of her back. Lord, how she moved him. He hadn't meant to come on so strong, but that single tear proved his undoing. It had triggered a desire too long denied. One he'd never expected to experience again.

Suddenly the void in his life became achingly clear. The only person who could fill it was Courtney. Courtney, a woman strong, real, unafraid of emotion.

He wasn't sure where his feelings for her were leading, but he hoped he didn't hurt her. God knows she'd been hurt enough by life already. He wanted to soothe her, cherish her, protect her.

His mouth softened, then trailed over Courtney's cheek, still salty from the tear he'd wiped away. He dropped tiny kisses down the slender column of her neck and lingered at the hollow of her throat where her pulse was hammering wildly. He slid his hands up her sides, lightly skimming her breasts. With his thumbs, he brushed the centers and found them already hardened against the thin material of her blouse. She trembled at the intimacy of his touch.

It took every ounce of strength Jeff could summon to draw his hands from the aroused peaks, but this was neither the time nor the place to make love. Tearing his mouth from hers, he nestled her head beneath his chin. "Ah, Courtney," he rasped, "I'm sorry."

Sighing, Courtney closed her eyes and allowed herself to revel in the tender embrace. How long had it been since she'd been held like this? Treasured? Sheltered? Gentled?

And, a memory at the back of her mind needled, *how long did it ever last?*

When finally she spoke, her voice was strangely quiet. "For kissing me?"

"Never." He tipped her face toward his and rubbed a thumb lightly across her bruised lips. "For being a little rough, maybe. But most of all for suspecting you. I was way out of line."

With both palms framing her cheeks, he once more pressed his mouth to hers. The tip of his tongue licked soothingly over her lips, dipping inside to slide provocatively back and forth. *To hell with right times and right places,* he cursed inwardly as he cupped her bottom and pushed her high against him.

Courtney gasped, then went limp. Knowing she had the power to excite Jeff was a heady sensation. With a rashness new to her, she tilted her hips and cradled him against her softness.

Jeff was about to deepen the kiss when Gladys Feldkamp's voice came over the intercom, jolting them apart. "Mr. Herrington, your father's on line one."

For a moment neither of them moved. Then as if in slow motion, Jeff released Courtney and stepped back. "We have to talk," he said huskily. "Don't go away."

As if she could, Courtney thought. As if she had the strength or will to move a muscle. Her legs were as wobbly as those of a newborn colt. They couldn't be counted on to hold her up, let alone carry her out the door.

She leaned back against the door frame for support and with trembling fingers tested lips that still throbbed from Jeff's kiss. What was happening to her? Was this what it felt like when, in Mary's words, the chemistry between a man and woman was right? Or did her emotions run beyond the mere physical? Could she be falling in love? She'd had so little experience with the emotion she couldn't be positive.

Her confused eyes followed Jeff as he calmly went to his desk and picked up the phone.

"What's up, Dad?"

"It's about that Hughes woman."

Jeff went rigid. "What about her?"

"Carol Miller at the *Daily* just got in touch with me. Seems our Ms. Hughes called her this morning, mad as a hornet about that ad and claiming she'd canceled it, but nobody there remembered. It got me thinking, maybe she's on the up and up, after all. Scuttlebutt has it their advertising department's been a shambles ever since Hal left."

Jeff's grunt was derisive. "I thought they were in worse shape when he *was* there." At one time, Hal Hawkins had been on the *Reporter*'s payroll, but Jeff had never cared for his work habits. As he saw it, the man's slipshod ways left too much to chance. As a result, he hadn't been sorry to lose the adman to a rival paper.

"I know there isn't much love lost between the two of you, but I always liked Hal. He had his faults, but he rarely made mistakes."

Jeff felt his stomach muscles tighten. "Meaning?"

"If Ms. Hughes told Hal to pull that ad, by all rights, it should have been trashed. Would have been, too, if Hal had been around. Anyway, to make a long story short, Carol recognized the logo and thought Hughes Designs was one of our subsidiaries. That's why she called. She didn't want any hard feelings. Under the circumstances, I suspect we did Ms. Hughes an injustice."

"My sentiments exactly. She's here now, if you want to apologize." Jeff's glance strayed to Courtney, whose eyes were wide with amazement.

"There? In your office?"

"Right. Shall I put her on?"

"No. I'd rather you bring her down to see me."

His father didn't wait for a confirmation. The line went dead, and Jeff replaced the receiver. "He wants to talk to you."

Courtney pulled herself erect. "Now?"

Jeff smiled as he ambled across the room to stand in front of her. She was looking for all the world like a woman who had been thoroughly kissed. Her lips were still swollen, her eyes slightly dazed. "Now," he repeated. "There's a bathroom through that door if you want to repair your lipstick." He ran a knuckle over his jaw. "When you're finished, I'd better shave."

Courtney couldn't suppress a grin. "Bad start to your morning?"

"You might say that." He gave her a playful swat on the derriere and shoved her into the small room. "But things are looking up."

She glanced over her shoulder and lowered her eyes tellingly. "Yes, things certainly are. Or at least they *were* a little while ago."

The interview didn't go nearly as well as Courtney had been led to believe by the one-sided telephone conversation she'd overheard in Jeff's office. She'd expected a friendlier reception, but while Jefferson E. Herrington, II, seemed sincere enough when he shook her hand and asked her to have a seat, he tended to be wooden and overbearing.

Straight off, he plunged into a lengthy monologue, explaining his position. "I'm sure," he finally concluded, "you can appreciate my thinking. However, Carol seems to believe the error was theirs, and that's good enough for me."

It wasn't an out-and-out apology, but Courtney knew it was as close to one as she was going to get. She felt like a starving man being offered crumbs in the guise of a seven-course meal. The words *I'm sorry* would, she decided, never pass this man's lips. Small wonder. They would be too apt to stick in his throat and choke him.

Out of the corner of her eye, she caught a glimpse of Jeff. Like her, he hadn't uttered a single word for the past five minutes. She surmised that he must take more after his mother. For all his intensity and drive, he had a sensitivity and gentleness lacking in the elder Herrington.

At last Courtney rose and pulled herself erect. "Ms. Miller is correct," she succeeded in interjecting. "The *Daily* was at fault. I kept my promise. I haven't used my old logo since I gave your son my word to change it."

For acknowledgement, he offered her a curt nod of his white head. "Thank you for coming by, Ms.

Hughes. I'm glad we've had a chance to clear up this misunderstanding in person.''

"So am I," Courtney returned, mirroring his formality.

As they made their way to the door, her heart went out to Jeff. She felt sorry for him, growing up with such an intimidating man. Though her mental picture of her own father was fuzzy at best, whenever she thought about him, she was surrounded by a warm glow. She couldn't imagine J. E. Herrington, II, ever leaving a child with that sentiment.

Once outside his richly appointed office, Courtney found the air incredibly lighter.

That had been eight days ago. Since then Jeff had been out of town. As they were returning from their meeting with his father, Gladys had waylaid him with a message, and the first thing Courtney knew he was stuffing papers into his briefcase.

"Family business," he'd explained. "I have to be in New York this afternoon. I don't know how long this will take, but I'll phone as soon as I get back." He'd rounded the desk and put his hands on her shoulders. "Will you be okay?"

"Of course," Courtney had said, warmed by his concern.

The memory faded as she gazed out the window of her apartment at the drizzly Sunday weather and despaired of enjoying a picnic with the Mitchells. She was glad now she'd postponed suggesting it, knowing that Julie and Jenny would pout over Mother Nature's refusal to cooperate. Even if the rain let up, the ground would be too soggy for a day in the park. Well, after church, she would simply spend an idle afternoon reading and maybe watching some TV. Perhaps she would also look over the sketches she'd finished for Jeff.

Thus far, she was more than pleased with the results—a mixture of ink drawings and watercolors that, she felt, accurately detailed the early presses and publishing houses. She hoped they also captured something of the character and mood of the times. She'd spent several hours researching in the main branch of Cincinnati's public library to supplement the materials Jeff had given her, and, as a result, had discovered a new interest in history. Today afforded the perfect opportunity to start satisfying it. Curling up with an interesting book on a rainy afternoon was an inviting alternative to spending the day outdoors.

Downing the last of her coffee, Courtney glanced at the clock. She would have to hurry if she wanted to make the eleven o'clock service.

Twenty minutes later she was drying off in the shower when her phone rang. She draped the towel around herself sarong-fashion and scurried to snatch up the receiver.

"Good morning."

Courtney started at Jeff's rich baritone. "Where are you?"

"Home. I got back about midnight. Once I settled the financial matters, I decided to stay over a couple of extra days in order to attend the anniversary party of some friends. Did I wake you?"

"No, I'm getting ready for church."

"And afterward? Are you free?"

"That depends." She twirled the phone cord around her finger and succumbed to a temptation to flirt. "What did you have in mind?"

"Since you put it that way—" he began on a suggestive tone.

"Forget I asked," she cut in, mentally scolding herself. Playing coy wasn't her forte, and she would do well
to remember it. "If you're referring to my plans, I
haven't any. Nothing major, anyhow."

"What? Not working?"

"Nope. Sorry to disappoint you, but I decided to take
some time off." She felt suddenly foolish for thinking
this was a social call. Jeff was probably behind after
being away for so long, and knowing she often worked
all weekend, had no doubt assumed they could make
headway on the book project. What did it matter? she
thought, dismally eyeing the raindrops as they trickled
down her kitchen window. With a lightness she was far
from feeling, she quipped, "I was looking forward to
getting outdoors, but I sure picked a great day, didn't
I?"

"Don't despair. It's supposed to clear by noon. You
know what they say about Cincinnati weather. If you
don't like it, stick around a few hours. It's bound to
change."

"In that case, I might go to Eden Park, after all.
Hiking's out, but I could stroll through Krohn Conser-
vatory. The indoor flower displays are always a treat."

"Would you consider a boat ride on the Ohio instead?"

"What?"

"Would you join me for a cruise on the beautiful
Ohio?"

"Are you serious?"

"You sound as though I'm asking you to fly to the
moon."

Courtney adjusted the knot in her towel and ran a hand through her hair. "I...it's not what I expected you to say, that's all."

"I admit the weather could be better," Jeff said, misinterpreting her remark, "but I'm hoping to take my boat out for a test run. Even if the rain keeps up, I want to drive down to see Al. Will you come along?"

Courtney needed no urging. "What time?"

"How about one? We can stop for lunch on the way."

By the time Courtney left church, the sun was shining and the day had taken on that peculiar clarity that comes after a night of heavy rain. Puffy clouds rode across the sky, and a light breeze stirred new leaves on a line of maples flanking the sidewalk. As she passed under them on the way home, she felt an occasional droplet of water hit her shoulders.

When she turned the corner onto her street, she was surprised to see Jeff waiting on the apartment steps. Julie was perched on one knee, Jenny on the other. They were dressed in their Sunday best, and she watched as he followed their animated conversation, his head turning from one to the other.

Without a doubt, Jeff was one of the most handsome men Courtney had ever met. His hazel eyes, hooded with heavy dark brows, gave him an alert, intense look, softened now by amusement over something Julie had said. Peeking from the top of his navy blue shirt were dark spirals of body hair that made her fingers itch to sample their texture.

When he started to imitate bird calls for the girls, Courtney's eyes fastened on his full lips. She remembered the feel of them on her own and experienced a sudden lurch of excitement. Swallowing, she quickened her step.

All at once Jeff must have caught sight of her coming down the walk. He looked up and smiled.

Courtney's heart nearly tripped over itself kicking into double time.

"Hi, Aunt Court!" the twins cried simultaneously.

"Hi, yourself." Her gaze swung to Jeff. "You're early."

He nudged the girls off his lap and rose. "A little, but, as you can see, I've been well entertained."

"I can imagine."

Julie thrust a piece of paper toward Courtney. Without urging, Jenny did the same. "Look what we did in Sunday school, Aunt Court."

"Such lovely colors!" She sank onto a step and circled an arm around each child. "Tell me about your pictures." Her eyes sought Jeff's, silently asking his indulgence a while longer.

"They're of the baby Jesus and his mother. She's got the same name as our mother," Julie informed her.

"That's right—Mary," Courtney confirmed.

"See, she's giving him a bottle in my picture," Jenny explained.

"And that's a donkey," Julie interjected, pointing to her own drawing. "They rode on donkeys in the old days."

"I particularly like the tail," Jeff remarked, and Julie turned adoring eyes on him. "Now in Jenny's picture," he continued, "my favorite part is the little bird flying overhead."

Jenny favored him with a radiant smile.

"I quite agree," Courtney said, training a critical eye on both drawings. "Very nice work. Your mommy's going to display these on the refrigerator door for sure."

"Want us to draw you one?" Julie asked.

"We can come up to your apartment and use your table," Jenny suggested.

"That's enough, ladies." The twins turned toward the sound of their mother's voice. "Aunt Courtney has company. You can visit with her another time." Her eyes went to Jeff. "I hope they weren't bothering you too much. I got a long distance call from my mother, or I would have rescued you sooner."

"I enjoyed them," he assured her.

Courtney looked puzzled. "Have you two met?"

"The girls introduced us," Mary said. "Jeff pulled up behind the building about the same time we did, and they pounced on him right away. They've been singing his praises ever since he read them those bedtime stories at your place." She shot Jeff an appreciative smile. "You were a good sport to let them con you into that impromptu tour of the neighborhood."

"It was my pleasure."

"Which I'm sure you've had enough of for one day." Mary offered a hand to her daughters. "Come along, you two. Let's get you out of that finery and into some play clothes. Then we'll have lunch."

"Can Aunt Court and Jeff eat with us?" Julie begged.

Jeff stooped down and put a hand on her small shoulder. "Thanks, but we already have plans for lunch. Could we take a rain check?"

"It's finished raining," Julie pointed out.

"He means," their mother intervened, "that they'll eat with us another day. Okay?"

"Okay," both girls agreed, albeit grudgingly.

After they'd disappeared through the door, Courtney said, "Give me a few minutes to change, and I'll be right with you." She started up the steps but spun around before reaching the top. "About lunch. You aren't thinking of any place fancy, are you?"

"You're not inviting me up?" he asked as if he hadn't heard her question.

"Later," she promised, knowing she would be a nervous wreck getting dressed with Jeff in the next room. "About lunch?"

He extended his arms. "Am I dressed for fancy?"

"No, but in those designer jeans you could probably go anywhere."

"These?" He glanced down at his legs. "They're Rudy's doing. He takes care of my wardrobe."

"Rudy?"

"My . . . handyman."

Courtney laughed. "Is that supposed to be a euphemism for a valet? Or butler?"

"Not in the strict sense. Anyhow, to answer your question, I thought we'd eat on the boat. I have a picnic basket in the car."

"A little something Rudy packed?"

"Nope. He's a health nut. I don't let him anywhere near my picnics. This is carryout from the deli."

Her smile widened. "Perfect," she said, warmed by the knowledge that he knew she would be more pleased by a sub sandwich than by exotic fare.

On being introduced to Al Schmidt, Courtney decided that he must have come from typical Cincinnati German stock. Big-boned and jovial, he was losing "the battle of the bulge," due as much, she suspected, to a penchant for beer as to advancing years. But the stomach that protruded over his heavy denims looked hard rather than flabby. Since he didn't appear the type to work out in a gym, Courtney guessed that his daily labor provided him with plenty of strenuous physical activity.

Al wiped his grease-stained hands on an old cloth, then peered at his right palm dubiously. "Maybe we better forego the formalities," he said as Courtney held out her hand. "If you don't mind."

"Not at all." She grinned. "Under the circumstances, I'd consider it more polite of you *not* to shake my hand."

They shared a laugh, and Courtney felt an instant kinship with the man. For all his rough exterior, Al's easygoing nature made her feel completely at home.

"Tell me," he said, "how did you meet this scalawag? You're not like the women he usually takes boating."

Courtney risked a sidelong glance at Jeff before returning her gaze to Al. "Is that a compliment? Or a complaint?"

"A compliment. And if he doesn't treat you right, let me know. I'll set him straight."

"Thanks a bunch," Jeff groused.

Al ignored him. "I've had lots of practice. Got five kids of my own. Ten grandchildren. Could be one or two more on the way, but nobody's admitting it yet. You come from a big family?"

"No," Courtney said simply. "An only child."

"Like Jeff here." He placed a wide hand on Jeff's shoulder. "I like to tease him, but he's all right. I oughta know."

"Could we change the subject?" Jeff pleaded, visibly uncomfortable.

Apparently on a roll, Al paid the request no notice. "He practically lived at our place until his folks sent him away to that fancy Boston prep school. He and my Frank were like brothers. Still are. Jeff always said he wished he came from a big family, too. By now I sorta expected him to have his own passel of kids. But he's getting a late start, don't you think?"

"You sound like my parents," Jeff gibed good-naturedly. "And would you stop talking about me in the third person?"

"It's past time he settled down," Al told Courtney, then looked at Jeff as if just acknowledging his presence. "By the way, Frank's coming home next month, so we're having a family party. You'll be getting an invite." His eyes slid to Courtney. "You're welcome to come, too."

"Thanks," she mumbled, struggling not to show how disturbed she was by Al's comments. The way Jeff took so naturally to Jenny and Julie, she should have realized that he would want children, but at the back of her mind she'd cherished the hope that his sophisticated lifestyle...

Courtney gave herself a mental shake. What in the world was she thinking of? She was a fool to even consider a permanent relationship with Jeff. Their backgrounds alone were enough to keep them apart. Determinedly she dragged her thoughts back to the conversation.

"Al's wife's a great cook," Jeff said to her. "You have to taste..." His words trailed off. "Hey, are you feeling all right?"

"Sure," she lied.

His arm went around her waist. "You look pale."

Al's nose wrinkled. "It's probably the smell in here. Let's get her outside. I've got your boat ready. Fresh air's what you need, missy."

Once on the river, Courtney put her misgivings aside and enjoyed the day. She turned her face into the wind, letting it whip her blond hair every which way. The sun was warm on her skin, but she was glad she'd remembered a sweat shirt. Summer was still seven weeks away, and the temperature was only in the high sixties.

They shared the water with barges, sailboats and other pleasure craft. A water-skier, wearing a wet suit, whizzed by and gave them a jaunty wave.

Over the chug of the motor, Jeff called, "Ready for lunch?"

"Anytime."

"We'll pull into that cove up ahead."

He maneuvered into a secluded shelter beneath a willow. Its newly budded branches partly hid them from river traffic, and Courtney was reminded of Civil War days. Perhaps slaves had made their way to freedom at this very spot where the river separating Kentucky from Ohio was not too wide.

After they'd dropped anchor, Jeff produced a cooler and pulled out a chilled bottle of sparkling grape juice. "There's coffee, too, if you'd rather have it. Or soft drinks."

"Juice is fine."

"I never carry anything alcoholic on the boat," he seemed compelled to explain. "It doesn't mix with water sports any more than with driving a car."

"No problem," she assured him, pleased at his sense of responsibility. "Like you, I'm not a big drinker."

He filled two stemmed glasses. "I do like a glass of wine now and then. Or a beer. On occasion something stiffer. But there's a time and place."

Though Jeff didn't elaborate, Courtney caught in the remark an undercurrent of pain and anger. Before she could pursue it, he proposed a toast.

"To the river. And reunions."

Courtney sipped, savoring the fruity flavor. "Is this a reunion?"

"Of sorts. I missed you, Courtney."

"You did?"

"Don't look so surprised. I guess I should have called. I considered it, but I don't like talking on phones. You can never say anything important over a long distance line, anyhow."

Courtney lowered her eyes and studied her glass. "What do we have to talk about that's so important?"

For an instant Jeff considered telling her about Vicky, about how this past week had helped him put his feelings for her into proper perspective. The anniversary party he'd attended had been for Vicky's parents, whom he phoned whenever he flew to New York. Since he hadn't visited the Coles in quite a while, touching base with them again made him keenly aware of how much they'd changed over the years. More significantly, how much he himself had changed.

Jeff wasn't the same man who had fallen in love with their daughter. His tastes, his outlook, his opinions—all had altered. Some of that was due to Vicky's death, but far more to the gradual process of maturing. If she had lived...but she hadn't. Though Vicky would always have a place in his heart, he suddenly wondered if he would still be attracted could he go back in time and meet her today. To his surprise, he discovered he didn't want to. Especially since he'd met the woman who now sat across from him.

Jeff smiled inwardly. Courtney was as different from Vicky as fine china from stoneware. But that didn't mean he loved her less. In fact, if the past few days had taught him anything, it was that he'd come to love her more. He and Courtney had weathered a couple of serious confrontations, surmounted some tough obstacles, whereas his love for Vicky had been untested, untried and, as a result, unproved.

Jeff's eyes touched Courtney's. Sometime soon she would have to know about Vicky, but at the moment her obvious tension made him hold his tongue.

"For starters," he said, deliberately keeping his voice light, "we need to decide where our relationship is going. But by the look on your face, I think I'd better feed you first." He opened a wicker basket. "I know for a fact that these sandwiches are guaranteed to soften the heart of the most reluctant of maidens."

"You think my heart needs softening?"

He handed her a sandwich. "I'll reserve judgment on that until later."

They dined on a sumptuous picnic of roast beef wrapped in small loaves of crunchy French bread, creamy potato salad and rich chocolate cake. By some unspoken agreement, they kept their conversation to safe subjects. Jeff talked mostly about his affection for the Schmidt family.

"Al gave me my most prized possession," he told Courtney. "For my thirtieth birthday he surprised me with a book on jazz, a real treasure he unearthed in a used bookstore. It's got fantastic illustrations."

He grew thoughtful, mentally comparing Al with his parents. The Herringtons preferred the more practical and impersonal expediency of money to gaily wrapped packages. Not since he was a small boy had Jeff received a gift from them that wasn't in the form of green bills. They seemed to be of the opinion that their son had no needs that couldn't be met by cold, hard cash. Just once he would have liked to know that they'd taken a little time and trouble to consider what would please him. He didn't care about size or price. A colorful tie. A pop record. A clever T-shirt.

The kinds of things Al gave him.

Because the Schmidts had always treated him as one of their own, Jeff, in turn, had tried to help Al out when business was slow. Not with charity, but by subtly funneling customers his way. Al was a top-notch mechanic, an expert on anything with a motor. He'd started with a garage and finally saved enough to buy the marina, which had enabled him to add the wealthy and privileged to his regular clientele. Jeff knew Al could use the money. He was saving most of his earnings to help finance educations for his grandchildren.

"I'd like to see it."

Courtney's request put an end to Jeff's musings. "What's that?"

"The book on jazz. Will you show it to me sometime?"

"Sure thing. Tell me, what was your favorite present?"

"Would you believe a bar of soap?" At his baffled expression, Courtney laughed. "The twins decorated it for me. With Mary's help, of course. They brushed gold paint around the border and stuck a decal in the center. Mary dipped it in paraffin to protect the design. I keep it in my dresser drawer as a sachet. I can't bear to use it. Something someone's made for you—particularly a child—is so...dear."

Replete, Jeff settled back against the deck chair. "I don't remember ever getting a handmade gift in my life, but I'm looking forward to a few when I have a family of my own."

Courtney felt her stomach drop. What would he think of her if he knew children didn't figure at all in her future plans? With shaky hands, she collected the last of the debris from their meal and tucked it into the basket.

"Such a neatnik," Jeff commented.

Courtney shrugged. "Force of habit. When I was young, keeping my things in order was the only control I could exert over my life. Besides, being tidy made me more welcome whenever I went to live with another family."

Jeff was touched by the chance remark. Courtney had spent most of her life feeling like a guest in somebody else's house. Suddenly he ached to give her a home of her own, to build a life with her. Without preamble, he heard himself boldly inquire, "Speaking of families—how would you feel about making babies with me?"

Courtney couldn't have been more shocked if he'd slapped her. Her face turned beet red, from anger or embarrassment, she wasn't sure.

"I didn't mean today," he said, unable to hide his amusement.

"Don't even joke about a thing like that."

"I'm not joking." He reached out and hauled her onto his lap. "I think I'm falling in love."

"Jeff, stop it! You don't know me well enough. If you did, you wouldn't—"

He bracketed her face with his hands and stilled her protest with his mouth. His lips were firm, persuasive, and in no time Courtney was kissing him back. How could he do this to her? she wondered vaguely. It was crazy. She couldn't allow herself to melt every time he molded his mouth to hers.

His hands trailed up her back and came around to circle her breasts. She let out an incoherent little cry as her nipples hardened and peaked against his palms.

"Ah, Courtney," Jeff whispered, his warm breath mingling with hers. "You drive me mad."

Even as Courtney told herself she couldn't let this happen, she sensuously raked her nails up his back and thrilled to his answering shudder. What was he doing to her? She'd spent all her adult years fighting the nesting instinct, keeping her emotions locked safely away or sublimating them by playing honorary aunt to other people's children. Now it was as if Jeff had discovered the key to her heart and was turning it ever so slowly and tantalizingly, exposing for all the world to see her deep-seated longing for a mate and a family of her own.

And yet that would never be, she forcefully reminded herself. Fear always outstripped her need. She was like the woman who won a trip to Hawaii but was too afraid to set foot on the plane that would fulfill her lifelong dream.

But with Jeff's tongue flicking in and out of her mouth, imitating a more intimate union, Courtney realized she *was* in danger of losing control. His lips, his tongue, his hands were doing disturbing things to her. She could feel his touch in the most remote nerve endings—places she had no idea were erogenous zones.

It wasn't fair to Jeff to let this continue, to let him believe she was a willing participant, but Courtney was unable to stop kissing him back. With a whimper of despair, she looped her arms about his neck. She couldn't give him up. Not yet. He made her feel so good, so protected, so desired.

But what if Jeff completely penetrated her defenses? What if she got pregnant?

Through a haze of desire, Courtney decided she'd better see her doctor. And soon.

A child was the last thing she wanted.

Chapter Six

By the middle of May, Courtney had completed all the illustrations for Jeff's history books and had easily won his approval of each and every one. With a speed that surprised her, he had the pen-and-ink drawings reduced to the proper size for reproduction. Courtney was pleased that his printer, Pete Baker, had been able to maintain a clarity of line, making it difficult to distinguish the originals from the reproductions. Indeed, they were good enough to be suitable for framing.

Duplicating the watercolors, however, was another matter altogether. Courtney had final say over the five she'd painted to enhance the historical text, and she was less than satisfied with the results. Despite the fact that an exceptionally high quality of paper had been used, some of the colors insisted upon separating. It was a common irritation, and the bane of printers and artists alike.

Though to the man on the street, the illustrations might appear pleasing, to the trained eye they lacked the subtleties of the original work. As a result, Jeff had set up a meeting in his office to discuss the problem with Courtney and Pete.

"Okay, Ms. Hughes," Pete said toward the end of the conference, "I see what you mean. I think I know a way to reduce the separation, but I can't promise perfection. After all, a reproduction's a reproduction."

"I understand. Just do your best. At least try to get rid of these particular overlays." Courtney pointed to several spots where the colors had bled, creating a fuzzy effect. "The rest I can live with."

"Consider it done."

"Thanks, Mr. Baker. I hate to be so picky."

"Picky? Lady, you're a dream to work with. After years in this business, believe me, I have a healthy respect for the artistic temperament. Seeing you're so reasonable, I'll bend over backward to give you my best."

"That's what I pay you for, Pete," Jeff reminded him.

"Exactly, Mr. Herrington." He gathered up the sample print runs. "Will that be all for now?"

"Yes. When can you have the new ones ready?"

"A couple of days."

"Fine."

They discussed a few more details before Pete took his leave. As soon as the door closed behind him, Jeff turned to Courtney.

"Why have you been avoiding me?"

"Avoiding you? I see you almost every other day."

"To talk business. That doesn't count. I've asked you out at least four times in the past two weeks, and you've always had an excuse. Why, Courtney? Did I say or do something to frighten you off?''

"I've been busy."

How could she explain that she was afraid of herself, of her own emotions? While she'd seen her doctor and started on birth control pills, she'd also done her best to deny her feelings, to put some distance between them. She'd even drawn up a list of reasons why she was wrong for Jeff. Why she mustn't encourage his attentions. Logic told her that their only true bond was this project. As soon as it was completed, they would gradually drift apart. Which was to be expected, given their totally divergent backgrounds.

It wasn't smart, she kept reminding herself, to let their relationship go any further than the few heated kisses they'd already shared. She couldn't become entangled in an impossible attraction. She had to protect her heart.

Why, then, had she bothered with the precaution of birth control?

Not until an hour ago did Courtney have a reasonable answer to that question. The moment she'd walked into Jeff's office she knew she was fighting a losing battle. She no longer had the strength to refuse him.

"Come here," he commanded softly.

Courtney's heart contracted. Her feeble attempts at rejection had hurt Jeff. She could see the pain in his eyes and because of it experienced a stab of guilt. God knows she hadn't meant to cause him any grief. She'd suffered too much herself to be the source of another's unhappiness.

She couldn't take her eyes from his as she walked into his arms. He locked his hands around her waist and kissed her brow, her nose, her cheeks, her lips. Tentatively, gently, making her crave more.

"Whatever plans you have for tonight, cancel them."

"Why?" The question quavered on a sigh.

"Because you're going to dinner. With me."

"Business or pleasure?" she breathed, feeling her legs buckle as he nipped the pulse point at her throat.

"Pleasure, purely pleasure." The tip of his tongue flicked out to test its erratic beat. "Always pleasure where you're concerned. Then on Saturday we're going to spend the afternoon at Kings Island. And Sunday, I'm taking you water-skiing."

"I don't know how to water-ski," she feebly protested, clinging to his shoulders to keep from falling.

"I'll teach you. And if you try to manufacture any more excuses why you can't see me, I'll tell Pete to mess up some more of your paintings. That way I'll be sure to get you back in my office. And my arms."

"You didn't!" Courtney found it difficult to think with Jeff's lips charting a path to her earlobe. "Oh-h-h, Jeff, don't do that," she said, trying unsuccessfully to twist out of his embrace. "You didn't...have him...not deliberately."

He chuckled and pulled her closer still. "Not...today. But," he murmured, peppering her neck with tiny love bites, "don't...put it...past me...in the future."

"That's dirty pool."

"Whatever it takes."

By the time his mouth finally returned to hers, she'd given up all thought of warding off his kisses.

It had been eons since Courtney had gone to an amusement park. She wondered if thrill rides had ever delighted her as much when she was a child as they did today with Jeff at her side. They'd already taken turns on the Eiffel Tower, which gave them a bird's-eye view of the park and surrounding area, and King Cobra, which took them in a loop, then spun them upside down. Instead of emerging with an upset stomach, Courtney dragged Jeff off to The Beast, one of the park's most exciting attractions. What, she reasoned, was a visit to Kings Island without a ride on one of its roller coasters?

There weren't many places Courtney liked to visit in memory, but she did have a vague recollection of being securely held by her father for the sudden downhill plunge of her first roller coaster ride. But that could hardly compare with the sensations that blossomed when Jeff's left arm closed protectively about her on their slow climb to the top of the first lift. Being a grown woman cradled by a man as devastating as Jefferson Herrington had a lot to recommend it!

Suddenly the car pitched forward, and her stomach took a vertical drop to the ground. They were racing toward what appeared to be a small dark hole. Courtney's scream died in her throat. She was too terrified to emit a sound. Or to breathe. The black hole gaped wider, and the next second they were careening through a narrow tunnel.

There were two more tunnels and an enclosed helix, angled at a sharp forty-five degrees. Courtney felt rather than saw the banked track. After the second incline, she shut her eyes and buried her head in Jeff's shoulder.

Jeff enjoyed having Courtney strain against him for support. The bones of her slender body felt fragile, almost childlike. She'd tensed up on the initial plunge. On the next, her vocal chords had allowed her no more than a single, frightened squeal. With a surge of protectiveness, he tightened his hold. For some reason he liked having her depend on him—if only briefly—for safety, reassurance. He'd spent so many years under the thumb of his father that it felt good being in charge. Not that he didn't wield a lot of power as president of Herrington Press, but he would never be completely in control as long as J. E. kept a hand, however remote, in the business. With Courtney he felt needed. And not merely now when the sensation of physical danger was manufactured. He believed that together they could complete each other, fulfill what was lacking in each other's lives. With his other hand, he reached over to clasp her head securely against his chest.

Far too soon for Jeff the ride ended.

"You can look now," he teased as the car glided to a stop.

Feeling slightly foolish, Courtney took a deep breath and sat up. She blinked as she opened her eyes to the light. "Are we having fun yet?"

Jeff took her hand and helped her out. "Want to go again? The line isn't too long for a change."

"I can wait—for another hundred years or so."

"Chicken."

"Sticks and stones—and roller coasters—may break my bones, but words will never hurt me," she improvised.

"Very well, how about something tamer? You a good shot?"

Courtney angled him a wry look. "There's a contradiction in that question somewhere."

"I was thinking of that booth with the wooden ducks. If you shoot them all down, you win a prize."

"I'd do better throwing a baseball at pop bottles," she said self-mockingly. "Which isn't saying much. I think I mentioned I never seem to hit where I aim. How about you?"

"Let's find out."

Walking toward the game area, Courtney remembered a time long ago when her father had knocked down a stack of glass bottles to win her a green rabbit. Funny, she hadn't thought about it for years. Whatever happened to that stuffed animal, anyway? Somehow, in all her moves, it had disappeared—like most of her possessions.

Instinctively, she fingered the locket at her throat. Her mother's locket. The one inheritance she'd managed to hang onto.

"Why so quiet? You weren't that frightened by The Beast, were you?"

Jeff's questions drew Courtney back to the present. "No," she admitted, "just thinking. I bet you're pretty good with a rifle."

"I used to be a fair shot. Never for game—killing birds and animals didn't appeal to me. But my father took me skeet shooting. Not for recreation, mind you. He felt it was important to hone one's reflexes. We'll see if I still have the touch."

He did, and Courtney had her choice of a Kewpie doll or a stuffed animal.

"What's your pleasure, my lady," Jeff asked.

"Since there aren't any green rabbits, I'll take that St. Bernard dog."

With a grimace, the man in charge of the game handed over the prize.

"What's this about green rabbits?" Jeff asked as they strolled down the midway.

Courtney told him the story, leaving out the part about the toy's mysterious disappearance. To steer the conversation away from her, she took hold of his arm and announced, "Now let me ask you a question. I'm dying of curiosity. What does the *E* in your name stand for?"

"That's easy. It—" When she pulled a wry face, he stopped short, then recognizing the unintentional pun, broke into a laugh. "Let me rephrase that. The *E*'s for Edward. When I was a kid, I wanted to be known as Ed."

"Why?"

He winced. "Because my mother insisted upon calling me 'young Jefferson'—her way of distinguishing me from my father—and everyone else followed suit. Even though Dad went by J. E., Mother disliked initials— thought they weren't dignified enough—and always referred to Dad by his given name. I suspect she may have hoped people would link us to Thomas Jefferson. Not that I would have minded being mistaken for his descendant, but Jefferson just sounded too pompous for a kid. So I latched onto my middle name. Much to my regret, I could never get it to stick. Only later—after I'd bloodied a few noses—did I succeed in getting family and friends to call me Jeff. Believe me, that was quite an accomplishment."

"I can imagine." Courtney's eyes connected with his. "I gather you don't appreciate being a third?"

He shrugged. "It's all right."

"It has such—" Courtney nuzzled her cheek against the stuffed animal and searched for the right word "—continuity. Family and all. That's nice."

"I suppose, but it lacks something in individuality."

"You feel the need for that?"

"In a manner of speaking. Being the heir of a prominent family has its restrictions."

"Poor baby."

Though her tone was light, Jeff felt suddenly ashamed. Here he was complaining when Courtney had no parents, no roots, no close kin. Even if the Herrington wealth hadn't insulated him against pain or tragedy, he couldn't justify feeling sorry for himself. Unlike Courtney, he'd been incredibly blessed.

Somewhat awkwardly he indicated the St. Bernard. "Will you give him a name?"

"What makes you think it's a him?"

"Size. That animal's much too big to be a girl.'

"You have a point." She pursed her lips, considering, then darted Jeff a mischievous smile. "How does Fritz the First grab you?"

"I'm not sure. Does that mean you expect more furry gifts from me in the future?"

"If you think I'm hinting about a mink, forget it. I like my animals alive—unless they're the stuffed toy variety."

"I quite agree."

She looked over a shoulder and lifted her eyes to his. "Is that your wallet or your conscience speaking?"

Jeff looped an arm around her waist and locked her to his side. "Neither. It's more a matter of preference. You can't put a price tag on love."

Yes, you can, Courtney silently disagreed, but her mind wasn't on a dollar sign. *You can ask something money can't buy, something the other's not prepared to give you. Such as babies.*

"Is anything wrong?"

Surprised by the question, Courtney brushed aside the gloomy thought. "What makes you think that?"

"You've gone all somber on me again."

"Hey," she said, keeping her voice cheerful, "planning a day at an amusement park is serious business. I don't want to miss anything."

"Okay, then, what'll be next?"

"While I'm deciding, how about an ice cream cone?"

"You got it." Grinning, he steered her toward the nearest concession stand.

Jeff suggested winding up the day at a small jazz bar where they tarried over a late-night snack. One of Courtney's questions led to another, and before Jeff realized what was happening, he was talking about his childhood, particularly how much he'd resented being sent off to boarding school.

"At first I felt rejected, but in time I accepted the decision as one made in my best interest. My parents wanted me to have a first-rate education."

Jeff could have counted on the fingers of one hand the number of people who knew about his strained relationship with his parents. He'd told Courtney, not because he was making a bid for her sympathy but because he had a strong desire to share everything with her. He wanted her to know him as well as he knew himself.

But when he took her back to her apartment, he purposely refrained from giving her more than a good-night kiss. After the other morning in his office, neither had mentioned again her tendency to avoid him, but Jeff suspected her wariness had something to do with his reckless comment about making babies. The remark had been a mistake, and he wasn't about to compound it. But curbing his natural instincts required almost more self-control than he possessed.

Jeff let her feel his frustration as he slid his tongue in and out of her mouth. Both of them were breathless by the time he forced himself to draw away.

"I'll pick you up about one o'clock tomorrow afternoon," he said in an effort to steady himself. "If this hot weather holds, we'll get a real jump on the water-skiing season."

"You forget that you're dealing with a woman who almost flunked phys. ed."

"I don't believe that for a minute. You'll catch on fast. It's almost as big a thrill as The Beast, especially when you learn to cross over the waves made in the wake of the boat."

Courtney's eyes rose heavenward. "I can hardly wait."

He tweaked the tip of her nose and was gone.

Courtney hugged Fritz against her middle and watched Jeff bound down her steps. She was touched by his efforts to make her feel comfortable with him. He could have shown off by asking her to the symphony or a fancy party, but he seemed to sense that she preferred him to keep their dating simple. After all, what was the point of meeting his friends when she knew their relationship was doomed?

Tomorrow they would spend a pleasant afternoon on his boat, and she'd make an attempt at learning to water-ski. And at keeping her heart safely locked away.

"That's it!" Jeff shouted from the helm of his motorboat. "Remember to keep the tips of your skis up."

Despite his encouragement, Courtney found the job of trying to put on skis while wearing a bulky life jacket a cumbersome feat. "And that's a deliberate pun," she mumbled to herself.

Jeff cupped a hand to his ear. "I can't hear you. Speak up."

"I think this requires more coordination than I can muster," she yelled above the idling motor.

"You're doing fine. Grab the line."

"Got it."

"Put it between your legs."

Courtney shivered, not so much from the cold as from the anticipation.

"Ready?" he called.

Crouched and gripping the handhold on the line that linked her to Jeff's boat, knees bent, the tops of her skis pointed up, Courtney braced herself for Jeff's acceleration. The boat pulled her slowly at first, then picked up speed.

"Now," he hollered.

Courtney straightened. To her amazement she actually rose up out of the water. One second she was on her skis, the next she was belly-up. As instructed, the moment she swamped, she let go of the line and waited until Jeff circled to help her get back in position.

After two more attempts, she finally knew the joy of a short ride over the surface of the Ohio. She felt like a bird. Daring, free, happy.

She loved it!

She swamped again.

This time when Jeff looped back, she grinned up at him. "I think I'm hooked. In more ways than one."

"Didn't I tell you it's a great sensation? You tired yet?"

"Hey, I'm just getting the hang of it. That taste of the real action only makes me want more."

The next time she stayed up so long that the muscles in her arms and legs began to burn. Reluctantly, she signaled her desire for time-out with a wave of her hand. As Jeff reduced his speed, she sank inch by slow inch into the water.

"Had enough?"

"Nope. Just give me a minute to recover." She yanked away the wet strands of hair plastered to her cheeks. "Stopping myself naturally was really something. Such a great sense of control!"

"What have I created? A sea monster?"

"A water worshipper! I want another long turn."

"Okay, one more time. But don't overdo it. The river's getting crowded, and you don't want to sap your energy. You need your wits about you. Climb back in for a minute, and we'll try to outrun some of this traffic."

"What are a few boats?" she asked, feeling cocky. "I don't want to go through all that business of putting on skis again. Only one more short ride. Please?"

Jeff frowned and assessed the degree of congestion. It wasn't too bad, but he would like it better if there were fewer craft out. Yet he didn't want to undermine her confidence. To his surprise, she'd even tried criss-crossing a couple of waves. "All right," he finally agreed. "But no stunts. Straight skiing behind me. We'll work on the more advanced stuff another day."

"Promise." Impishly, she gave him a mock cross with the tips of her skis.

Jeff laughed and revved up the motor. Courtney popped out of the water like a pro. The wind grabbed at her cap of curls, tossing them in wild array about her face. With the sun caught in her short, feathery hair and excitement radiating from her smile, she couldn't have looked more enticing. Equally as riveting were her long legs, shown to advantage by the French cut of her emerald suit. Jeff was torn between guiding the boat and keeping an eye on Courtney. He could look at her all day and never be bored.

For a moment he concentrated on steering out of the way of a speedboat, then glanced behind him, only to discover that Courtney had disappeared. Alarmed, he hastily scanned the area for a sign of her skis. If she went under, she was supposed to hold them up to mark her spot and warn other boats of her whereabouts. When he didn't see them, he panicked. Instantly his heart set up a furious thundering in his chest.

Courtney gulped water, choked and sputtered. While Jeff wasn't watching, she'd gotten carried away in her exuberance and tried to lift one ski out of the water. Because she wasn't ready for the fancy footwork, she'd quickly lost her balance.

Bobbing up, she gasped for air. Somehow both her skis had slipped off. She was groping for them when out of nowhere came the roar of a motor. Turning her head, she was momentarily paralyzed by the sight of a powerboat bearing down on her. As it filled her vision, her body was jolted by a spurt of adrenaline. Reflexively, she shot her arms up in warning just as the high-speed craft swerved to miss her.

Jeff's stomach lurched. He'd spotted Courtney barely a second before the other pilot had veered off course. As swiftly as he could, he maneuvered his way back to where she was swimming. His heart was still hammering wildly as he leaned over the side of the boat and pulled her from the water.

"Let me get my skis," she wailed.

"The hell with the skis," he snapped, his fear giving way to anger. "You almost got yourself killed."

"I'm sorry. I couldn't resist—"

"You're shaking." He removed her life jacket and wrapped a blanket around her. "Don't move. I'll get the skis. Then we're out of here."

Jeff dived into the water as much to cool his temper as to retrieve his equipment. He would have liked leaving the damned things where they were, but they might cause an accident. Once he was back on board and had stored the ladder and ski line, he headed upstream.

Neither of them spoke until they were safely anchored in a quiet niche. Like the day of their picnic, overhanging willows provided both shade and privacy. While Jeff silently poured her some coffee from the thermos, Courtney marveled at how adept he was at discovering these hideaways. Did he purposely seek them out when he needed to escape from the hectic world of publishing?

"Thank you," she said as he handed her the plastic mug. She took a tentative sip, then glanced at him. The peaceful setting was at odds with his emotions. She'd angered him before, but never like this. His lips were set in a grim line; his shoulders were rigid. Blue veins stood out in his neck, and his jaw appeared carved in granite. Clad only in a black bikini, he looked for all the world like a savage warrior.

Using her free hand, Courtney pulled the blanket more securely around her. "I'm sorry," she ventured, remorseful that her foolhardiness had spoiled their day together.

"Don't ever do that to me again. God, Courtney, I thought I was going to lose you."

"I'm sorry," she repeated. "I guess I went a little overboard." When he didn't return her smile at the wordplay, she tried again. "But I was having so much fun. I can't remember when I've had such a relaxing day."

"Relaxing?" Jeff raked a hand through his thick hair. "I'm shaking like a leaf."

Guiltily, Courtney laid aside her cup and went to him. Circling his waist, she touched her lips to his bare chest. "I was being very selfish. Forgive me."

A shudder ripped through him, and his hands tunneled into her soft curls. "It's all right, baby. Nobody's hurt. Everything's all right."

It was as necessary to convince himself as to reassure Courtney. A second before the boat had swung sharply around her, his mind had conjured up another time, another accident.

"Thank God that navigator had quick reflexes. If he'd been drinking—" Jeff stopped himself and squeezed his eyes shut, blotting out the image of what might have been.

He brought his arms around Courtney and pulled her against him. He needed the closeness. Needed to feel the warmth of her body, the steady rise and fall of her chest, the beat of her pulse at his temple. Tipping up her head, he ran a thumb along the curve of her jaw and slowly lowered his mouth to hers.

The kiss was tender and consoling. Without uttering a sound, Jeff's lips told her how much he yearned for her, how much she was cherished. His hands played over her sun-warmed skin, both worshipping and heating the sensitive flesh.

A soft sigh trembled from Courtney's lips as she linked her fingers at the nape of his neck and clung to him like the lifeline he'd become. When it had happened she didn't know, but he was her center, her universe. She couldn't think anymore about leaving him—no matter how inevitable their parting. All she could focus on was the fullness of his lips as they claimed hers, the crush of her breasts against his hair-roughened chest, the spread of his legs imprisoning her thighs.

Jeff slid his hand lower, splaying his fingers against her bottom to bring her hard against his arousal. He lowered the straps of her maillot, and the top fell away. His palm rotated over her nipples before his mouth skimmed down her throat, over her collarbone, along the mound of her breasts. When his lips covered one pink tip, she arched her back and cried out.

For a fleeting moment Jeff wondered if he was taking advantage, if she was vulnerable from the shock, if he should break away. But he'd been more shaken than Courtney. And her lips, her hands were telling him she wanted this as much as he did.

A myriad of sensations overtook her. Courtney never knew she could feel so vulnerable, yet so protected. She wanted to give as much as she took; she wanted to please as much as she was pleased. Jeff's body was tense with restraint, and she knew he was purposely holding himself back. That more than anything made her throw caution aside. She slipped her fingers beneath the waistband of his bikini and edged it over his hips. She felt rather than heard his moan and met it by boldly invading his mouth.

If anything, the danger had heightened their senses, making them more attuned to each other. Their tongues darted and dueled. Their knees bent, and somehow Courtney ended up with her back on the wooden deck

FREE! gold-plated chain

You'll love your elegant 20k gold electroplated chain! The necklace is finely crafted with 160 double-soldered links and is electroplate finished in genuine 20k gold. And it's yours FREE as added thanks for giving our Reader Service a try!

Silhouette Special Edition®

FREE-OFFER CARD

4 FREE BOOKS

FREE GOLD-PLATED CHAIN

FREE MYSTERY BONUS

PLACE HEART STICKER HERE

FREE-HOME DELIVERY

FREE FACT-FILLED NEWSLETTER

MORE SURPRISES THROUGHOUT THE YEAR—FREE

☑ **YES!** Please send me four Silhouette Special Edition® novels, free, along with my free gold-plated chain and my free mystery gift as explained on the opposite page.

235 CIS R1YT
(U-SIL-SE-08/90)

NAME _____

ADDRESS _____ APT. _____

CITY _____ STATE _____

ZIP CODE _____

Remember! To receive your free books, gold-plated chain and mystery gift, return the postpaid card below. But don't delay!

DETACH AND MAIL CARD TODAY!

MAIL THE POSTPAID CARD TODAY!

BUSINESS REPLY CARD

FIRST CLASS MAIL   PERMIT NO. 717   BUFFALO, NY

POSTAGE WILL BE PAID BY ADDRESSEE

SILHOUETTE BOOKS
901 FUHRMANN BLVD
PO BOX 1867
BUFFALO NY 14240-9952

NO POSTAGE
NECESSARY
IF MAILED
IN THE
UNITED STATES

of the boat. She was vaguely aware when Jeff grabbed a floating mattress and wedged it beneath her.

"Are you sure?"

"Yes, I'm sure," she breathed.

He braced himself above her and brushed a damp tendril from her forehead. "Good. And in case you're wondering, you don't need to worry. That is... I guess there's no delicate way to put this, but I've never...I've always been ... careful."

"So have I."

He smiled. "Give me a minute. I can protect you."

She caught his wrist as he started to push away. Unable to meet his eyes, she shyly confessed, "I've already taken care of that."

"Oh, Courtney. You can't know how that makes me feel."

"Hush," she ordered, "and kiss me. I think I'm developing a fetish for your lips."

"Is that all that interests you?"

"Right now," she admitted unsteadily, "I'm in no condition to catalog your virtues." *Or,* she silently amended, *to list all the reasons why I'm in love with you.*

There was no doubt in Courtney's mind that she did love Jeff. Against all odds, it had happened. She'd gone and fallen in love. And with a man she couldn't have. But she no longer had the strength to fight it. Maybe Jeff's reaction to her brush with death today had weakened her will. Or maybe it had prompted her to own up to her feelings. At the moment she didn't care.

Without hesitation, she closed her fingers intimately around him, eliciting a harsh intake of air. "But I have noticed another part of your anatomy seems to be clamoring for my attention."

"I was wrong. You're not a sea monster. You're a siren."

"Stop talking and make love with me."

"My pleasure."

The prelude to intimacy was as tender as it was passionate. Lost in their own private world, they gave themselves up to sensuous exploration. Her fingertips charted each muscle and sinew of his well-honed body. His lips adored very inch of her soft flesh. A slow heat built wherever they touched until neither could bear separation a moment longer.

Together at last, they climaxed in an explosion that left them both spent and shaken.

Afterward they lay huddled beneath Jeff's blanket and watched the sun edge lower in the sky.

Courtney was the first to break the silence. "We should be getting back."

"What's the hurry? You got a hot date tonight or something?"

"I had a hot date this afternoon. Tonight is up for grabs."

"In that case—" He reached for her and covered her mouth with his.

When they finally broke for air, Courtney sighed. "This could become addictive."

"Be careful. That kind of talk turns me on."

"Really?" She rolled on top of him, then gasped, startled to learn he wasn't lying.

His fingers circled her neck. "You can't say I didn't warn you," he said and pulled her mouth to his.

Chapter Seven

Dinner...with your parents?" Nervously Courtney wound the phone cord around her little finger. "And the ballet?"

"Yes, the ballet," Jeff affirmed. "You know, women in tutus, men in tights. Dancing together on a stage." His voice took on a pronounced huskiness. "It can be very sexy."

"I know what a ballet is!" Courtney snapped.

"Well, that's a relief. For a second there you sounded as if I were inviting you to witness an execution."

"It may well be. Mine. Especially since your mother and father will be sitting with us."

"Come on, sweetheart. They're not ogres. This benefit is important to them. Mother's always been one for causes, and the Children's Home happens to be her pet project."

"Is that why you're taking me? Because I once stayed there?"

"You know better. But now that you mention it, I couldn't have picked a more appropriate date. It's the perfect time for you to get to know my folks."

"*Folks* is hardly the word I'd choose to describe your parents. If I remember correctly, your father has a distinctly regal air. He's definitely not the down-home type. And I bet your mother would feel quite comfortable sipping tea with Queen Elizabeth."

"As a matter of fact—"

"Don't tell me. I'd rather not know about how she hobnobs with the high and mighty."

"So we're listed in the Social Register. Big deal. Say yes, Court. It's time you stepped into my world."

Courtney was struck dumb by Jeff's use of her nickname. Recovering her voice, she observed, "You've never called me that before."

"What?"

"Court."

"Isn't that what you prefer? What your closest friends call you?"

"I guess so."

"Don't get me wrong. I think Courtney's a beautiful name. But the shortened version sounds more... intimate." The hushed overtone of the last word was decidedly suggestive.

"Jeff. Somebody might be listening in."

"I don't care if they are. I don't care if the world knows how I feel about you. In case you haven't noticed, I'm kind of stuck on you, Court. For lots of reasons. Damned few people have your kind of guts."

"That's very flattering—I think."

"It was meant to be."

"But I'm not ready for a public announcement concerning our private lives."

"I promise to be the soul of discretion. On one condition—that you agree to the ballet. After dinner," he tacked on, knowing full well how much she enjoyed food.

"That's bribery."

"All's fair in love and war."

"You're a hard man, Herrington. Very well, I'll go. But I'll be a basket case between now and then."

"Hmm. That sounds like a good excuse to sweep you off your feet and carry you into the theater."

"If you do," she said with sham sweetness, "I'll call you Jefferson."

Her threat prompted an exaggerated groan. "Best behavior. Cross my heart."

Cradling the receiver, Courtney reflected that she could probably have found some way to worm out of Jeff's unexpected invitation if he didn't hold her in the palm of his hand. But she didn't want to disappoint him. She loved him too much. Nor could she bear to miss an opportunity to be with him.

Their time together was growing short.

Courtney smiled at Jeff, then twirled slowly around. The soft fabric of her new and only silk dress caressed her stockinged legs. She felt feminine and slightly daring in the shocking pink, cocktail-length gown that dipped to a low V in the back but modestly skimmed her collarbone in front. The long sleeves and fitted bodice complemented her slender form, and the black leather heels added several inches to her stature, bringing her head even with Jeff's broad shoulders.

"Do I pass?" she asked, uncertain if her bare back would meet with his approval. Though she had some reservations about the style, she'd been unable to resist the dress and on a whim had bought it.

Jeff's appreciative whistle lent her confidence, a feeling she knew wouldn't last. But for the moment, she cherished it.

"Lady, you more than pass. You go to the head of the class in that little number."

"It doesn't bare too much skin in the back, does it?" She had no desire to cause Jeff embarrassment by appearing in something inappropriate. Though Mary had all but signed a written guarantee that she looked every inch the elegant woman, Courtney still had her doubts. "I have a basic black I can change into if you think—"

"You take off that dress, and we'll never make it out of this apartment."

She blushed. "Then I guess it will have to do."

"You look spectacular. I'll be the envy of every man at the benefit."

"Humph. I bet you're the youngest guy there. All the other men will probably be pushing a hundred if they're a day."

"Don't count on it." He snaked out a hand and grabbed her wrist. "Come here and let me mess up your lipstick."

Warmed by his admiration, Courtney did her best not to feel too smug. "I don't think that's a good idea."

His lips hovered over hers. Against them, he murmured, "You're right. I could never stop with a kiss." He ground his hips against her. "See what just looking at you does to me."

"Jeff! For shame."

"Shame has nothing to do with it. As I'll demonstrate after the ballet."

She laughed to cover the tremor that raced up her spine. "I think it's time we got on our way."

When Courtney opened the door, she was taken aback to find the twins ready to ring her bell.

"Julie. Jenny. What are you doing here? Goodness, is your mother sick?"

"No." Mary's voice came from the stairwell. "But they wouldn't give me any rest until I let them see you. Do you mind?"

"Of course not."

"You look just like Cinderella," Jenny piped up, awe unmistakable in her childish voice.

"And Jeff's the prince," Julie giggled.

Mary nodded her assent. "You make a handsome pair. I like the tux, Jeff."

"Thanks, but, to be honest, I prefer jeans."

"Well," she clucked, "we all must make these little sacrifices."

Jeff's grin was lopsided. "Methinks the woman's envious."

"Smart ass," Mary returned, but her smile was warm.

Jenny wagged a finger. "Mommy said a bad word."

"See what you started?" Mary chided Jeff. To Jenny she announced, "Mommies aren't infallible."

Julie yanked on her skirt. "Can we go get ice cream now?"

"What a perfect exit line. Have a good time, you two." The wink she sent Courtney said worlds.

The charity committee, their families and special guests were invited to the gala dinner held at one of

Cincinnati's finest hotels. It was an imposing crowd of the rich and glamorous that greeted Jeff and Courtney as they entered the dining room. A waiter showed them to their table where the elder Herringtons were already seated.

Jeff's father rose at their approach. "Ms. Hughes. So nice to see you again."

Courtney extended her hand. "Mr. Herrington."

"May I present my wife. Grace, this is Courtney Hughes of Hughes Designs. You remember my mentioning her."

"Of course. How do you do, Ms. Hughes."

The corners of Grace Herrington's mouth turned up in a meager smile. If her curiosity had been aroused, it was carefully hidden behind a mask of composure. Courtney wasn't given a chance to ponder what might be going through the woman's mind since introductions to the rest of the party at the table followed. There was a youngish couple—Elizabeth Kendall and David Donahue—as well as three others. One turned out to be Herbert Williams, a city councilman and, as Courtney's luck would have it, Nat Hamilton's opponent in the November race.

"Mr. Williams is a close family friend," J. E. Herrington explained somewhat stiffly. "As is his wife, Frances."

"I'm pleased to meet you both. Mr. Williams, Mrs. Williams."

Frances was a plump middle-aged matron with a kindly face. She returned Courtney's genuine smile while allowing her husband to speak for her. "The pleasure is ours, my dear."

Courtney accepted his hand and tilted her head. "Are you sure? I must tell you that I'm the one designing your opponent's campaign literature."

Herbert Williams's brows rose in surprise. "You don't say?"

"Oh, but I *do*," Courtney avowed, determined not to spend the evening tiptoeing on eggs. But from the dubious expression with which Mrs. Herrington eyed her, she wasn't certain she'd acted wisely. *Nice going, Courtney,* she admonished herself. *First tactical error of the evening, and it turns out to be a double whammy. With your usual bluntness, you've managed to irk Jeff's mother and alienate his father's best friend.* To make amends and soften the announcement, she hastily added, "Nat Hamilton's a friend of my favorite art teacher. That's how I got the job."

"Is that right?" Williams smiled. "I may be in trouble. I've seen some of your work."

"You have?" Courtney gulped, astonished at the councilman's good-natured response. What a charmer! Small wonder Williams was so well liked in political circles and a favorite of the voters. She'd heard Nat was in for a close race, and she was beginning to see why.

"Yes," he responded. "Since my grandfather was one of those early Cincinnati publishers Jeff's celebrating in his latest book, he shared some of your illustrations with me. I'd say Nat's fortunate to have you on his team."

"Keep talking like that, and I may vote for you yet."

Williams laughed. "Wherever did you find this enchanting creature, Jeff?"

"She's not a creature, Herb," Jeff politely informed him, "but a very bright as well as beautiful woman."

"You're quite right. I stand corrected."

Jeff acknowledged the apology with a courteous smile. "To answer your question," he continued, "we met over a business matter. But that's another story."

"I must hear it sometime. Meanwhile, I'd say it's our good fortune to have you as a dinner companion, my dear."

"Thank you," Courtney replied, beginning to relax despite Grace Herrington's frown. So what if she wasn't batting a thousand according to Her Eminence's social standards? David Donahue had engaged Mrs. Williams in conversation, and neither of them was behaving as if she'd disgraced herself. As for the councilman, he appeared genuinely delighted by her candor, even if he was merely putting on an act.

Like it or not, Courtney could never pretend to be other than what she was—an honest, forthright, middle-class working woman. She might as well get her background out in the open, too, and was considering how to broach the subject when Herb Williams handed her the perfect opportunity.

"Have you always lived in Cincinnati, Ms. Hughes?" he asked pleasantly.

"Yes, I was born here. In fact, for a few weeks I was placed in the very home that the ballet is benefiting."

"Now that *is* a coincidence," Herb said genially.

"Not so," a sultry voice from behind contradicted. "I know Jeff. He leaves nothing to chance."

"Amelia!" Jeff's head snapped around at the same time that he rose from his seat. "How are you?"

"Fine, darling." She bussed him on the cheek, then let her fingers trail down his neck and over his collar. As if it were an afterthought, she swiveled her head toward Courtney. "I don't believe I've met your... companion."

"Courtney, this is Amelia Meyer. Amelia, Courtney Hughes."

Courtney died a little inside. She recognized the name. This was the woman Jeff had been seeing when they met. Arranging her features into a smile, she said, "Jeff's mentioned you."

"He has? Now that's a surprise. But then we do go way back." Amelia pivoted so that her breasts brushed Jeff's sleeve. "Don't we, Jeff?"

"Dr. Meyer and Dad were college roommates," Jeff inserted for Courtney's benefit. "But don't let us keep you, Amelia. Where are you sitting?"

"Why, right across from you, darling." With a flourish she indicated the one empty seat at their table.

The other men stood, and Jeff's father pulled out Amelia's chair. All the while Jeff wondered if his mother had manipulated the seating arrangements. He wouldn't put it past Grace to have switched place cards in order to throw him and Amelia together. His mother reinforced the suspicion when he observed her leaning forward to cover the younger woman's hand and smile warmly.

"Amelia," Grace Herrington said, "it's so good to see you again."

"Just like old times, isn't it? With one exception, of course." She stared icily in Courtney's direction before returning her attention to Grace. "But then Jeff does like to play the field. We must be patient with him."

Courtney saw a muscle in Jeff's jaw twitch. Was Amelia telling the truth? Was she simply another diversion in a long line of diversions?

Exactly what did she expect? Hadn't she told herself all along that they were wrong for each other? Didn't she know what they had together was only temporary?

She felt Jeff's hand on her knee and jerked away. Though Amelia was still smarting from Jeff's desertion, she clearly expected to win him back. And with just cause. She was definitely more his style. If nothing else, her sleek black gown made a resounding statement about class. Probably a Dior. Or whoever the current designer of choice happened to be. What did Courtney know? She couldn't tell a Gucci bag from a leatherette imitation. How could she ever hope to compete with a woman like Amelia? A woman from a privileged background.

Why was she even considering throwing her hat in the ring, anyway? Just looking at Amelia gave her an inferiority complex. She felt like a broken fingernail on a perfectly manicured hand. And one whiff of that heavenly perfume the woman wore was enough to cinch the image.

Courtney squirmed uncomfortably. Suddenly her long-sleeved, full-skirted pink frock seemed frumpy.

"Excuse me," a waiter said, interrupting her thoughts and draping a linen napkin across her lap. The server following him set a shrimp cocktail before her.

Somehow, Courtney managed to swallow her food and pretend to be enjoying herself. With Herb Williams and Jeff's father carrying the brunt of the conversation, she was mercifully spared having to say very much.

But afterward, she was unable to recall a single item on the menu. For all she knew, she might have spent the evening dining on cardboard.

On the drive to the theater, Jeff coaxed, "Don't let Amelia get to you. She still hasn't forgiven me for not marrying her, but all that we had in common were workaholic fathers and a desire to make a better life for our children."

"It went that far? You discussed children?"

"Not in so many words, but we complained a lot about our absentee fathers. And about getting sent away to boarding school. We both appreciated the fact that neither promoted a warm family life. But discuss marriage and family? No. Besides, one doesn't discuss things with Amelia."

Courtney permitted herself a wan smile. "I noticed."

"Even if we had married, it would have been to please our parents. Both sets are eager for grandchildren. And since they're good friends, well, they'd hoped to have them in common. Added to that, Amelia feels her biological clock ticking away, and she's ready to find a mate. In our circle, most of the men her age are already taken. And she would like someone from . . . someone who understands her tastes."

"In other words, someone with the right pedigree."

"That's one way to put it."

"Someone like you."

He stopped for a light and turned to face her. "I was convenient. Seeing another woman on my arm reminded her I'm no longer available. When Amelia isn't having an attack of jealousy, she'd be the first to admit that we were never in love."

"From her performance this evening, I wouldn't have guessed it. She gave me the impression that you—"

"That I played around a lot but always came back to her? Not true, but I suppose to preserve her ego, it's what she'd like to think. You may find it hard to believe, but under different circumstances Amelia can be quite pleasant."

"I'll take your word for it," she said, softening the retort with a smile.

The light turned green, and Jeff crossed a busy intersection, then picked up the thread of their conversation. "Before we leave this subject, I want you to know something else. I may have done my share of dating, but that doesn't mean I made a practice of hopping into bed with every woman I asked out."

"So you were selective." Courtney shrugged as if she couldn't care less. "It's none of my affair. I don't know why we're even having this conversation."

"Don't you? Tell me, Court, what's really eating you? Are you still troubled by Amelia? Or is it my playboy reputation you can't dismiss?"

"I don't see why you bother trying to justify yourself to me." She bent her head and toyed with the strap on her evening bag. "This isn't going to work."

"What isn't going to work?"

"Us. You and me."

"How can you be so sure?"

"How can you be so obtuse?" Courtney shot back, cloaking her vulnerability in anger. "Wasn't it obvious tonight? I don't fit in."

"What's fitting in?"

"Being to the manor born for one thing. Suffering from a two-for complex doesn't cut it in your crowd."

"What the hell's a two-for complex?"

"Reading menus from right to left. Always looking for bargains. Trying to stretch your pocketbook by getting two things for the price of one."

To her surprise, he threw back his head and laughed. "Oh, Court, the wealthy aren't immune to that malady. How do you think some of the robber barons built those fabulous fortunes? Certainly not by being careless with money. When it comes right down to it, everybody loves a bargain. The trick is to know when you've found a genuine one."

"That leaves me out. I can't tell real diamonds from paste, sable from fake fur—"

"That stuff's boring, not to mention insignificant. It doesn't even make the top ten thousand—not in any scheme of real values." He reached out to take her hand in his. "Whether we do or don't wear designer suits is immaterial. The only thing that matters, the only important thing, is how well we *suit* each other. And have no doubt about it, Ms. Hughes, you suit me just fine."

Touched by the compliment but afraid to let herself hope, Courtney fell back on humor. Reclaiming her hand, she protested, "Oh, you publishers do have a way with words."

As if to prove her point, Jeff murmured in a low voice, "To be specific, you fit me like a glove."

A fiery blush stole over Courtney's face. "You have a dirty mind, Jefferson Herrington."

"Wrong. I have a very provocative woman. And if I weren't driving a car in city traffic, I'd pull over to the side of the road and show her just how deeply she affects me."

The ballet passed in a blur of music and color. Jeff's parents remained stiffly correct and tolerant of her presence, but after Courtney had allowed Amelia to ruin her dinner, she refused to let them spoil the rest of her evening.

Since it was quite late by the time the dancers had taken their half-dozen curtain calls, Courtney was surprised when Jeff turned east rather than west in the direction of her apartment.

"Aren't you going into the office tomorrow?" she asked.

"I skip an occasional Saturday morning. How about you? Anything pressing?"

"Nothing that can't wait."

He grinned. "Are you reforming?"

"Do pigs fly? No, I'm finally about caught up. Having finished a commission for a certain history of printing."

"I was hoping that might free up some of your time. Then you won't object to spending the night at my place."

"Awfully sure of yourself, aren't you?"

He threw her a sideways glance. "You've never seen my house. I'd like to show it to you."

Courtney smiled, pleased that he wanted to share another facet of his life with her. "I'd like that," she said before teasingly charging, "even though you've confessed to an ulterior motive. But what will Rudy think?"

"Probably the same thing that Herb did. 'Wherever did you find this enchanting woman?'" he mimicked.

"I believe he called me a creature."

"I assure you, Rudy has better manners. But if he should slip up, I promise to set him straight."

Jeff's home was far more magnificent than Courtney had imagined. The downstairs was spacious and, though no light—either natural or artificial—filtered through the sheer draperies, she had an impression of airiness. Simple but dignified modern furnishings managed to combine taste with comfort. Plump cushions invited guests to sink onto them. Thick rugs tempted visitors to kick off their shoes. Low wooden tables encouraged them to prop up their feet.

And color! Jeff's home celebrated a profusion of shades. From dark indigos to soft powder-blues, bright reds to muted pinks, kelly greens to aquamarines, deep golds to sunshine yellows, and somehow all the tones blended together like a giant bouquet of flowers.

The combinations were an artist's dream, and Courtney eyed them with full appreciation for the decorator's palette. It crossed her mind that Julie and Jenny could play here without constant reminders to be careful.

Still, it seemed a waste for a single man to occupy so many rooms, and Courtney was frank enough to say so.

"Sometimes I feel guilty about that," Jeff admitted. "When I had the architect draw up the blueprints, I wasn't planning to live alone for long."

"You weren't? Who was—?" She broke off, not certain she wanted to hear the answer.

"She died," Jeff said with such directness that the breath caught in Courtney's throat.

For a long moment silence hung between them. Suddenly Courtney felt her legs would no longer support her, and she sank onto a couch. "I'm so sorry. You never mentioned—"

"That was unfair of me, I know." Jeff loosened his tie and dropped down beside her. "Victoria's a part of my past. I won't lie to you. I'll never forget her, but years ago, I realized I had to let go and live in the present."

"Tell me about her," Courtney whispered.

"We met in the East when we were college seniors. Both of us were terribly idealistic—we had that in common. Before long we were also very much in love, but we decided to postpone marriage until we'd had a chance to get started on our careers. Vicky was a modern woman, and she was determined to find her niche in the banking world. Though she wasn't totally committed to having a career, she did want an opportunity to prove that she could make it on her own.

"To accommodate me, she found a position here in Cincinnati so that we could be together. We gave ourselves two years before we planned to marry. Our parents were ecstatic when we officially announced our engagement and set a date.

"Together we chose the plans for this house, but I suspect it was more my dream home than hers. Vicky wasn't much into building or decorating. At any rate, it was to be ready by the time we returned from an extended honeymoon. As fate would have it, she saw only the bare skeleton of what it was to become."

"Oh, Jeff. What happened?"

"A month before the wedding she was coming home from work when a drunk driver— She died instantly."

Courtney reached over and closed her hand around his. "I had no idea." Or, she wondered vaguely, had she? All along didn't she suspect some sad secret that lent Jeff the depth of character she so admired? His attitude toward alcohol was another clue. What had happened to him explained a lot about the attraction he held for her. His private grief matched her own, but she'd resisted exploring it, sure she had to be mistaken.

To all appearances, Jefferson Herrington was a man who had the world by the tail, who'd always lived a charmed life, whose humor and vibrancy gave no hint of past suffering. Suddenly she felt ashamed. Ashamed for thinking she'd been the only one deprived, the only one denied happiness.

Jeff knew he should have told Courtney about Vicky, but the right time had never presented itself. After a while bringing up the past was overshadowed by the present. By what the two of them shared. He'd almost broached the subject that first day on the boat when he'd pulled out the bottle of sparkling grape juice instead of wine, but the day was so lovely, he'd hated to cloud it with a personal sorrow. Now, looking at her stricken features, he cursed his silence.

Freeing his hand, Jeff brought his arm around her shoulder and pulled her close. With his cheek resting against Courtney's temple, he went on. "After the funeral, I stopped construction on this place and left the city for a year. When I came back, I decided to finish what I'd started. As a kind of assertion that all was not lost—that I was alive and that Vicky would want me to live my life to the fullest—I ordered the house completed.

"My parents left me alone until I was about thirty. But, as I said, they were hoping for grandchildren—to carry on the family name and tradition—and since I was their only child, it was my duty to provide them. They started nudging women in my direction. Amelia in particular. Naturally, they were quite discreet. A dinner party here, a birthday celebration there. I could see what they were up to, though. And a part of me resented it." He lifted a curl at Courtney's temple and let it fall back into place. "Unfortunately, I could never feel anything but a kind of casual friendship for Amelia. God help me, because I wanted a family, too, I almost settled for that. Which would have been an injustice to both of us."

Such strong emotion welled up inside Courtney that not even his reference to Amelia—or his desire for children—could dispel it. She'd lost her parents, but Jeff, too, had suffered. He'd been denied the woman he loved, the woman he'd planned to spend his life with. And like Courtney, he'd toughed it out and somehow survived. He'd picked up the shattered pieces of his life, gone on with his work, made a contribution to his profession.

Personally, too, he'd triumphed. His home was not only a celebration of color. It was a celebration of life.

Courtney felt the sting of tears behind her lids and tried to blink them back. She didn't want Jeff to misunderstand, to think she pitied him. Quite the reverse. What she was feeling was more akin to pride.

She lifted her face to his, communicating with her eyes more eloquently than she could with words. "I'm glad you told me."

"I've wanted to let you know for a long time. Because until you came into my life, I never thought it would be completely whole again."

"I don't know what to say."

"You don't have to say anything. Yet." He took her arm and pulled her to her feet. "Come on, I'd like you to see the rest of my home."

The leisurely stroll through the remaining rooms restored some normalcy to their mood, but by the time they reached Jeff's bedroom, the tension was back.

"Here's where the tour ends," he said, closing the door.

When his lips met hers, Courtney melted against him. His kiss was soft but desperate. With his hands and his tongue, he brought to her a passion that flooded her senses. She was filled with him—the lingering taste of mint on his lips, the manly scent of his after-shave, the slight abrasion of his beard-stubbled chin, the hardness of his chest.

Courtney's heart overflowed with love. She'd never felt as close to anyone as she did to Jeff. She longed to comfort him, to pleasure him. Her hands delved into his thick, dark hair, soothing as much as caressing. She dropped tiny kisses over his brows, his jaw, his neck. Freeing the buttons on his shirt, she moved her lips over his chest, lingering to trace each male disk with her tongue.

"Ah, Court, love, you drive me crazy." He brought her face to his for a long, wet, greedy kiss. With one hand he molded her breast while he undid the zipper at the back of her gown with the other. Slowly, painstakingly, he slipped it from her shoulders, down her arms, over her hips. In seconds it lay in a pool at her feet.

He deftly unhooked her lacy bra and discarded it. His hands whispered over her bare body, admiring, worshipping. Her panties and hose went the way of her bra until she stood nude and trembling before him.

"You're so lovely, Courtney. So very, very beautiful."

He trailed his lips over her breasts, down her torso to her flat stomach until he was kneeling before her, arousing, tantalizing, driving her mindless.

In a sensual haze, she was only vaguely conscious when he started to work on his own clothing. "No," she protested sinking down before him. With shaking fingers, she pushed his coat and shirt from his shoulders, then unsnapped his trousers. When she attempted to slide down the zipper, he stayed her hand.

"Let me."

Getting to his feet, he quickly divested himself of his remaining clothes, then lifted Courtney into his arms and carried her to the bed. She linked her hands around his neck as he threw back the spread and gently lowered her to the mattress.

Coming down beside her, he turned her in his arms. His mouth tugged at her nipple, and Courtney gasped as bolt after bolt of sensation shot through her. His fingers skirted up her legs and tangled in the triangle of hair at the juncture of her thighs. Her breath came faster and faster.

Jeff tensed at the sweep of her palms over his flat stomach and narrow hips. Air hissed through his teeth when her mouth followed the arrow of hair to its bushy source. Her lips brushed him intimately.

He groaned and hauled her up his body. "I can't take any more of this, woman."

"Then come to me. Now."

"Not until I return the favor."

His lips flowed over her, pausing at her throat, her breasts, her navel until she arched toward him, begging him to end the sweet torment. But Jeff couldn't get enough of her. Every part of Courtney was precious to him, special. She'd brought such joy, such compassion, such excitement into his life. If he lived to be one hundred, he would never be able to tell her how much she meant to him.

When at last they came together, Courtney wrapped her legs around him and matched his rhythm. As one, their tightly clasped bodies climbed higher and higher until release came in a blinding rush, and they cried out with the wildness, the sweetness of their union.

Chapter Eight

No! No!"

Jeff was jerked awake by Courtney's moans. Bolting up in bed, he found her flailing about wildly. Her legs kicked at his ankles, her fists pounded his chest. Instantly he pulled her into his arms.

To prevent her from fighting him, he tightened his grip. Rocking her trembling body, he crooned into her ear, "Wake up, love. Don't be afraid. It's Jeff. You're safe here with me."

He pushed damp curls from her forehead and cradled her as carefully as if she were a small, defenseless child. "It's only a bad dream. That's all."

When she quieted down, he eased them to a sitting position and reached around to switch on the bedside lamp.

Courtney's lids came open. Blinking at the light, she stared dazedly into hazel eyes, narrowed with concern.

Several seconds ticked by before she remembered where she was. "Jeff?"

"Yes, sweetheart. It's me. You're in my room. My bed. You were having a nightmare."

"Oh, Jeff." She flung her arms around his neck and buried her face in his chest, willing away the frightening images. Reality, she told herself, was the feel of sleep-warmed skin beneath her cheek. Reality was a cloud of wiry hairs tickling her nose. Reality was strong, firm muscles pressed against her breasts. Reality was the familiar, masculine scent that was Jeff's and Jeff's alone.

But the haunting visions that had shocked her awake were too recent, too vivid. With chilling clarity, they whirled over and over again behind her lids. It didn't matter whether her eyes were open or closed. Like instant replays caught in an endless memory loop, they defied her every attempt to escape.

"Oh, Jeff," she cried again. "Hold me."

He clasped her more tightly, pillowing her head against his hair-roughened chest. "I am holding you, love. I am."

Unable to stop herself, Courtney wept unabashedly. After a while the steady rise and fall of Jeff's breathing had a calming effect, and her sobs subsided.

He sensed the instant she began to relax. Still keeping her in the protective circle of his arms, he loosened his hold and kissed her dampened brow. "Better?"

"I need a tissue," she got out between ragged sniffs.

Jeff snatched one from a box on the night table and pressed it into her hand. With the edge of his thumb he wiped the tears from beneath her eyes. "Better?" he repeated.

"I feel like such a fool."

"Nonsense. It happens to the best of us. But I must say," he gently scolded, trying vainly to coax a laugh, "I'm not terribly flattered that my lovemaking gave you bad dreams."

She angled him a watery smile and caressed his cheek. "No way."

"But that was a nightmare you were having, wasn't it? Or do you always wake up fighting the bed covers?"

She did laugh then, though the sound was a trifle rusty. "Not often."

"I'm glad to hear it." He smoothed a hand up and down her arm. "But how often's not often?"

She shrugged noncommittally.

"Talking it out will help."

Jeff spoke with such assurance that Courtney wondered if he might have been plagued with terrible dreams after Vicky's death. Though it had been several weeks since she'd last wakened in a cold sweat, off and on, ever since her mother's death, she'd endured the same recurring nightmare. Sometimes a newspaper article or a TV show would trigger a bad night. She suspected that Jeff's revelation about Vicky had prompted this evening's embarrassing episode.

Jeff continued to gently stroke her arm. "What terrified you, Courtney?" he again prodded. "Let's talk about it."

"I don't know if I can."

"Try. When did these nightmares first start?"

Finally, Courtney told him, explaining that in her sleep she relived over and over the loss of her parents, particularly her mother, who, ironically enough, like Vicky, had died in an automobile accident.

"Didn't anyone ever ask you about the dreams? Or see about getting you some counseling?" Jeff inquired when she'd finished.

"The Grangers tried to help, and for a while, it was better. But then I was sent to another foster home, and—"

"They came back," Jeff finished for her. His heart went out to Courtney. Every time life looked up for her, every time security was just within her grasp, something else happened to rob her of happiness, to undermine her confidence in the future.

He shifted his body slightly. "As you grew up and became more independent, didn't the nightmares fade?"

"Not really. They changed."

"How?"

"Now, I'm the one who's killed. Sometimes I'm driving, sometimes it's a man. I know we're married, but he doesn't have a face." At least, she silently amended, he didn't have a face until tonight. Tonight his features were appallingly familiar. Tonight the man's face was unmistakably Jeff's.

Another violent shudder ripped through her, and she struggled for control.

"Oh, my darling. My poor darling."

At his mournful chant, Courtney felt a surge of anger and drew away. "Don't pity me, Jeff. I can't stand to be pitied."

"Nor do you deserve to be. But I'm not pitying you, Court. I'm sympathizing." He capped her head in his large palm and drew her close. "You see, I can relate to what you're feeling. I've been there. In that same kind of private hell. I've never told anyone this, but after

Vicky was killed, I kept reliving that dreadful moment the police came to my door."

"Oh, Jeff." Pleased he'd trusted her with the confidence, she smoothed a finger over his eyebrow. "Was it the middle of the night?"

"No, it was a lovely summer evening. The sun was just dropping below the horizon, and there wasn't a cloud in the sky. No reason to think anything could be wrong with the world. Vicky was only a mile from her apartment when..." His voice trailed off before he continued. "But accidents can happen in broad daylight, beneath a cheerful sun, close to home. At the time I found that hard to accept.

"What's more, I kept blaming myself. If it hadn't been for me, Vicky wouldn't have been on the road then, driving alone. She would have been sitting in a restaurant, having dinner. With me. I was supposed to meet her after work, but at the last minute I got held up and had to cancel our date. When I called to tell her, she said she didn't mind, that she had some catching up to do at the office. Afterward I figured she must have stayed there and worked a little over an hour. That's all it took to—"

Lovingly, Courtney caged his blue-shadowed face, her thumbs working the painful memory lines away from his brow. "But you can't blame yourself for that. You couldn't have known. The guilty one is the drunk driver. Not you."

"I finally came to grips with that. One day I woke up and saw the light. Instead of feeling sorry for Vicky, who'd died so young and so full of promise, I was focusing on myself. Wallowing in my own misery. And in the process, shutting out the rest of the world. That's when I realized I could no longer live my life on what-might-have-been." He lifted her chin for his direct gaze. "By the same token, Court, you can't live yours on what-might-be. There's no profit in borrowing trouble."

"Don't think I haven't told myself that. A thousand times. But there's a big gap between the mind and the emotions."

"Granted. Still you have to bridge it. What are you really afraid of, Court? It's not riding in a car. You do it every day with no visible sign of tension."

Courtney wondered if she dare tell him, but before she could stay her tongue, the words rushed out. "I don't want to marry and have children." With the admission came a sense of relief. But, oddly enough, no lessening of panic.

"Forgive me if I find that hard to believe."

"It's not that I don't *want* a family," she hastily amended, "but I can't shake the belief that if I do have one, they'll be left the way I was. Homeless. Penniless."

It wasn't what Jeff expected to hear, but, now that he thought about it, he might have guessed as much from the nature of her nightmares. Tucking Courtney's head beneath his chin, he attempted to dismiss her fears. "Nonsense! You're acting as if you believe there's some strange hex on you that's going to make history repeat itself."

She shivered. "Sometimes it does."

"Oh, my love, it's time you let yourself be happy," he said, almost echoing Mary's advice. "You've paid your dues—if there is such a thing. Which I seriously doubt."

"I wish I could believe that."

"You can. But first you'll have to stop thinking so much." He kissed her softly. "Let yourself go. Just feel."

"Feel?"

"Umm-hmm. Like this."

Slowly, languorously, Jeff comforted, then aroused her. There was nothing reckless in his touch, only a tender, seductive courting. Provocative lips nibbled and trembled over her face and down her neck; lazy fingers grazed along her sensitive skin. Courtney had never felt more sheltered, more revered, more a woman.

Jeff watched as pleasure built and overtook her. Once, twice, three times, she cried out. Only then did he permit her to take the initiative.

Courtney moved her hands up Jeff's chest and over his broad shoulders. She charted his firm biceps, his wide rib cage, his narrow waist, the long sinews of his legs. She was eager to memorize every inch of his muscular length. Though taut with desire, he held himself still as her fingertips ran over his hard body.

Her tongue teased one earlobe, then slid along his bearded jaw to trace the tempting fullness of his lips. Her own hovered and rubbed. At his quivering response, she settled her open mouth on his and poured her soul into the kiss.

The thought slammed through her that this could be their last time together. It wasn't what she wanted, but then she had little choice.

When he was telling her about Vicky, Courtney realized just how vulnerable Jeff was. He might be rich, handsome and successful, but he wasn't immune to heartache. She had the power to hurt him. And she couldn't bear that. She'd suffered too much hurt herself. But she was treading a thin line. Jeff had already admitted he was falling in love. What if he should go a step further and ask her to marry him, to have his children? Wouldn't she cause him less pain to walk away now than to refuse him later? To give him up, she knew, would nearly kill her, but the last thing she wanted was to bring even more anguish to the man who lay beneath her, the man whose lips she was devouring like a woman starved for passion.

Jeff tasted the urgency in Courtney's kiss. In one smooth motion, he flipped her over and took back the lead. At that instant he was certain he had the power to heal her. God, how he wanted to! Fate had given him a second chance with Courtney, and he couldn't let her go. Somehow he would convince her they belonged together. But now wasn't the time for talking.

Jeff brought his mouth to hers in a bruising kiss. Their lovemaking grew frantic, demanding. Their hands and lips flew over each other in a frenzy of desire. Courtney's hips arched up to meet him and with one hard thrust he crushed her against the mattress.

Instantly all thought vanished. Moving to an ancient rhythm, they lost themselves in each other. Heat shimmered along their skin, blood pounded through their veins, their hearts beat in wild unison. As one, they drove higher and higher toward a soul-shattering convulsion that finally took them both.

Afterward they lay quietly side-by-side, Jeff's arm circling her shoulder.

"I have no words to tell you how I feel right now," he said, a raw edge to his voice. With the pads of his fingers, he tenderly brushed at her bangs.

Still unbalanced, Courtney turned her face into his shoulder. She felt protected, safe. She was grateful to Jeff for having given her a secure harbor—if only for a little while. Just before she drifted into sleep, she spoke against the curve of his neck, "I love you, Jeff."

But her confession was smothered and only reached his ears as an incoherent mumble.

On the terrace the following morning, Courtney encountered the wiry Rudy, who didn't bat an eye at her presence. She wore one of Jeff's terry robes—her pink silk evening dress seemed inappropriate attire at least before noon—but Rudy acted as if she'd simply dropped by for an early morning swim in Jeff's pool and stayed on for breakfast.

"More toast, miss?" he asked, offering her a silver tray with neatly cut light-brown wedges.

"No, thank you, Rudy. I'm fine."

"Very well. I'll leave the coffee pot. Mr. Herrington's still on the phone, but he should be back in a minute. He always takes a second cup." Rudy grimaced slightly, his disapproval of caffeine apparent.

Courtney curled her bare toes on the flagstone beneath her. "I'll pour it when he comes then."

"Very good. If there's nothing else, I'll see to my chores."

"Is Rudy always so proper?" Courtney asked when Jeff reappeared.

"Not on your life. He's on his best behavior. He didn't even blink when I asked him to fix eggs. My usual breakfast is a bowl of high-fiber cereal laced with skim milk. I suppose you noticed that wasn't butter on your toast."

"Whatever it was, it was delicious," Courtney allowed, relieved to be making small talk. Her hand shook slightly as she poured his coffee. She'd had little experience dropping a lover—none breaking with a man she had no desire to leave—and she wasn't sure how to go about signaling Jeff that she wanted to cool their relationship. Coward that she was, she preferred to let things ride and hope he wouldn't do anything to force her hand.

Her hope was short-lived.

Their night of lovemaking had put Jeff in a particularly jovial mood, and before he'd finished his second cup of coffee, he walked over to her chair, dropped down on one knee and took her hands in his. "Courtney, I want to know when you're going to make an honest man of me."

"Jeff, what are you doing?"

"Proposing, of course. Isn't it obvious?"

She gave a nervous laugh and attempted to tug him up. "Be serious."

His expression sobered. "I couldn't be more serious. I love you, Courtney. I'm asking you to marry me."

"But you can't…it's…I mean, we don't know each other all that well, and—and . . . I barely met your parents—"

"I'm not asking you to marry my parents. I want you to marry me." He pulled her to her feet and into his arms. "It's so wonderful, so natural having you across from me at the breakfast table. Exchanging laughter, understanding. I want you here every morning. And I want to wake up each day and find you curled next to me in bed." He lowered his forehead to hers, and his voice took on a husky note. "I've told you things no one else knows. Not even Al, and he can drag a lot out of me when he has a mind to. Last night you shared some very private feelings with me, too—and I'm not talking about your body, sweet as it is. I've never felt this close to anyone else, and I think we know each other well enough to make a commitment. Don't you agree?''

"I-it's so sudden."

"No, it isn't. This has been building for a long time, Courtney. Ever since we met. I'd rather hoped you felt it, too."

She couldn't lie to him. "I did. I do."

He smiled. "That's good. Because I'm having trouble imagining my life without you. You rob me of breath, sweetheart. Every time I look at you."

"Oh, Jeff, what can I say?"

"I'd kind of hoped for a yes before you had much chance to think about it. But if you insist, we can wait until after Frank's party to make the official announcement."

"Frank's party?" she asked, grateful for the diversion.

"You remember Al's mentioning that he was coming home. The party's next week." He ran a knuckle down her cheek. "You will come with me, won't you? I think Al would take it as a personal affront if you didn't show up."

Courtney felt herself weakening. What was one more date? After last night she was too emotionally drained to argue. Their parting could wait a week or so. By then she would have marshaled her courage enough to make the final break.

"Sure," she finally agreed. "I'll go."

"Great," Jeff replied, willing to drop the subject of marriage. For now. He probably should have waited longer to ask her, but after last night they'd seemed so attuned to each other that he'd yielded to impulse.

Frank's party was the ace up his sleeve. His friend was sure to bring his wife and small son with him. Jeff had seen Courtney with the Mitchell twins, and he knew she loved children. All that was left was to convince her that she was missing a lot by not having some of her own. It was a long shot, but he was counting on Frank's three-month-old baby to melt her resolve. With her defenses down, he would be able to pump some reason into her pretty head. He would make her see she could rest easy over that crazy notion about leaving her children destitute orphans.

His mouth turned up in a triumphant grin. It probably hadn't yet occurred to Courtney, but with his financial resources, he could ensure their offspring a comfortable home and secure future.

The Schmidts lived in a narrow, two-story frame house, a style typical of many older homes dotting Cincinnati's seven hills. The sides facing the neighbors had few windows, leaving plenty of space indoors for arranging furniture, particularly in the bedrooms, which, Courtney surmised, must have been rigged up like dormitories to accommodate the Schmidt clan.

They were a friendly, noisy bunch, as were the friends who had gathered to welcome Frank home. While pale-colored bratwurst browned on outdoor grills, conversation—along with soft drinks and beer from the city's breweries—flowed freely. Many of the older children played cards at several tables scattered about the living room. The younger ones scurried about among the adults, furtively helping themselves to the German potato salad and baked beans that had been set out on the buffet table or to hard pretzels from the baskets that had been placed around the house.

When Jeff introduced Courtney to Al's wife, the buxom Lillian Schmidt threw her arms around the younger woman and gave her a hearty squeeze. Then she set her apart and looked her up and down. "You're as pretty as Al said. He told me all about you." She winked at Jeff. "I'd keep this one if I were you."

"I'll take that under advisement, Lil."

"You'd better. You're not getting any younger, you know."

"I'm not over the hill yet."

"Listen to him," she said, directing the comment to Courtney. "You'd never know he's pushing forty, would you?"

"Pushing forty!" Jeff objected. "Aren't you stretching my age a bit? Last time I looked, I was thirty-four. You should remember. You baked me a birthday cake."

She rested her chin on a palm. "Was that this year?"

"You know it was, dearie-mine."

"Do tell. But if you're going to sweet-talk me, I guess I'll let it pass."

"Somewhere," Jeff complained, "I lost the point of this conversation."

"You never could keep up with me," Lil boasted. "Not for all your fancy Harvard education."

Jeff gave the older woman a playful cuff. "I'm not going to argue with that."

She chuckled. "Come along and get some food. You always were partial to my potato salad."

"Later. First, I want Courtney to meet Frank and Edna. Where are they?"

"Frank's outside helping Al grill the meat. I think Edna's upstairs nursing little Kurt. He's sure a cute one. Chubby with rosy cheeks. Looks just like Frank when he was a baby."

"I can't wait to see him," Jeff said. "Tell Edna we'll be in the backyard."

Jeff took Courtney by the hand and led her through the crowded rooms toward the patio. She was glad she'd come to the party when Al made no secret of how pleased he was to see her and have her meet Frank. She was also introduced to several of his brothers and sisters and an assortment of grandchildren.

Courtney could understand Al's pride. He had a fine family. Of his offspring, Frank appeared to be the favorite. He was a handsome, well-built man, as light as Jeff was dark. His blond hair was thick and straight, his blue eyes clear and candid. Fair of skin, he had the ruddy complexion of his German ancestors.

"So this is the woman who tried to become a champion water-skier in one day."

Courtney winced at Frank's comment. "I see that's one story I'm never going to live down."

"Afraid so. We heard all about your spill in the Ohio. You gave Jeff quite a scare."

Remembering that day and its aftermath, Courtney's cheeks flushed. "I scared myself."

"Well, you're certainly no worse for wear. You may, however, show signs of aging by the time this party's over. Have you ever heard a noisier crowd?" His gaze ran around the spacious yard. Several teenagers were playing badminton in one corner, while a larger group was participating in a croquet game that had spilled over into the adjoining lawn.

Al began methodically turning the sausage on the grill. "Noise means they're having fun."

Just then a sharp clang went up from behind the garage. "Horseshoes," Frank explained. "The only reason the neighbors don't complain is because they're all here."

Courtney smiled. "I think it's nice. You must feel pleased that everyone turned out to welcome you home."

"I am, though I think Mom's cooking is what really enticed them."

"Grandpa," a small girl interrupted, "Grandma says to tell you she's really for the brats."

"Coming right up. Guess I'd better get these inside. Mind putting on some more, Frank?"

"Not at all, Dad. If you see Edna, send her out. I'm eager for these two to meet your new grandson. You haven't seen him yet, have you, Jeff?"

"No, Edna was giving him supper when we arrived."

Frank glanced toward the house. "What do you know? It looks as if he's had his fill. There she is now."

A small, dark-haired woman shouldered through the screen door. In her arms she carried a sturdy bundle. When she caught sight of her husband, she smiled and started toward him.

Frank put his arm around his wife's waist. "Edna, darling, meet Courtney Hughes. She's with Jeff. Courtney, my wife, Edna. And our son, Kurt Jefferson Schmidt."

Both Courtney and Jeff met the announcement with surprise.

"Buddy," Jeff said softly, "you didn't tell me. I'm honored."

"I hoped you'd be pleased. We'd like you to be Kurt's godfather."

"I'm doubly honored." He stretched out his arms. "May I hold my new godson?"

Edna handed him over, and Courtney was touched by how tenderly Jeff took the baby.

"I envy you," he said to the proud couple. "You have a fine boy here."

"Thanks," Frank responded. "But don't hog him. Give Courtney a turn."

Jeff watched Courtney's face as she accepted little Kurt from him. Her features softened as she brushed a finger against his round cheek. When her eyes closed briefly, blissfully, Jeff was certain he'd scored a victory.

"Admit it," Jeff urged as he pulled in along the curb by Courtney's apartment, "you adored holding that baby. We practically had to pry him from your arms so you could eat your supper."

"Of course, I loved holding him. He's precious."

"I rest my case."

"What case are we talking about?"

Jeff killed the motor and pulled the keys from the ignition. "Let's discuss this inside."

As they silently climbed the stairs to her apartment, Courtney reflected on the past few hours. It had been a wonderfully warm family evening. No one could be with the Schmidts for long without falling under their gregarious spell. She could well understand why Jeff had spent so many hours there as a boy. In contrast to his parents who were stiff and proper, the Schmidts were natural and unreserved. They expressed their feelings openly and freely. They embraced each other and the world.

Though the world they embraced was far different from the one Jeff normally moved in, he fit into it as easily as he did the rarified atmosphere of his parents' world. For that alone, Courtney couldn't help but love him.

Jeff had an uncanny knack for bringing out the best in people, for making them feel appreciated and special. With him, Courtney was another person. Already, she sensed a crack in her resolve never to have children of her own. The past week she'd caught herself thinking about what a child of theirs would be like. The prospect of marriage, a home and motherhood thrilled her.

But it frightened her more.

Jeff took her key and opened the door. As soon as they were inside, he tugged her into his arms. His lips played with hers as he spoke against them. "How about it, Courtney? Are you going to marry me?"

"Jeff, I explained. I know you want children, and I'm not sure—"

"That you want them? How can you deny that? Especially after tonight?"

"It's true, Jeff, I loved little Kurt. I love Julie and Jenny, too. But loving somebody else's children and wanting your own are two different things."

"For some people maybe. People who are devoted to their careers or prefer to remain single. But those aren't your reasons, Courtney. You have maternal instinct written all over you. You long for the home life you missed, and you know it. You're not going to let some silly, irrational phobia, some crazy unfounded nightmare stand in the way of our happiness, are you?"

She brought her palms to his chest and shoved away. "How dare you belittle my fears!"

"I didn't mean to." He sighed, exasperated. "I just want you to listen to reason."

She walked over to the window and looked down at the dark street below. "You're pushing, Jeff."

"Damn right, I'm pushing," he fairly shouted in frustration, then more calmly, "Look, Courtney, if you want to wait a few years before we start a family, build up your business first, fine. We have plenty of time." When she didn't respond, he went on. "Why can't you get it through your head that our situation is entirely different from your parents'? Your father left your mother without means—"

"That's not true," she snapped. "He left us well-off."

"Well-off? I don't understand. How, then, did you end up a ward of the state?"

"My mother lost everything. Every last penny. But it wasn't her fault. She was the victim of poor financial advice and an unscrupulous broker."

"Oh, sweetheart, I'm sorry, but—"

"That's why she died. To make ends meet, she often worked double shifts at one of those twenty-four-hour groceries. She wore herself out. One night on the way home, she fell asleep at the wheel."

Jeff came up behind her and circled her waist. "Oh, Court, love, you've had a rough time of it. But, don't you see, it'll be different with us? There isn't much chance of that happening to my inheritance."

"I want to believe that, Jeff, but I'm afraid." She tried to wriggle out of his embrace, but he wouldn't let her. "It's not only the nightmare. I don't expect you to understand...I know this sounds foolish, but I feel too good with you, too right. It can't last. We come from different worlds."

He turned her in his arms. "You're talking nonsense again."

"No, Jeff. It's better to break it off. Now."

"You'd rather trade our future together for...for what? Some false idea of security? Court, do you know how selfish that sounds?" He paused, his eyes narrowing thoughtfully. "Or is it that you don't love me enough."

"The trouble is, I love you too much."

"Prove it. Marry me."

"I can't."

She closed her eyes against the hurt in his. She didn't open them again until the door clicked quietly shut.

Chapter Nine

Closing the door without a word was a deliberate act. Jeff wasn't going to beg—no matter how much he was tempted to coax and cajole. What's more, he couldn't trust his voice not to break over a simple good-bye.

But once outside Courtney's apartment building, he gave in to a deep sense of despair. Together they could conquer her forebodings; he knew they could if she would just give them half a chance. If she would simply let their love be the guiding force. But she seemed determined to deny it. And to deny him.

Dejected, Jeff climbed into his car and fired up the engine. He felt a certain kinship with the legendary knights of myth and folklore. The warrior was always assigned some impossible task to win the freedom of the captive maiden. He had to slay a fire-breathing dragon, outsmart a hideous monster, puzzle his way through a maze of horrors. But in the end he triumphed when the fair damsel fell gratefully into his arms.

Of course, it was fantasy that gave the fiendish symbols of evil shape and substance. The same was true for Courtney. Only the monster that held her captive was her own anxiety. She was trapped in an endless circle of what-ifs. But no matter how tangible the danger loomed in her imagination, it could not be dispatched with a single brave thrust of the sword.

"Damn!" Jeff swore aloud, slapping a hand against the steering wheel. How did a man fight illusory terrors? How did he conquer demons that weren't real?

He wanted Courtney, wanted her more than he'd ever wanted any other woman, Vicky included. Theirs had been a love of youth and idealism. With Courtney the passion was fuller, richer, more mature. But no less exciting. And it had little to do with sex.

Jeff needed her. It was as simple as that. And maybe, given their backgrounds, as irrational as Courtney's unwillingness to take a chance on their love. How could he, Jefferson E. Herrington, a man who—at least when Rudy wasn't looking—dined on lobster Newburg and filet mignon—how could such a man ache for a woman who survived on pizza and deli sandwiches? Their preferences in food were as disparate as their life histories. By all logic, they should have nothing upon which to build a lasting relationship.

But somehow, to Jeff, none of that mattered. The important thing was that he loved Courtney. She understood him as no one else ever had, understood him precisely because she'd grown up as far from his world as the sun from the earth. An orphan who had been shuffled from one home to another, she could empathize with the lack of warmth he decried in his own life.

Vicky had been too young, too starry-eyed to suspect the emotional deprivation of his youth. About the only time his parents had been sensitive to his feelings was at Vicky's death. They'd agonized over her loss, mourned her as deeply, he believed, as if she were their own daughter.

But over the years, Jeff had found no one to take her place, and they'd started to prod him. At first subtly, then more and more openly. When he failed to marry any of the women his parents deemed suitable, they grew impatient, advising him not to get hung up on false notions of love. Similar backgrounds, they'd argued, were more important than chemistry. Though they didn't say so, Jeff knew their own marriage had settled into one of indifferent tolerance. As far as he could determine, they expected his to do the same.

But Jeff wanted more. He wanted the warm caring that was part and parcel of the Schmidts. In Vicky he might have found it, but a cruel twist of fate had snatched her from him. Now he'd been given another chance with Courtney.

Maybe it was a classic case of opposites attracting, but Jeff longed for Courtney to complete him, to have his children, to warm their home with her humor and resilience, to make his life richer than he could ever have believed possible.

Unfortunately, she was afraid to be happy with him, afraid of what he could offer her, of the close family they could build together. Would she, Jeff wondered, ever come to her senses and realize that their love was strong enough to overcome whatever blows life might deal them? Realize that what they shared was too damned powerful to be defeated by vague uncertainties and absurd fears? Realize that their very differences made them perfect for each other?

As Jeff pulled into his driveway, he told himself not to lose hope.

Courtney had lived most of her twenty-eight years on hope, but to guard against disappointment, she'd schooled herself to anticipate the worst. And with just cause. Why look for happiness, she'd reasoned, when misery was always waiting just around the corner?

But despite all the grief life had visited upon her, Courtney hadn't been prepared for the sense of desolation she felt when the door clicked shut behind Jeff. It was over. He was gone.

She'd lost him.

For a time she stood motionless, her arms locked across her stomach, her eyes staring out the window. Then slowly she made her way to the sofa and collapsed onto it. Pain seared her heart; tears burned her eyes. She tried blinking them back, but first one, then another and another trickled down her cheeks, opening the floodgates of grief. She covered her face with her hands and sobbed—for herself, for Jeff, for the family she would never have. She wept until her body went limp with fatigue, until she was too drained of energy to wring out one more tear.

When the first streaks of dawn appeared on the horizon, Courtney told herself to get up and go to bed. She was badly in need of some sleep. Her eyes were puffy and grit-sore, her face red and raw, her nasal passages swollen shut. But she had difficulty making herself move off the couch.

So what, she asked herself, was she going to do? Sit around all day and lick her wounds? If so, she would be running the danger of a renewed crying jag. Is that what she wanted?

The mental upbraiding at last brought Courtney to her feet. First she went to the bathroom where she tried to clear her nose, but no matter how noisily she blew into the tissue, she felt as though she were suffering from a bad attack of hay fever rather than from a broken heart. She leaned over the basin and repeatedly splashed her face with cold water, which somewhat restored her spirits. Feeling marginally better, she was patting dry her tear-chafed cheeks when she was overcome with a sudden need to talk to someone.

If she didn't share her sorrow, she would go crazy.

"My God!" Mary gasped when she opened the door to her apartment. "What happened, Court? You look like the Grim Reaper!"

"Gee, thanks, Mary. You sure have a way with compliments."

Her friend stepped aside. "Come on in. I think you'd better dump some of that load you're carrying. And for once you're in luck. The twins are next door."

Five minutes later Mary was leaning forward on her couch and regarding Courtney with a look of disbelief. "You did what?"

"I said no to his proposal."

"Are you out of your mind, girl?"

Courtney laced her fingers together and squeezed until her knuckles were white. "I'm trying to be sensible."

"You call turning down the most eligible bachelor in the city sensible? Especially when he's a hell of a nice guy and you're crazy about him? Not to mention that he's nuts over you." She held forth a restraining hand. "No, you can't deny it, Court. The feeling's mutual. I've never seen a couple more in love."

"Don't make this harder for me than it is, Mary. I need you to understand."

"I'm trying, but it isn't easy." She peered intently at Courtney. "You don't have a fever, do you?"

"I'm perfectly healthy." And she was—if she discounted the pain that filled her chest.

"In body maybe. But I can't say much for your mind. Something's muddled your reasoning."

Courtney stiffened. "That's a low blow, Mary. Can't you tell I'm doing my best to *think*, to listen to my head instead of leading with my heart?"

Mary's brows lowered. "For the life of me, I can't imagine what sanity has to do with love."

"In this case a lot. What I don't have can't be taken away from me."

Mary threw up her arms and slumped back in her seat. "Now you've totally lost me."

"Don't be dense. Jeff's a—a blueblood, and I'm...I'm more like blue-collar. I simply can't face the prospect of losing him."

"What gives you the idea you're going to lose him?"

"No matter how much he thinks he loves me, it's a distinct possibility. Sooner or later, I'd say or do things that would embarrass him. Plus I'd be thrown into the company of all those sophisticated and elegant women. When the novelty wore off, he'd find me irritating rather than amusing."

Courtney failed to mention that should she be unable to master her fear over having children, his irritation would turn to anger. Then he would realize he'd made a dreadful mistake in marrying her, and they would go their separate ways.

Instead she added stubbornly, "It could never work between us. So I'm saving us both a lot of heartache by breaking it off now."

Mary didn't bother with tact. "Now I know why you went into art. You certainly don't have a head for logic. Just because Jeff comes from old money and you grew up in foster homes doesn't mean you two don't belong together. Or that you're destined for a divorce court."

"But the odds are against us."

"Convince me. Go ahead, give it your best shot."

"For starters, his parents. They're sure to come between us."

"Yeah, I guess you're right. Now that you mention it, I've noticed how Jeff's a real mama's and papa's boy. He's got no backbone at all—"

"Mary! That's not true, and you know it!"

"Ha! Don't you remember how he let his father walk all over you, how he didn't make the slightest effort to come to your defense? Lucky for you, his lawyer was lazy about slapping you with that lawsuit. But no thanks to Jeff. He didn't hold the hounds at bay to save your fanny. Yep, you're right. The guy's a real twit."

Courtney managed a weak smile. "Honestly, Mary, I'm not imagining trouble. His mother made it clear I don't belong."

"Oh, were you and Jeff planning to move in with the Herringtons? Or have you set your sights on joining her clubs, working for her charities—not that you couldn't make a contribution with your talent in graphics—or had you figured on modeling yourself in her image?"

"Now you're being ridiculous! You're deliberately trying to bait—"

"Look, Court, you and Jeff have your own life to lead. Jeff's no fool. He knows his parents. If he's not concerned about how they'll accept you, then you needn't be. Trust his judgment."

"I wish I could. But I can understand how his mother feels about me. Jeff and I have so little in common."

"So? Who says a husband and wife have to be Xerox copies of one another? Take it from me. Paul and I couldn't have been better matched if we'd been paired by a computer. And know what? We bored each other to death."

"Still, you have to have something to build a relationship on. Something more solid than an interest in baseball and jazz."

Mary smiled. "You forgot physical attraction."

"Don't think that's easy to dismiss. But it's not enough."

Mary moved closer and draped an arm around her friend's shoulders. "Out with it. What's the real problem, Court?"

Unbidden, tears again sprang to Courtney's eyes and slid down her cheeks. "I'm scared, Mary. Scared for me, even more scared for Jeff. I'm a disaster waiting to happen. Misfortune follows me around like a lost puppy. I'd just bring Jeff grief. And he doesn't deserve that."

"No, he doesn't. But I have to tell you that's the most hare-brained argument you've come up with so far."

"Not to me, it isn't." She still couldn't bring herself to tell Mary about the nightmares. But she did reveal Jeff's loss of Vicky. "So you see," she concluded at Mary's sympathetic look, "Jeff's been hurt enough by life already. In time, our differences are bound to cause trouble. I can't believe they won't."

Tell me I'm wrong, Courtney's heart silently begged.
I love him so much.

But Mary's eyes refused to meet hers. She heaved a
heavy, resigned sigh. ''If you feel that strongly, then do
him a favor.'' Her pause hung between them—a silent
challenge. ''Don't see him again.''

May slipped into June, and Courtney neither heard
from nor tried to contact Jeff. For days, she hovered
near the phone, expecting him to call. But he never did.
Nor could she bring herself to dial his number. Though
she must have picked up the receiver a dozen times or
more, she always hung up before she hit the last few
digits. Mary was right, she kept reminding herself. Unless Jeff initiated a meeting, she ought to stay out of his
life.

Difficult as it was, Courtney threw herself into her
work and did a fair job of distracting herself. Once she
was called to Herrington Press to give final approval on
her sketches and watercolors. She met with Pete Baker
in the room adjacent to Jeff's office, but Jeff himself
was nowhere in sight. Though her eyes kept targeting
the closed door, he never walked through it.

She was sorely tempted to ask Gladys Feldkamp if he
was in the building. But she had no idea what she would
say to him. And now that the book project was completed, they had nothing to discuss. There was no reason to see him at all.

Courtney's days dragged by with a dismal sameness,
but early in June she did receive one piece of good news.
A paper she'd submitted had been accepted for reading
at the Book Publishers of Ohio convention. The conference was to be held at Cincinnati's Hyatt Regency at

the end of the month. Preparing visual aids to supplement her talk helped fill her already heavy workdays.

Her nights she spent alone. Other than Mary and the
twins, she saw only her clients, the grocery clerk at the
corner market where she shopped, the newspaper boy
and on Sundays her pastor and fellow church members.

From time to time the *Reporter* carried a picture of
Jeff on the society page. Courtney always felt a stab of
pain when she saw a gorgeous woman at his side. It
didn't help that he never escorted—or never seemed
to—the same beauty twice. Just seeing his smile touch
another woman's face was torture. Soon she made a
point of avoiding that section of the paper altogether.

Mercifully Mary never mentioned Jeff. She didn't
scold Courtney for being foolish, nor did she attempt to
change her mind. Instead she continued to include her
in family activities and to propose pleasant diversions
when she sensed the going was tough. An evening at the
movies, a late-night glass of wine and girl talk, a dis-
cussion about the latest best seller, or a romp with Jenny
and Julie in the park—all played a part in driving away
the blues when she plummeted to rock bottom.

Courtney was grateful. Mary's quiet acceptance of
her decision was comforting and communicated the
depth of their friendship more than any words possibly
could.

And Courtney had never needed a friend more than
she did now.

As the weeks plodded on, the misery that tore at her
heart dulled to a hollow ache. Sometimes a whole day
went by before some slight reminder—a preliminary
sketch for Jeff's books, a jazz piece on the radio, a

glance at Fritz the First—sparked her memory and brought with it a wave of regret.

Only one incident reminded her of how Jeff had the ability to stir her anger as well as her love.

At breakfast she was flipping through the *Reporter* when she came across a feature on Herbert Williams, Nat Hamilton's opponent in the fall city council race. Recalling Williams's graciousness when she'd been seated next to him the night of the benefit, she read the profile with interest, then with mounting irritation.

During the course of the interview, the reporter slipped in a question that, Courtney felt, was deliberately calculated to malign Nat's character. He asked Williams about a rumor that his opponent had cheated on a law school exam.

"No comment," Williams was quoted to respond.

"Is that," the reporter pursued, "because you're uncertain about the truth of the allegation or because you are known to shy away from mudslinging?"

Williams's answer was succinct. "Both."

"Yellow journalism," Courtney complained to Bill over a deli sandwich that noon. His opinion of the piece ran counter to hers. Yet how good it felt squaring off face-to-face with her old friend. Though they'd kept in contact by phone, Bill had been tied up with an important design project at Queen City Graphics, and this was the first time they'd gotten together in over six weeks.

Bill shook his head. "I disagree, Court. Maybe it was a little biased in Williams's favor, but carefully worded."

"Sure. Herrington Press wouldn't invite a slander suit." For a moment a smile played at the corners of her mouth. "Eldridge would hyperventilate."

"Eldridge?"

"Their lawyer."

"Oh, yes, the one who threatened you about the logo." Between bites of his sandwich, Bill offered a different point of view. "Look, I know you designed Hamilton's political materials, but that doesn't automatically mean his character's as sterling as the First Family's silver. Come on, Court, 'fess up. Why have you singled out the *Reporter* for criticism? I thought you made your peace with Mr. J. E. Herrington. At La Maisonette, no less," he said in his best French accent.

"We went out a few times, yes."

"Went out?" Bill nearly choked on his pastrami. "As in dating?"

"You could say that," Courtney evaded.

"Geeze, the orphan and the millionaire. Sounds perfect for a TV series. And?"

"And what?"

"Did he show you a good time? Or—" his eyes contracted to icy slits "—did he hurt you, Court? Because if he did—"

"Don't be ridiculous. He was both kind and considerate. Honestly."

"But that doesn't mean he couldn't have led you on, then dropped you like a hot potato once you finished working for him."

Courtney colored over Bill's word choice. Remembering how Jeff could raise her temperature with a look, she covered her sudden flush by blotting her lips. What would Bill think if he knew she'd been the one to do the rejecting? She felt a little guilty for not confiding more in him, but during their occasional phone conversations, Courtney had invariably steered the talk in other directions. Though she thought of Bill as one of her best friends, for some reason she couldn't bring herself to discuss her love life with him. Not the way she had with Mary.

Hoping her easy smile would throw him off, Courtney laid her napkin beside her plate and hedged, "Impossible. You know me, I'm not into relationships."

"If you're not holding a grudge against J. E. Herrington, why are you so irked?"

"The man may have been nice to me, but that's not grounds for shelving my good judgment where he's concerned. I don't like shoddy journalism—whether from friend or foe."

Bill picked up his soft drink. "I wouldn't call that article shoddy reporting. Cliff Toland wrote it. When one of Cincinnati's top newsmen claims his information came from a reliable source, I believe him. As far as I'm concerned, if Hamilton's guilty, the public has a right to know."

Courtney's response was a disgruntled snort.

"What's eating you, Court? You've been trying to hide it, but I can tell something's wrong. You've lost your...twinkle. You having financial problems again?" He started for his checkbook. "If you need a little money to tide you over, I can lend you up to a thousand. My savings account's never been fatter."

Courtney stretched her arm across the table to stop him. "You're a dear, Bill, but for once I don't have to worry about my checks bouncing. The business is in the black."

"What is it, then? Aren't you feeling well?" He put a palm to her forehead. "Maybe you should see a doctor."

She batted his hand aside. "Can't a person be grouchy once in a while without getting the third degree?"

"Once in a while, but you haven't given me a genuine smile this whole hour."

"Oh, Bill, I appreciate your concern, really I do. But I'm fine. Maybe a little overworked, but what else is new? Believe me, I can handle it."

"If you say so." Bill made no further comment, but Courtney could tell he wasn't convinced.

Courtney sat beside the podium, fidgeting with her notes. She took a deep breath, then scanned the packed convention room in search of Bill's friendly face. She was half-pleased, half-anxious about the large crowd. This was her first professional appearance before her peers, and she considered it a double-edged honor. It was flattering and at the same time frightening. She worried that she might not pass the trial-by-fire when she was questioned by fellow artists and publishers after her talk. She knew some job seekers would be doing their best to impress potential employers by putting her on the spot.

Moistening her lips, she listened while Leon Hawkins, the session moderator, introduced her. She'd worked with Leon at Queen City Graphics, and they'd gotten on well.

He began by cataloging Courtney's experience, then proceeded to list her awards and credits—matters that she herself had barely given much thought to. Like a proud father, he cited her professional experience and announced that she'd recently established her own business.

"Ladies and gentlemen," he concluded with a theatrical flare, "I give you our expert on graphic design, Ms. Courtney Hughes."

Embarrassed by the lengthy biography, Courtney took the podium, thanked Leon and quipped, "I have to admit I hardly recognized myself in that glowing introduction. At one point, I began to wonder if there were another Courtney Hughes in the crowd."

The spontaneous ripple of laughter that followed took the edge off her nerves. When all was again silent, she began to speak. By the time she'd finished her opening remarks, she'd started to relax.

Before long Courtney was actually enjoying herself. She could tell from the audience's response that the visuals she was using to illustrate her points had sparked interest. Out of the corner of her eye, she caught an encouraging nod from Bill, the smile of an interested audience member, the thoughtful note taking of a college student and then . . . a flash of hazel eyes.

Suddenly her mouth went dry. She reached for the glass of water on the lectern and prayed that her imagination was running away with her. Jeff couldn't be here—not in her session. Even if he was attending the convention, surely he'd seen her name listed on the program. Swallowing the cool liquid, she chanced a covert glance in his direction. It was Jeff all right, looking more handsome than ever in a lightweight blue suit.

Courtney's heart skidded to a halt, then began a wild hammering. Why hadn't he avoided her presentation in favor of another in the same time slot?

Slowly, she lowered the glass, gripped the sides of the lectern and took a moment to steady herself before launching into her conclusion. Somehow, she managed to get through the summary of her main points and deliver her punch line with adequate force.

As the applause began to dwindle, Courtney hunched her shoulders forward and tugged at her white linen blouse, acutely aware of the trickle of perspiration slowly sliding down the valley between her breasts. When Jeff left the room, she sighed in relief. With him gone, she would be in better shape to field the questions thrown at her.

During the cocktail hour preceding the banquet, Courtney ran into Bill.

"Great job," he praised. "You knocked 'em dead this afternoon."

"Is that your unbiased opinion, Mr. McLean?" She smiled and hooked her arm through his while her gaze traveled over the reception room. Assorted cliques of men and women were discussing the various sessions or engaging in small talk. Here and there couples were openly flirting, some undoubtedly pairing up for the evening. Courtney supposed every convention saw its share of casual relationships. She'd already had to discourage several men from being overly friendly and was thankful to have Bill as a buffer.

Patting her hand, he declared, "Absolutely. Although for a minute there you had me worried. You turned white as a sheet. I thought you forgot what you were going to say next."

"Was it that obvious?"

"Only because I know you. You feel all right?"

"Fine. I guess I was eager to get the whole thing over with."

"Old Hawkins did you proud. What an intro!"

Courtney turned crimson and picked up a glass of Perrier from one of the buffet tables. She still felt too shaky to chance anything stronger than sparkling mineral water. "Don't remind me."

"Hello, Courtney."

Startled by the deep baritone, she pivoted to find Jeff standing behind her. "Hello," she got out.

"I enjoyed your talk," he said, one side of his mouth tilting in the engaging smile she remembered so well.

"Thanks."

He turned to Bill and stuck out his hand. "I don't believe we've met. Jeff Herrington."

Bill did a double take, his head swiveling between Courtney and Jeff. "J. E. Herrington? Of Herrington Press?"

"J. E.'s my father. But, yes, the same family."

Bill shook his hand. "Bill McLean. Nice to meet you."

A waiter carrying a tray of assorted hors d'oeuvres interrupted the exchange. As the men stepped apart, Jeff asked, "You a friend of Courtney's?"

Bill speared a chicken liver wrapped in bacon. "Of long standing. We went to college together."

"I see."

"We also worked together at Queen City Graphics."

"Is that so?"

Courtney stood numbly by, listening, watching. Was there actually a hint of jealousy in Jeff's eyes? The idea both surprised and amused her. At an awkward pause in the conversation, she asked, "How is the history book coming along, Jeff?"

"On schedule. The first copies should be ready in a couple of months."

"That's good."

Just then someone bumped her shoulder. Perrier splashed over the rim of her glass and dripped down her fingers.

"So sorry," a portly gentleman apologized.

Courtney gave her hand a quick shake. "No harm."

"Why don't we move over there?" Jeff handed her a napkin with one hand and motioned to a less congested area with the other. "Where we can talk."

"Okay," Courtney agreed with some reluctance, wondering how she could put an end to this encounter. It was agony to be this close to Jeff, yet deprived of the touch of his hand on her arm, the brush of his thigh against her hip. Half-turning as if to escape his magnetic pull, she called over her shoulder, "Coming, Bill?"

Jeff's eyes were steely. "Don't let us keep you, McLean. I'm sure you'd like to circulate."

"Uh, come to think of it, I need to find my office mates. We agreed to sit together tonight." Before Courtney could stop him, Bill had disappeared into the crowd.

"That was rude, dismissing Bill like that. He's a nice guy."

Jeff gave an affirmative grunt and took her arm. "Let's split."

"What?"

"You don't have to sit at the head table or give another speech, do you?"

"No, but—"

Jeff took her glass and set it on a tray by the door. "Then you're free to leave. We can talk in my room."

"Your room?"

"I'm spending the night at the hotel."

"Aren't you afraid we may walk in on someone?"

Jeff smiled at the added touch of green in her eyes, a color that had nothing to do with her muted eye shadow. "If you're asking about a woman, no. Give me a little credit, Courtney. I'd never do anything to embarrass you. I'm alone. I've got an early morning meeting in town and decided to save myself a back-to-back drive.''

"But—''

"No more buts. You're beginning to sound like a stuck record. What's the matter? Did you use up all your vocabulary in that speech this afternoon?''

Angry, Courtney tried to dig in her heels. "You can't do this?''

"Do what?'' he asked, dragging her toward a bank of elevators.

"Just waltz back into my life as if you'd never left.''

He jabbed the up button. "You're the one who called it quits.''

The barb struck a nerve, sending her chin up a notch. "True, but, I don't remember your putting up much resistance. So why should we talk now?''

A muscle in his jaw tightened. "Because we're long overdue for...a chat. Get in.''

They didn't speak the rest of the way to the seventh floor. Courtney asked herself why she'd allowed him to railroad her into going to his room. She should have set up a ruckus the likes of which Jeff Herrington had never seen.

Then a small smile crept over her lips. She just might do that yet. She had a bone to pick. Over Nat Hamilton.

Chapter Ten

Courtney stood just inside the door of Jeff's hotel suite. To his way of thinking, she'd never looked more desirable.

She was still wearing the white blouse and maroon linen suit she'd had on during her presentation, but both had lost their former crispness. Instead of being a detraction, the fine creases and wrinkles lent her a touching vulnerability. For evening she'd dressed up the ensemble by draping a colorful scarf around her shoulders and anchoring it with a gold stick pin. The light caress of silk softened the tailored lines of her jacket and heightened her femininity. As did her tousled wheat-colored curls. On the elevator ride, she'd repeatedly pushed a hand through her short hair, disturbing its neat arrangement and creating a style far sexier than one tamed with a brush. Though her lips could have used a fresh application of pink gloss, he liked her better this way—with just a trace of color. What little remained, he had an overwhelming urge to kiss off, leaving her mouth moist and bare and even more inviting than it appeared now.

But Courtney was in no mood to be kissed. She may have been achingly appealing, but she was also madder than a wet banty hen. Her lower lip puffed out in an ill-humored pout, one leg lunged off-center and both fists capped her slender hips. She didn't utter a sound, but beneath thick, dark-brown lashes her eyes nailed his in silent defiance.

Jeff arched a brow. "What got your hackles up?"

"I'm in no mood for games," she said testily.

"I can see that." He walked toward the conversation area and took a seat. "For the record, I hadn't intended to play any."

"No? Then why do I feel like a recalcitrant pup that's been made to heel?"

Jeff returned her intense glare with a smile. "I apologize for the caveman tactics. To be frank, something snapped inside me when I saw you with another man." His expression grew serious, his tone low. "I'm still not over you, Court. I don't expect I ever will be."

"I find that hard to believe," she said, folding her arms across her chest in an attempt to deny the truth of his disclosure. "If the pictures on your paper's society page are any indication, you bounced back after our break fast enough."

He flipped his hand in a dismissive gesture. "Mere social functions where my presence was required rather than requested. It was less awkward to go with someone—anyone—than go alone."

"I wouldn't know."

"Wouldn't you? Does that mean you're pretty thick with this McLean fellow?" His eyes narrowed. "Is it serious? Are you sleeping with him?"

"Of course not!" she sputtered, straightening with a jerk.

Relieved, he ran an index finger across his lower lip. "Interesting. But from where I stood, you two seemed pretty cozy. All those wide smiles—you could have been posing for a toothpaste ad."

"Hold it right there! Bill and I enjoy each other's company, but that's as far as it goes! He's a friend. Nothing more."

"Then why did you latch onto him as if you couldn't bear having him out of your sight?"

"Since when is it illegal to link arms in public?"

"It's not, but that kind of behavior does make a statement."

"So?"

"So it follows that you must have wanted anyone interested to believe you were involved. Am I on the mark?"

"If you're suggesting I was trying to make you jealous, think again."

"I'm not that conceited. What I do think is McLean was a convenient way to fend me off. To quote my old psychology professor, you were using the man 'to ease a social situation.'"

Courtney winced. His accusation hit too close to home. Shrugging, she allowed, "Maybe, but I wasn't using Bill. Not in a literal sense and certainly not to avoid you. But even if that were my motive, he wouldn't have minded. He'd have been glad to play along. I told you, Bill's a friend. And friends are always willing to help each other out."

A satisfied grin spread across Jeff's mouth. "Precisely my point."

"You are the most aggravating man! What point?"

"That appearances can be deceiving. I'm no more involved with the women I've been escorting than you are with McLean."

"Oh?" Her chin tipped upward. "I'm sure your love life's none of my affair."

"A minute ago, you seemed quite interested in it. Now you're pretending you don't care. Let's talk about that."

"I have nothing more to say."

"Then let me do the talking." Jeff patted the place beside him. "Come on, don't stand there by the door." When he noticed her wavering, he entreated, "Please, Court, hear me out."

Courtney was about to turn on her heel but remembered she hadn't yet confronted Jeff about the slanted report on Nat Hamilton. Telling herself she would stick around for that reason alone—not because she had the least curiosity about his social life—she plopped down on the couch, making sure to sit far enough away so she wouldn't feel his body heat or catch a whiff of his aftershave.

Jeff yearned to pull her into his arms. No woman had ever caught his interest and held it as Courtney had, no woman had ever seemed so authentic, so spirited or quite so vulnerable. But he knew better than to crowd her.

He stretched an arm across the back of the couch and chose his next words carefully. "I thought you were magnificent at the session today. Creative, entertaining, innovative."

Of all the things Courtney had been waiting to hear, praise for her talk was the last. Disarmed, she nearly choked on her mumbled "Thank you."

"On the contrary, I should be thanking you. I learned a lot."

"Did you?" A tinge of skepticism laced her voice.

"Yes, I did. And all of it wasn't about graphic design."

"Really? Such as?"

"I know now why I've been hurting so much these past weeks."

"You did...do?" she corrected, unnerved as he edged nearer.

His gaze was intent, burning through her reserve. "I've been starved for the sight of you, for the sound of your voice. I've missed your wit, your intelligence, your warmth. Believe me, Court, I haven't thought of much else. My days have been empty without you."

Courtney closed her eyes against the anguish in his confession. Her mind drained of everything except him. Why did he have to make it so difficult for her? "Oh, Jeff, I've missed you, too," she quavered, too shaken to dissemble, "but—"

"There's that word again. Why don't we forget about the buts. Put the reservations and the fears on hold." He slid his arms around her. "We've been given this evening together. Shouldn't we make the most of it?"

Before she could protest, his head lowered, and his lips brushed against hers, not demanding but coaxing. The touch was electrifying, and her mouth quivered for more. She mustn't let this happen, couldn't let this happen, she told herself, but with his tongue flicking at her lips, his warm breath feathering over her cheek, his fingers spreading through her hair, she was too weak to fight the sensations he aroused.

"Our parting left a bitter taste in my mouth, Courtney," he whispered. "Help me wash it away. Be my love, if only for this night."

He kissed her again, sweetly, tenderly. How could she deny him? How could she deny herself? A hot wave of desire coursed through her, and with a helpless whimper, Courtney linked her arms around Jeff's neck and kissed him back. She groaned as his tongue slid over hers, then swept the sensitive roof of her mouth. She trembled as his hands skimmed up and down her back. She became weightless as he tipped her head and rained kisses along her jaw and over her neck.

Jeff reveled in the feel of her. She was so soft, so fragile, and her small body melded so perfectly with his. How had he survived these past weeks without her? Knowing he couldn't bear to let her go again, he poured all his longing and need into the kiss. Tonight he intended to love her slowly and thoroughly. With his mouth, his hands, his body, he would wipe from her mind any thought of ever leaving him.

Courtney wondered how it was possible to love a man as fiercely as she loved Jeff, and yet know she must let him go. This night of passion would change nothing, but that made her no less determined to have it. Impatient with the barriers between them, her breasts aching for the feel of his hands, she freed the tail of his shirt and began fumbling with the buttons. She was so intent on her task that she was barely aware when Jeff dealt with the pin holding her scarf or when he removed her jacket and slipped her blouse from her shoulders.

At last his palms coasted over her breasts, covered only by twin triangles of lace. "Your skin is like satin. Incredibly creamy. So very, very smooth. I love to feel it, to slide my fingers over it. Here. And here. And under here."

A fine trembling took her. Courtney moaned and arched into his touch. Jeff teased each pert tip with the pads of his thumbs, causing them to pearl with desire.

"So sweet," he murmured. Through the skimpy material covering them, he dropped damp kisses around one rosy aureole, then the other.

Courtney gasped with pleasure. "Take it off," she pleaded. "I don't want anything between us."

Deftly he disposed of the bra, and Courtney rubbed her breasts against his hair-roughened chest. At Jeff's throaty groan, she pulled back and lowered her mouth to trace the flat disks with her tongue.

"You're killing me," he rasped and cupped her chin to bring her mouth back to his.

Courtney had no idea how Jeff rid them of their remaining clothes, but by the time they reached the bedroom, she was quivering with desire.

"Oh, Courtney, I love you so much, so very much," he breathed, coming down beside her. His hands, his mouth, his tongue traveled over her body, memorizing every detail.

She, too, couldn't touch him enough. There was comfort in the strength of his body poised and tensed above hers, delight in the tantalizing sweep of his fingers from her neck to her toes, warmth in the fervor of their kisses.

The moment of climax was so intense that tears sprang behind Courtney's lids and an unconscious cry escaped her lips. "Oh, Jeff. I love you." A second later she felt his own shuddering release.

For a long time neither moved. When the after-shocks subsided, Jeff raised himself up on his elbows, surprised to see two large tears coursing down Court-ney's cheeks. Tenderly he framed her face and caught the drops with the edge of his thumbs. "Did I hurt you?"

"Oh, no. It was just so wonderful."

"For me, too, sweetheart. So very good." His lips met hers for a gentle kiss before he rolled to his side, taking her with him. As he folded her in his arms, he wondered if she knew what she'd cried out in her moment of passion. The words were like a healing balm to his soul, and lightly he brushed a stray tendril from her cheek.

Together they slept deeply and well.

Courtney awoke in a cold sweat, totally disoriented. She felt a leg shift against hers and bolted upright. In her mind she was pinned in the wreckage of a car, next to a lifeless body. The body of her husband. The body of Jeff.

She seemed to be tangled in her seat belt. She ripped at the nylon bands, desperately trying to free herself. Finally she managed to liberate her arms, only to find her legs ensnared. As she clawed at the restraints, she woke with a start. Slowly her eyes began to focus.

At last it dawned on her. She wasn't in a car. She was lying in a bed.

The few seconds it had taken for the terrifying images to flash through her mind had seemed to Courtney like an eternity. While her heart pounded frantically and her breath came in short, quick gasps, the remnants of her nightmare slowly receded.

Blinking several times, she tried to remember where she was. The room was dark and unfamiliar, but through the window she spotted a sliver of moon. Her hand groped among the sheets until it came upon hard, muscled flesh.

The body beside her moved, and an arm flopped across her lap. Courtney shuddered with relief. She was with Jeff, safe in his hotel room bed. Miraculously he slept on, unaware of the torment she'd once more passed through.

Her insides still churning, her brow cold and damp, Courtney arranged the covers over Jeff and eased out of bed. She made her way to the bathroom, closed the door and flipped on the light, squinting until her pupils adjusted. After turning on the faucet, she ducked her head and splashed cool water over her eyes. If only she could wash away the image of Jeff's face, the hazel eyes that held hers just before the terrible impact of her dream.

She groped for a towel and blotted her damp skin, wishing she had something to steady her nerves. She considered going into the sitting area and reading, but she was bone-weary. What she needed was rest. Yet she was afraid to fall sleep again. Afraid the nightmare would return.

Filling a glass with water, she spied Jeff's bottle of vitamins on the counter. A rueful smile crossed her lips. No doubt Rudy had made sure he'd packed them. Maybe taking one would help her. Wasn't vitamin B-something supposed to be a natural sedative?

Courtney uncapped the bottle and shook one of the tablets into her palm. As she prepared to swallow it, she froze. The capsule jogged her memory and brought a chilling thought. Good lord! How could she have forgotten? Shortly after she and Jeff had broken up, she'd gone off the pill. What if tonight they'd made a baby?

With a trembling hand, she recapped the bottle, then—as if the vitamin could ward off pregnancy—gulped it down. Her whole body started to shake uncontrollably, and she was bending over the sink again when strong arms closed behind her. Startled, she jumped.

"It's just me, darling." Jeff tightened his hold and pulled her against him.

Her body sagged, her head dropped, and she turned her face, pressing her cheek into his warmth.

"You're shaking," he said, his voice low with concern.

"I can't seem to stop."

Jeff rested his chin atop her head and set up a steady rocking motion. In the bathroom mirror Courtney saw his arms locked beneath her breasts, her back tucked against his firm chest. She took comfort from the secure fusion of their bodies, moving in steady cadence as Jeff swayed them back and forth. Soon her eyes drifted shut, her breathing deepened.

"I'm okay now."

He shifted her in his arms and dropped a light kiss on her forehead. "Come to bed."

She let herself be led back into the darkened room and gently urged onto the mattress. Jeff joined her, drew up the sheet and pulled her into his protective embrace. "Tell me about it," he urged.

"Same old story." Courtney's eyes shut. She was tempted to talk about the man's face, how it had taken on a frightening clarity. She longed to give voice to her terror, to hear Jeff scoff and make light of it. She also wanted to say how frightened she was about getting pregnant. But when she opened her mouth to speak, the picture imprinted on the back of her lids was too morbid to describe.

Instead of words, a helpless whimper escaped her.

"Oh, sweetheart. It's nothing but a bad dream."

"Why does it seem so real?" *Why,* she asked herself silently, *does going off the pill seem like an omen?*

"Give it time."

Courtney knew he was right. In the light of day, the nightmare would fade. And as far as her worries over a baby were concerned, only the next few weeks would tell if this had been the wrong day. She couldn't dwell on that now. Nor did Jeff seem willing to allow her.

He stroked her arms with calm assurance. He cupped her neck and kissed her brows, the tip of her nose, her chin. His fingers strayed along the curve of her jaw and directed her mouth to his. The kiss was tender, caressing, healing.

"I love you, Jeff," she said.

"Oh, Courtney, darling. I like hearing you say that. I love you, too. Let me kiss away your hurt, make you better." Before long his lips trailed a hot path over her skin. An involuntary tremor pulsed through Courtney, but it had nothing to do with fear.

Soon comfort turned to desire, desire to passion, and she lost herself—and for a time, her dark fears—in Jeff's love.

When she awoke the next morning, she knew she'd been wrong. Her nightmare hadn't ebbed with the dawn of a new day. If anything, she was more afraid than ever.

For the better part of an hour she and Jeff had been arguing about their future. Finally, with a look that pulled her apart, he said, "I can't give you more than I have, Courtney. If my love isn't enough to conquer your misgivings, then maybe the fault's with you. Maybe you simply don't love me enough."

"But I do. I love you too much. Can't you see that's the problem? I'm afraid if we marry, my nightmare will become reality."

Jeff heaved a weary sigh. He'd tried every avenue of persuasion he could think of, but Courtney was too emotionally paralyzed by her past to be swayed. Only one other solution had sprung to mind, but he proposed it tentatively, knowing it was his last resort. "If that's the sole obstacle to our future, how about this? What if we agreed not to have a family? Would that make a difference?"

Courtney hesitated. Endless seconds crawled by before she soberly shook her head. "I couldn't ask that of you. And even if I could be so selfish, it would ruin your relationship with your parents. They're looking forward to grandchildren, and they're bound to resent us—or worse—for deliberately denying them. Besides, a childless marriage would destroy our love."

"You can't know that."

"No, I can't. Not for sure. But I don't want to take the chance, Jeff. I'd rather cherish what we've already had together than risk watching it turn into something hateful or ugly. This way we can look back and feel good about us, about what we shared."

His eyes closed in resignation. "Then it appears we've reached a dead end."

At a loss, Courtney brushed awkwardly at her rumpled skirt. "Not a good choice of words."

"Sorry, but it's how I feel inside."

She lifted a hand to his cheek, and for a moment their gazes met and held. Jeff searched her eyes, seeking, waiting, measuring. When his head began a slow descent toward hers, she panicked. Her hand fell away, and she took a step back. The spell was broken.

"I may be a damn fool, but I'm not willing to give up on us, Courtney. Not yet. My offer still holds—marriage without children. The ball's in your court." He threw his suit coat over a shoulder and started for the door. "If you're willing to accept it, let me know. But don't take too long. I won't wait forever."

He turned the knob and was gone.

"Higher, Aunt Court! Higher!"

Courtney pulled back the park swing and let it fly. Jenny's delighted squeal was matched by her twin when Mary gave Julie a firm push that lifted her skyward.

"So, are you and Jeff back together again or not?" Mary asked while keeping an eye on her wiggling daughters. "No trying to stand up, Julie. Sit still, both of you, or you'll have to get off."

Courtney's own gaze was riveted on her small charge; she knew that at any minute she might have to bring the swing to a halt. "Listen to your mother, Jenny. You have a few years yet before you can try out as an Olympic gymnast."

When both girls settled down, Mary repeated her question. "So what's the status of your love life?"

"How about yours?"

"I asked first. I don't mean to pry, but you did say you ran into Jeff at the conference. What's up?"

"Was that a Freudian slip?"

"Was that an evasion? No fair clamming up on me now. Are you two going to get married or not?"

"Nothing's decided," Courtney admitted, unwilling to say more. To discourage further questions, she gave her attention to pushing Jenny in a gentle, rhythmic arc.

"Young lady, I warned you! No standing up!" Mary stopped the swing, pulled Julie from the seat, then towed her to a nearby bench for a stern lecture.

The mechanical rise and fall of the swing was lulling, and Courtney's thoughts drifted back to the previous weekend and her bittersweet reunion with Jeff. She was in anguish about what to do. One part of her wanted to say yes to his proposal; another told her it would never work.

"Aunt Court, you're not pushing."

Jenny's voice brought Courtney back to reality. "Oh, sorry, angel." As she gave the wooden seat a light shove, she realized that Mary was standing beside her, eyeing her speculatively.

"You daydreaming about the possibility of becoming Mrs. Jefferson E. Herrington the Third?"

"Since we're into rubbernecking," Courtney returned in an attempt to tease, "how's it going with what's-his-name?"

"Dan?" She flicked her hand in a so-so gesture. "He's good company, but I can't say he's Mr. Right. I think the twins intimidate him."

Courtney's grin was droll. "I can't imagine why."

"I'm not hard to please. All I have in mind is a tall, good-looking, well-muscled male with a strong paternal instinct. Any candidates to suggest?"

Courtney could think of one, but she forced herself to enter into the light banter. "I could design an ad for you. Or how about a billboard? I do good work. Just ask Nat Hamilton."

"Speaking of Nat, did you see this morning's paper? His political career may be headed for an abrupt halt. And I was so sure he'd be running for Congress in a few years."

"Mommy?" Julie pouted. "Can I swing again?"

"You know what I said. You're grounded for a week. But it's time for Jenny to get off, too. I need to start supper."

As the four of them strolled toward home, Courtney picked up on Mary's comment about Nat. Last weekend, the moment Jeff took her into his arms, she'd forgotten about her complaint. Now she was glad, since the rumor about his cheating had been confirmed. "I feel terrible about Nat. I sure had him pegged wrong. And he seemed like such a nice, upstanding guy."

"People aren't always what they seem."

"So I've been told," Courtney said, recalling Jeff's admonition not to judge him by what appeared in the gossip columns.

"At any rate, nobody's perfect."

"I guess not. But it's a shame. One mistake and a career's ruined."

"When a man runs for public office—even just a city office—he can expect to have his life examined under a microscope. Hamilton should have foreseen that."

"Did you read the quote from one of his supporters? He sounds as if he's going to be out for blood. I smell more trouble ahead."

"Politics. A dirty business. We probably shouldn't count Hamilton out yet. More often than not these days the bad guys end up heroes."

Courtney took Julie's hand while Mary grasped Jenny's. When the light changed, they crossed the street.

"Says something about our society, doesn't it?" Courtney mused.

"Yeah, and newspapers are in the thick of it. Media mania. Thank God for publishers like Jeff. At least the *Reporter* doesn't sensationalize. I can't see Herrington Press paying Nat to make a quick buck on his biography. No wonder old J. E. wants to keep the Press a family business."

It was another reason, Courtney realized, why an heir was so important to Jeff and his parents.

As Mary opened the door to their apartment building, she missed the grief-stricken expression on Courtney's face.

The Fourth of July held no fireworks for Courtney. It was just as well because her tattered emotional system was long overdue for a day of rest. She'd spent the better part of two weeks trying to talk herself out of her phobia, but to no avail.

During her sophomore year in college, Courtney had taken a psychology course. After the lecture on the significance of dreams, she'd decided to visit one of the psychologists on the Counseling Center's staff. From those few sessions, she'd learned to live with her fears, but to conquer them, she knew, was up to her.

"You must," Dr. Collins had advised, "get out of your imagination and into the real world. Otherwise your past pain is going to act as a barrier against present happiness. There's a possibility that a small part of you wants that. That you're hanging onto the past, hiding behind it, using it as an excuse to protect yourself from risking further hurt."

"Makes good sense," Courtney had agreed. She'd been able to accept the doctor's words intellectually, but her emotions refused to match her reason.

With Jeff, she'd very nearly closed the gap. When she was with him, she felt alive, strong, protected. She'd even seriously considered the possibility of having a child. But she couldn't promise Jeff—not without a nagging shadow of doubt—that when the time came, she would be able to have a baby.

And after her conversation with Mary, she was more certain than ever that she could not deprive Jeff of children. His need for them went beyond emotional fulfillment, beyond any desire he might have for a kind of personal immortality. It was tied in with a well-deserved pride in the reputation of Herrington Press, a reputation carefully built and preserved by his family over the past hundred years. That's why Jeff's pet project—the history of printing in the city—meant so much to him. Not only was it a way of honoring his forefathers but also of preserving the values he cherished for his heirs. Added to that, he was perfect father material. A man who doted on children deserved some of his own.

How, she pondered, was she going to go on without him? He'd opened her heart, taught her to feel again. Something she hadn't allowed herself since she was a small child.

Yet, ironically, because of him the nightmares came more frequently, more vividly than before.

Still, Courtney reflected, she owed him an answer. Was it fair to keep him in limbo awaiting her decision? Shouldn't she have the guts to tell him she wasn't brave enough, to make the break final, to set him free? Was she dragging her heels because she couldn't bear to see him pictured in the Sunday paper with another society beauty?

The questions shamed her and served as a catalyst. She would do it, she decided. She would drop by his office tomorrow.

Sitting tight until he heard from Courtney was ripping Jeff apart. Each day he went to work in a daze, wondering if he'd done the right thing to walk out on her. But he'd been so sure she would stop him. Or at the very least phone him later. It wasn't like him to break off with a woman, only to come back for more. But then other women weren't Courtney Hughes.

He loved her, and she loved him. Why wasn't that enough? In time, their love would overcome her anxieties, he was sure of it. Why wouldn't she take the chance with him?

Jeff slumped back in his desk chair and scrubbed a hand over his face. This mental turmoil was beginning to interfere with his work. His desk was cluttered with odds and ends awaiting his decision, and his father was down the hall expecting him to go over more papers.

He would take care of things with his father first. J. E. liked to finish by one o'clock, have a leisurely lunch, then drive to the club and get in a few holes of golf before dinner.

"Gladys," he spoke over the intercom. "I'll be in my father's office for about an hour. If Ms. Hughes should call... uh, tell her I'll get back to her."

Courtney couldn't imagine what all the confusion was about in the hall leading to the Herrington Press executive suite. A number of staff members had gathered in a circle and were talking excitedly. She poked her head in the reception area, but Gladys Feldkamp was nowhere in sight.

She'd just about decided to take a seat and wait for Jeff's secretary to reappear when a lanky man ran out of the elevator and dashed past her. "Is it true?" he called to the group ahead. "Did someone take a shot at Herrington?"

Courtney's head snapped around and the breath backed up in her throat.

"J. E. or Jeff?" another man yelled, following close on the heels of the first.

"Jeff," a feminine voice from the crowd answered.

"Gunshot?"

"No, a clip on the jaw."

"They catch the guy?"

"Yeah, Jeff decked him. He pulled him into J. E.'s office. They're calling the police now."

"What's it about?"

"Don't know."

At that moment Jeff emerged from behind a closed door, working a palm over the side of his face. When a cheer went up, he lifted his hand to silence the men and women.

"You okay, Jeff?" somebody asked.

"Peachy. Why don't you all get back to work?"

Before the crowd could disperse, the lanky man tossed him another question. "Who was the guy who threw the punch? Somebody said it was a disgruntled member of Hamilton's staff. That right?"

Jeff grinned. "News sure travels fast."

"What do you expect? This is a newspaper, isn't it?"

"Hell," another man piped up, "I didn't know city politics were so hot. You'd think Hamilton was running for President."

"Was the scoundrel a relative?"

"Naw, I can't see my brother-in-law sticking up for me like that."

"Who says it was a brother-in-law?"

"Hamilton doesn't have a brother."

Jeff held up his hands. "Okay, enough. Back to your desks."

Immediately the gathering began to disperse, some of the men giving Jeff a supportive slap on the back. As they walked away, Jeff spotted Courtney standing down the hall. His face brightened. He was beside her in a few swift strides.

"Court! What a surprise!"

"I picked a bad time, didn't I?"

"A little excitement, that's all."

"God, Jeff, for a second I thought you'd been killed."

"Nothing so dramatic."

She raised a hand and ran her fingers over the bluish mark on his jaw. "You're hurt."

He gave her a tilted smile. "You should see the other guy."

Jeff took her arm and led her inside his office. "I can't talk now. The police should be here any minute, as well as the ambulance." At her raised brow, he explained, "My assailant is still out cold. Can you wait?"

"Oh, Jeff, I'm so frightened."

He took her in his arms, his heart leaping with hope. "Hey, it's nothing."

She gave herself only a few precious minutes in his embrace, then stepped away. "I can't wait, Jeff. What I have to say won't take long."

At the formality of her tone, every muscle in his body contracted. "Okay."

"I love you, but I can't marry you." If anything her resolve was stiffer than ever, since the incident had underscored her worst fears.

"That makes a lot of sense."

"I know I must sound like a hypocrite—especially after—" her hand fluttered helplessly "—this, but I'm not right for you. I've thought it over. And over and over. I simply don't want a child. And you do. We have enough differences between us, we don't need that, too."

"Don't you think we can work things out? Together?"

A siren screamed in the distance. As it drew nearer, its ominous tone seemed a fitting accompaniment to the tension that arced between them.

"I want to believe it, but . . . I'm sorry, Jeff."

He stuffed his hands in his pockets. "Is this goodbye?"

She nodded. "I wanted to make it official."

"Mr. Herrington." Gladys's voice came over the intercom.

Jeff went to his desk and pushed a button. "Yes, Gladys."

"Both the police and the ambulance have arrived. I directed them to your father's office. I understand Jack the Clipper still hasn't come to."

"Thanks, I'll be right out." He couldn't bring himself to smile at his secretary's uncharacteristic levity.

Chapter Eleven

As she wiped up the kitchen counter, Courtney blew at a damp lock of hair clinging to her brow. Had there ever been a worse heat wave on record? Hot, humid air hung in the Ohio Valley, making the nights as scorching as the days. Sleeping was difficult, if not impossible. A mixed blessing, she thought, since she was less likely to suffer one of those detestable nightmares. Whether it was the lack of a good night's sleep or whether she was going through a period of remission, she didn't know, but mercifully the horrid dreams had ceased.

Courtney moistened a paper towel and held it to her forehead. Her apartment was getting unbearable. Working all day in air conditioning, then coming home to her stuffy, close quarters drained her energy. She'd considered going out and buying a window unit, but decided to wait for the fall sales. With her luck, a cold snap would hit as soon as she had cool air pumping through her rooms.

Courtney dropped the towel into the garbage, rinsed off the dish that had held her cottage cheese and crackers—all she could stomach on such a steamy night. When had she ever been this affected by the weather? If she didn't feel quite so draggy, she would climb in her car and drive to the shopping mall or the movies to keep cool. She hadn't felt really up to par for well over a month. A lot of what she ate didn't agree with her, and off and on she'd endured bouts of nausea. Weeks ago she'd switched from colas to ginger ale. Mom Granger had sworn by ginger ale to quiet an upset stomach, but so far it hadn't done the trick.

Obviously breaking with Jeff had hit her even harder the second time around. Otherwise why was she physically sick? She was so rundown that she'd totally skipped her last period. The heat didn't help matters. Some days she could barely force herself to go to work.

More than once it had crossed her mind that she might be pregnant, but a quick check of the calendar convinced her that she and Jeff had made love on what should have been a safe, infertile day. Now with her August period a week overdue, she was beginning to think she couldn't blame her woes entirely on emotional distress and the weather. It was possible she had some sort of lingering virus. All she knew was she couldn't run a business when she felt this lousy. Nor could she put off the inevitable much longer. First thing tomorrow, Courtney promised herself, she would call Dr. Stacy's office and make an appointment.

In the living room she turned the fan to high, settled onto her couch and wondered if there was anything worth watching on TV. Probably still reruns. The new fall line-up wouldn't start for several weeks yet.

She reached for the newspaper and scanned the headlines before deliberately turning to the comics. Of late, she'd been avoiding most of the feature sections. Too often she happened across Jeff pictured with Liz Kendall, one of the lovely women seated near Courtney at the charity gala. According to the society editor, Jeff had nabbed his latest conquest from under the nose of David Donahue, Liz's escort that evening, and rumor had them ready to walk down the aisle.

How could she blame him? Hadn't she wanted him to find someone else? Even so, a small part of her hoped he would still be a little bit miserable over their breakup. But if he was, he hid it well. Her sole consolation was that he hadn't returned to Amelia Meyer. Despite her impeccable bloodlines, Courtney didn't think Amelia was right for Jeff.

Never a day passed that she didn't think about him. Right after he'd been assaulted, she'd searched the news for some mention of the event. After a great deal of rummaging, Courtney had located a short article buried on the *Reporter*'s back pages. It pleased her that Jeff had declined to press charges and that no mention was made of his attacker being connected to Nat Hamilton. How like Jeff to play down the incident. Probably also thanks to him, no mention of the episode was ever made in the rival *Daily*.

Unable to appreciate the antics of her favorite cartoon characters, Courtney let her newspaper sail to the floor. Leaning back against the couch pillows, she listened to the twins romp across their living room overhead. Too bad their energy didn't come in capsules.

At the thought of swallowing a pill, her stomach suddenly turned over. Unable to fight back the nausea, she cupped a hand over her mouth and lurched to her feet. How dare her stomach reject food as bland as cottage cheese and crackers! On her way to the bathroom, she told herself that she really must see her doctor.

"Elizabeth Kendall is on line one, Mr. Herrington."

Jeff thanked his secretary and picked up the phone. "Liz, what can I do for you?"

"As of today, not a thing!" Her voice fairly dripped with excitement. "I'm happy to report our little scheme's working."

"You mean David finally took the bait?"

"Hook, line and sinker!"

"It's about time!"

"Amen to that! I suspected he might be about to break. Did you notice him last night? He was so jealous that I could swear his skin took on a greenish tint!"

Jeff laughed and propped crossed legs on his desk. "Now that you mention it, David has been glaring daggers at us lately, but what makes you think he's ready to be reeled in?"

"Because ten minutes ago he sent me a dozen red roses and a five-pound box of candy. *Godiva* chocolates," she added, her sultry tone a pointed reminder of the legendary lady who'd ridden nude through Coventry. "Is there a message there or not?"

"I'd say he'd either like you to gain weight, or else he wants you to let your hair down."

Liz giggled. "Before or after I take off my clothes?"

With a grin, Jeff let his feet hit the floor. "I'll leave that decision up to you. Now if he doesn't try to punch me out for stealing his woman, we're almost home free.''

"Don't worry. When you were talking to your father last night, he asked me just how far our relationship had gone. I acted suitably offended and told him it was none of his business. He saw fit to warn me about your love 'em and leave 'em reputation, but I told him not to fret, that I was well aware of your lady killer image.''

"Thanks for the character reference. David may come after me yet.''

"I don't think so. He's not the violent sort. And I managed to slip in a hint that the last fellow to take a punch at you landed in the hospital with a mild concussion.''

Jeff groaned. "Not something I like to broadcast about, but in this case I'll overlook it. The only way I want to bring David to his knees is in front of you. With an engagement ring in his pocket.''

"That moment may not be far off. He's asked me out for tonight.''

"Does this mean our date is off?''

"I already took the liberty of canceling your dinner reservation.''

"If we hadn't planned all this, I'd take offense. As it is, I couldn't be happier for you.''

"Thanks, Jeff.''

"Thank you, Liz.''

She sounded bewildered. "For what?''

"For keeping me company during a hard time. I hope you don't take this the wrong way, but it was a relief to go out with a woman who expected nothing more than dinner and some good conversation.''

"Don't be so modest, sweetie. If I weren't already head over heels in love with David, I'd be tempted.''

"You're a special woman, Liz. I hope David appreciates how lucky he is to have you."

"What a nice thing to say! It's been fun, Jeff—or as fun as something like this can be. Let me know if you ever need anything. I owe you."

"Be happy, Liz."

After hanging up the receiver, he wished he could take his own advice. He was still as miserable without Courtney as Liz had been without David. If only he could come up with a scheme that would win her over, even one as crazy as the plan Liz had cooked up. At the back of his mind, he'd nursed a secret fantasy that by helping Liz, he might do himself a favor as well. But he wasn't surprised it hadn't turned out that way. Courtney would never be lured as easily as David had been.

From his desk Jeff picked up a copy of his leather-bound history of printing. The first edition had arrived yesterday. He paged through the text, pausing at each of Courtney's illustrations to recall how they'd mulled over the sketches.

Would the pain ever dull? he wondered. Would there come a time when Courtney wasn't the very first thing he thought of in the morning? Would he ever forget what she looked like? What she felt like in his arms?

Thoughtfully, Jeff closed the book and put it back on his desk. As he sat pondering the embossed leather cover, he regretted that Courtney wasn't there to share his pride in their "baby." His mouth twisted to one side as the word popped to mind, but the more he thought about it, the more appropriate it seemed. Producing a book had a lot in common with giving birth. In their own ways, both a child and a literary creation were gifts of the self.

Certainly Courtney had put her best into the project. She deserved to see the finished product. Even better, she ought to have a copy of her own. Though most all the initial books were spoken for, he would send the one on his desk to her. Yet packaging the volume and mailing it with a formal note seemed cold and impersonal. He ought to deliver the book and his thanks in person.

Jeff scrubbed his knuckles over a cheekbone. He wasn't ready to face Courtney. Not yet. As long as he didn't see her, he could always pretend that there was a chance for them—however slim. Sometimes—though less frequently of late—when he thought he couldn't bear another second of living without her, he allowed himself to indulge in the hope that she might change her mind.

One corner of Jeff's mouth slanted up. He'd thought he was finished with self-deception, but Liz's good fortune must have renewed his faith in happy endings.

He snatched up the history book and tucked it in the back of his bottom desk drawer. Courtney would have to wait for her copy. Right now he wasn't up to having his hopes dashed again.

Courtney sat nervously in the large waiting room and counted the number of patients before her. Her doctor's appointment was for four o'clock, and here it was already nearly five. Her stomach felt dangerously squeamish, probably because she hadn't eaten since noon, but it was just as well. She would hate to embarrass herself by throwing up on the examining table.

Bored, Courtney picked up one of the several newspapers lying beside her. It turned out to be an issue of the *Reporter*, and fearing a visual reminder of what she'd thrown away, she tossed the paper aside in favor of an outdated magazine. She wasn't much interested in fashion and glamour, but it would pass the time less painfully than having Jeff's name or picture creep up here and there.

Courtney glimpsed at the wall clock. Five after five. She could be thankful for one thing. The doctor's office was air conditioned.

"Chicken soup! Mary, have you checked the temperature lately? People don't eat soup during a heat wave."

Mary stood at Courtney's door, holding a small pot in her mitt-protected hands. "The weather has nothing to do with it. When you're sick, you need chicken soup. Now kindly step aside so I can deposit this in your kitchen."

"Sorry," Courtney said, ushering her in. "But what makes you think I'm sick?"

"Don't you remember begging off going to the movies last night? Because you didn't feel well?"

"So? I'm not alone. The heat's got everybody down."

"They aren't all rushing to the doctor."

"How did you know I went to the doctor's?"

Mary set the dish on the counter and announced smugly, "I have my sources."

"Such as—?"

"I happened to be driving by Dr. Stacy's this evening and saw you leave her office. What's the matter, honey? You've looked washed out for weeks. Is it depression?"

"Good guess, but slightly off target." Tears welled behind Courtney's eyes, and she turned toward the refrigerator, so Mary wouldn't see. Pulling out a carton of milk, she tried to keep her voice steady. "What ails me, chicken soup isn't going to fix. But I appreciate the thought."

Mary's brow knitted in concern. "What did Dr. Stacy say? Is it serious? You don't need surgery, do you?"

Turning, Courtney gave her a wan smile. "No, but you're getting warm."

"God, Courtney, don't keep me in suspense. What is it?"

"I'm not going to have an operation, Mary. I'm going to have a baby."

Mary's eyes widened and her hand flew to her chest. "You're what?"

"I'm pregnant."

"I want to say that's wonderful, but...I don't know. Under the circumstances, I'm not sure." Without another word, Mary lifted the carton of milk from Courtney's hand, returned it to the refrigerator and led her into the living room. When they were comfortably settled on the couch, she suggested, "I think we need to have a heart-to-heart."

"Don't worry about me, Mary. I'll be fine. Hadn't you better see to the girls? It's not like you to leave them alone."

"You're not getting out of this that easy. For your information, Jenny and Julie are downstairs helping Mrs. Keller make ice cream. I told her I was coming up to see you."

Courtney sought her friend's eyes. "I'm not trying to put you off, Mary, but I'm still in shock. My thoughts are so scattered I don't know if I can put together a coherent sentence."

"So far you're doing fine." She laid a hand on Courtney's shoulder. "Tell me, how do you feel about having this baby?"

"Terrified. For a while this afternoon, I came close to pushing the panic button."

Mary hesitated before asking, "What are you going to do?"

"I haven't gotten that far. For the time being, nothing."

Mary gave her friend's shoulder a pat and reclaimed her hand. "You're wise not to act in haste. You're too upset to make a decision you might regret—later."

Courtney's eyes came back to hers. "I know what you're thinking, Mary, but you needn't worry. I want my baby."

The simple admission required no soul-searching. After an initial surge of alarm and disbelief, she'd broken down and wept tears of joy. Logic, Courtney realized, had nothing whatever to do with her reaction. She was ruled by pure emotion. And bemused by the irony of life. She'd given up the man she loved because she was afraid to bear him children, yet she'd gotten pregnant, anyway. And what happens when she finds out she's going to have a baby? Does she explore alternatives? No way. She's far too busy being thrilled!

Courtney sighed. "I'm not sure how I'm going to manage as a single parent. Wouldn't you know it? My baby isn't even born yet, and already the little dear's half-orphaned—"

"Not exactly. A call to Jeff would fix that."

Courtney shook her head. "How can I go to him now and tell him it was all a mistake and that I want him back? I love him too much to keep hurting him that way. Besides, last time I looked he was practically engaged to another woman."

"But he deserves to know. Surely you intend to tell him."

"When it's the right time. But I'm afraid we'll have to go it alone—the baby and me."

"That's crazy. You love Jeff, and I bet he still loves you. It's not fair to keep this news from him."

"Perhaps, but what if he doesn't love me anymore? What if he decided a clean break was the right thing after all? What if he's serious about someone else? I know Jeff. If I **told** him about the baby, he'd do the honorable thing and marry me—whether he felt anything for me or not."

"Okay, I can't force you to do something you don't want."

"Maybe. But nothing's ever sure, is it?"

Mary's shoulders dropped in defeat. Accepting the futility of further argument, she struggled for a light tone. "You know what they say—the only things you can count on are death and taxes."

Unwittingly, Mary had just given her the perfect opening for mentioning her private fears. Seeking reassurance, she ventured, "True. That's what worries me. Life's so...uncertain."

"What are you getting at, Court?"

"I can't help...that is, what if something happens to me? I know Jeff will take care of the baby, but he isn't immortal, either. What if something should happen to him, too? The way it did to my parents."

"The odds have to be astronomical. But if by some fantastic quirk of fate, you have the bad fortune to be that one in billions or whatever the chances may be, what's the worst that could happen? The Herringtons would certainly see that their grandchild is cared for." Mary lifted her hands, palms upward. "Look at it this way—you had nobody, and you turned out all right."

Courtney gave her a half-smile. "That's debatable, but I'm too vain to argue."

"If you had, I would have countered with my clincher."

Courtney cocked an eyebrow. "Which is—?"

"Would you rather not have been born in the first place?"

"No," came the ready reply.

The more Courtney thought about it, the more Mary's arguments made sense. Despite the problems she'd faced growing up, she'd managed to make something of her life. At least by her own standards. She'd worked her way through college, established a graphic arts agency and was building a successful business. She liked her friends and for the most part, she was content with her life. As content as she could be without Jeff, but somehow she would go on.

By no stretch of the imagination could she be described as deprived. Instead of beating her down, misfortune had made her stronger. If she'd suffered any damage at all from growing up an orphan, it was her fear of bringing children into the world. And now that she was pregnant, even that had magically evaporated.

Hours later, as Courtney slipped into a light gown, a strange sensation swept through her. For the first time in weeks she didn't feel lonely. She had someone with her. Someone dependent on her. Someone to lavish with love. Someone who would love her back. Though she couldn't yet detect the baby's movement, she ran a hand lightly across her stomach and smiled to herself.

* * *

As the weeks passed, Courtney began to look forward to impending motherhood with even keener anticipation. She tried not to think about how foolish she'd been to allow fear to shatter the happiness she'd shared with Jeff. But it was too late to change that now. She couldn't go back. The only way she could triumph over her mistakes was by endowing their child with her hard-won wisdom.

By the end of September she could see subtle changes taking place in her body—a thickening of her waist, a fullness in her breasts. When the nausea and listlessness finally eased, she actually felt pretty good. Mary had even complimented her on her healthy glow. Soon, she decided, she would need to look into purchasing a few maternity clothes.

Early in October, Mary and Courtney were grocery shopping when Mary quietly hinted, "It's time, Court."

"Time for what?"

"Time to tell Jeff about the baby."

Courtney put back the bunch of carrots she was examining and frowned. "I can't. It'll mess up his life." Lately she'd been giving that possibility a great deal of thought. She couldn't help wondering how Jeff would react to her unplanned pregnancy. True, he wanted a child, but that didn't mean he'd still welcome her as the mother of his baby. Especially after she'd walked out on him. Nor could she dismiss the likelihood that he and Elizabeth Kendall might by now be officially engaged.

"Don't you see? You're going to mess it up sooner or later. And later won't necessarily be easier. If anything, it'll be harder."

"I've waited so long, how is he going to feel?" The question was put to herself more than to Mary. Jeff's involvement with Liz complicated matters. Their romance was public knowledge. What would he think if she broke the news about their baby just as he was ready to walk down the aisle with another woman?

"Well?"

"What was that?" Courtney asked, suddenly aware that her friend was waiting for a reply.

Mary gave a quick shake of her head. "I hate to play on your weakness, but you do need to begin planning for the child's future. Jeff would want that. You know he would."

Nodding, Courtney met her earnest gaze. "I suppose you're right. I'll give it some serious thought."

Mary wheeled her grocery cart around. "That's a start."

Courtney pulled on an oversized sweater and bloused it over her baggiest jeans. If she left the snap open and the zipper partway down, she felt comfortable. The large bulky sweaters that were all the rage provided just the right camouflage for her newly rounded stomach.

Pregnancy must be a real upper, she decided, because she was feeling terrific this bright Saturday morning. There was a slight nip to the air, a perfect day for a long walk in the neighborhood park. She thought about taking the twins, then remembered they were spending the weekend with their father.

As she bent to tie her tennies, she reflected on the little girls. She wasn't sure how she and Mary were going to explain the baby to them, but maybe they were too small to wonder about daddies. Especially since they saw their own father only a couple of times a month.

A knock at the door brought Courtney to her feet. "Coming," she called. Before unbolting the lock, she checked the peephole. Her eyes widened in astonishment, and for a split second she considered not acknowledging her visitor. But just as quickly she rejected retreat. Slowly she turned the knob and allowed the door to swing open.

"Hello, Courtney."

"Jeff. What can I do for you?"

God, it was good to see her! Shifting his weight from one foot to the other, he suggested, "To begin with, you might invite me in."

"Sorry." Flustered, she stepped back and let him enter. "How have you been?"

"Okay."

He didn't look okay. He was thinner than she remembered, and his eyes were hollow, his face haggard. A knot of fear twisted inside her. Was he ill? Then his mouth turned up in the dazzling smile that never failed to melt her heart, and she decided he'd been working too hard.

"You look great, Court." Better than great, he thought. She looked fantastic. It piqued him a bit that she'd gotten over him so quickly. He, on the other hand, was feeling dreadful. He ate so little that Rudy was beginning to nag. And despite throwing himself into his work until he was ready to drop at night, he hadn't slept well since they'd parted.

Courtney responded to the compliment with self-consciously murmured thanks, then, fumbling for something to say, sputtered the first thing that popped into her mind. "How's work?"

"Fine," he allowed, startled by the question. "Here, I brought you something." Feeling as ungainly as a teenager, he extended his arm. "The book."

Not until that moment did Courtney realize he was clutching a small brown volume. When he offered it to her, their hands brushed, and she felt a familiar rush of pleasure.

"Oh, it's finished!" She ran her fingertips over the smooth leather. "How lovely. I like the title."

"*Pressed for Time* seemed appropriate. The subtitle's inside—*A History of Printing in the Queen City.* Go ahead, open it up."

Carefully she turned back the leather cover and examined the cream-colored pages. She let out an excited breath as she scanned the credits. "You included my name!"

"Of course. As illustrator."

"I've never seen my work in a book before."

"It's a thrill, isn't it?"

Fascinated, she studied the first illustration, then lingered over several more before she realized they were both still standing. She signaled him to take a seat. "I'm forgetting my manners. Would you like something to drink? Coffee maybe?"

"That would be nice."

"Is decaf okay? It's all I have."

"That's fine."

She placed the book on her dining table while she went to prepare the coffee. When she returned, she said pleasantly, "It'll be ready in a few minutes. Meanwhile, would you excuse me while I examine the history?"

"By all means. That's why I brought it."

Courtney took her time perusing the volume. She felt Jeff's eyes on her, but she couldn't bring herself to meet them. She should be making small talk, but she couldn't force out the words. Instead, she pretended complete absorption in the book.

Jeff was delighted to sit and watch her. Sun coming through a nearby window caught in her pale hair and illuminated her face, giving it the translucence of fine china. Her long, dense lashes shadowed her eyes as she slowly turned page after page. He wished he had her artistic talent. He'd like to sketch her just the way she looked at that moment. Perfect.

Courtney glanced up. "Perfect," she said as if she'd been reading his mind instead of the book. "It's a gem."

"Thanks to your illustrations."

"Hardly. Your printer deserves all the credit. The reproductions are an art in themselves." She lovingly stroked a page. "The font styles, the quality of paper, the binding—it's a collector's item."

"That was the general idea. Your approval means a lot to me, Courtney."

"I'd be hard pressed to come up with any criticism," she allowed, touched that her opinion mattered to him.

"This is the first book I've overseen alone. All the others Dad's had a hand in. I guess I was a little uncertain if I could pull it off. If it would meet Herrington Press standards."

"And did it?"

"Dad was pretty lavish with his praise—lavish for him, anyway...."

"I'm glad." Feeling uneasy beneath his steady gaze, she suggested, "I'll get the coffee."

Jeff followed her to the kitchen and accepted the steaming mug. "So tell me, what's new in your life?"

At the question, her hand jerked, and hot coffee sloshed over the rim of her cup. "I've been meaning to talk to you about that."

"Have you met somebody?" he asked anxiously. Was that why she seemed so radiant? Had she fallen in love with someone else? Had she and that Bill fellow finally clicked?

"Do you mean, is there a man in my life?"

He nodded, suddenly unable to speak.

She gave him a noncommittal shrug and ran her reddening fingers under the faucet. The gesture wasn't a deliberate attempt to lead him on, but it did occur to her that she could be carrying a male child. Frustrated at her clumsiness, she snapped off a paper towel to wrap her hand and observed irritably, "I noticed you didn't let any grass grow under your feet."

"What's that supposed to mean?"

"Isn't Elizabeth Kendall about to become Mrs. J. E. Herrington the Third? If you haven't already made her your wife."

"Hardly. She's in love with David Donahue."

"Well, you could have fooled me! Every time I picked up the *Reporter*, you were escorting her to some function or other."

"I know we were pictured together on a few occasions, but I was only helping Liz make David jealous." He permitted himself a smug grin. "You'll read about their engagement in tomorrow's paper."

"Congratulations!" Irritated that she'd agonized for weeks when all along Jeff's big romance was nothing but a sham, she wadded the towel and tossed it onto the counter. Involuntarily she winced at the searing pain her show of anger caused.

"Damn it, Courtney, let me see that hand—you've burned yourself."

"Never mind!" She turned aside and sucked on the injured flesh."

"Mulish woman! You can't just go through life afraid to let anyone share the responsibility for your well-being!" He knew he was overreacting, was talking about a great deal more than a few scalded fingers, but he couldn't help himself. It hadn't occurred to him that Courtney would be hurt by his mock involvement with Liz. He'd thought she wanted him out of her life, that she didn't give a whit what he did. Though he regretted he'd upset her, at the same time her reaction brought him a glimmer of hope.

Courtney spun away and braced her hands on the counter. "Oh, come off it, Jeff. You're making me sound as though I'm little Miss Self-Sufficiency."

Jeff slammed down his cup. "Aren't you?"

"No, I'm . . . I'm good and ticked off. The least you could have done was tell me."

"About what?"

"You and Liz," she bit out. "Did you have to behave as if you were having such a good time?"

"Do you know how hard that was for me? To pretend I was enjoying myself when all the while I wanted to be with you?" He balled his hands into tight fists. "Hell, I'd say my performance deserved an academy award!"

At his confession, her anger evaporated as rapidly as a drop of water under a blazing sun. "There's no need to shout. I'm not hard of hearing."

The softness of Courtney's admonition brought Jeff up short. He stepped around the table and came up behind her. His hands went to her shoulders and began a gentle kneading. "Sorry. I didn't mean to yell. I just happen to care about you."

When he gently turned her to face him, his contrite expression melted her heart. Smiling, she asked, "Don't you know parents shouldn't argue in front of their baby?"

Visibly confused, he stammered, "I fail to see...what baby?"

"Ours. Yours and mine."

"Ours? Ours?" he repeated more forcefully. "Are you saying that—?"

"I'm pregnant." She lifted her sweater and tugged on the waistband of her jeans. "See? That's why these don't fit."

"Pregnant?" Staggering backward, Jeff closed his hand about a chair rail. "I think I'm going to faint."

"Mothers faint, silly. Not fathers."

"Courtney, how did this happen?"

"The usual way. After we, or rather, I decided we shouldn't see each other again, I flushed my birth control pills down the toilet. Then at the convention—" her face flushed a becoming red. "—I didn't stop to think about the possibility of getting pregnant until afterward. And it shouldn't have happened. That is, I didn't think it was the right time, but going off the pill when I did...I guess I screwed things up, huh?"

"No way, sweetheart. Dumping those pills may have been the smartest thing you ever did." He took her in his arms and rested his cheek against her temple. "But I thought you didn't want a baby."

She went still. "You mean you're surprised I didn't do something about it when I found out."

Jeff placed a palm on each side of her face and tipped back her head until their eyes collided. "Nothing could have been further from my mind. Whether you realize it or not, Courtney Hughes, you have strong maternal instincts." He watched her eyes mist over, and his voice caught. "I never stopped hoping they would win out in the end."

Courtney broke into a wide smile. "I guess you're right. Funny, how quickly I changed my mind when I learned I was going to be a mommy."

He pulled her close. "When did you find out, Court?"

"A couple of weeks ago."

"A couple of weeks!" Jeff held her away from him and regarded her through half-closed eyes. "And just when did you plan to tell *me*? Or weren't you going to?"

"I was working up my nerve. I thought you were ready to marry Liz. I wasn't sure you'd be too pleased."

"Do I look unhappy?"

"No. No, you don't."

"When are you going to get through your pretty head that you're the woman I love? You, Courtney." Hugging her to him, he promised, "We'll get married right away."

She rested her forehead against his chest. "Oh, Jeff, are you sure? I think you should know I'm still a little afraid. I'll probably be a worry wart the rest of my life." Leaning back, she grinned sheepishly. "As soon as I saw that you'd lost weight, I started having an anxiety attack. I wondered if you were sick."

"Nothing's wrong with me that marrying you won't cure."

"Jeff Herrington, I love you."

"I love you, too, Courtney. God, how I love you!" Slowly his head began to lower toward hers. "In case you've forgotten how much, let me refresh your memory."

Chapter Twelve

Jeff covered Courtney's mouth with his. The moment their lips made contact, a small, broken cry escaped her. She plunged her fingers into his thick, dark hair, re-learning its texture, delighting in its feel. At once she was swept under by a wave of need so powerful that she wanted to drown in it. Drown in Jeff. Too long denied, Courtney arched into him, desperate to bring him nearer, frantic to weld her body to his. They were a part of each other now as they'd never been before. The proof of that oneness nestled within her.

Courtney's eagerness tore a ragged groan from Jeff. His mouth widened, his kiss deepened. If he could, he would have swallowed her, sucked her into his body, his soul. He was a starving man, and Courtney was the only one who could satisfy his hunger, a hunger that had gnawed at him for weeks, months, years. His entire life.

They couldn't get enough of each other. Courtney locked her hands behind his neck, dragging him closer, making his mouth her prisoner. They clung together like two lost souls, each afraid of breaking the hold, each terrified of being set adrift without the other, of losing what they'd found again.

With their lips still fused, their hearts pounding against their ribs, Jeff brought a hand under Courtney's knees and lifted her into his arms. His lips coasted over her brows, her nose, her cheeks. Her mouth was bereft without his, and she placed a hand at his jaw to force his lips back to hers. The kiss left them both shaken.

"God, Courtney, I was sure I'd lost you. I'm never going to let you go again. Never." He dropped his forehead against her temple, struggling for control. "I want to strip away these clothes, to feel your silky skin against my body. I crave being inside you, deep inside, but I'm trembling so much I'm afraid I won't be able to hold back. I may hurt you. And the baby—"

"It's all right, my love. Neither of us is that fragile. It's what I want, too. My whole body's on fire."

Jeff demanded no further encouragement. With long, swift strides, he carried her to the bedroom, then gently, reverently placed her on the mattress. He had to make a conscious effort to steady his shaking hands as he began to undress her.

Courtney's bulky sweater had a line of buttons down the front. As Jeff freed them one by one, he forced himself to go slow. When he'd opened the last button, he parted the soft knit. His breath caught as he viewed her breasts, bursting from the confines of a small, lacy bra.

When Courtney saw the direction of his gaze, she smiled. "One of the benefits of motherhood. I need a larger size."

"Lovely." Releasing the front clasp, he allowed the creamy mounds to spill into his palms. He took special delight in caressing their smoothness, testing their heaviness. His thumbs flicked over both rosy nipples, and he smiled at the hard thrust of their pointed tips. Slowly he lowered his head and bathed each center thoroughly before taking it into his mouth and sucking gently.

"Will you nurse the baby?" he murmured.

Courtney nodded, unable to speak as a hot shaft of desire speared from her breasts to her loins.

"I'm going to like watching you." His voice was clogged with emotion.

Courtney ran her fingertips from his shoulder to his hand. Even through his shirt and pullover, she could detect the hard muscles that bunched beneath her touch. "Take this off. I want to feel you next to me."

Smiling, he obliged her. When both his sweater and shirt lay on the floor beside her own clothing, Courtney reached for him. Still sitting, he lowered his chest against hers. The bare contact was electrifying. She moaned and rubbed her breasts against the crinkly body hair that spread across his upper torso.

"I like the way this feels," she said, "but I'd enjoy it even more if I were on top."

To his surprise, she pushed him onto his back and straddled his thighs. Languorously she let her breasts graze his skin. At his moan of pleasure, she dipped her head and circled first one flat male disk, then the other.

Her tongue was a ribbon of soft velvet trailing over his heated skin. Jeff groaned and gripped the rumpled

covers in his hands, afraid to touch her, afraid he would
be tempted to rip off their remaining clothes and take
her too fast.

"Sweetheart . . . no more."

"I like to make your nipples harden, see your body
respond to me the way mine does to you. But if you
don't like it—"

"I like it—too much. It's sweet torture. But I'm not
going to be able to restrain myself much longer."

"I don't mind."

"I do. I want this to be very special. For both of us."
In one swift movement, Jeff rolled her beneath him.
"Your turn again."

He untied her canvas shoes and removed her white
socks, pausing to massage and kiss each of her toes.
Then he slipped her jeans down her legs, leaving her
clad only in a scrap of nylon and the locket he'd never
seen her without. His eyes were drawn by the flash of
gold, and he lifted the necklace with one finger. "Who
gave you this?"

"It was my mother's. It's all I have left of her and my
father. Their pictures are inside."

He flicked open the heart-shaped charm. Though he
could barely make out their features from the tiny por-
traits, he could tell that Courtney's parents were a
handsome couple.

"Mr. and Mrs. Hughes," he said, speaking to the
photos, "I love your daughter more than life itself, and
I want you to know I'm going to marry her. I promise
to take good care of Courtney and our baby. It doesn't
matter to me whether we're blessed with a girl or boy,
but—if it's okay with Court—I hope this child won't be
our only one. I'm sorry you haven't lived to see what a
beautiful woman your daughter's become and what a

terrific mother she's going to be, or that you'll never get to rock your grandchildren to sleep, but that's something you had no control over. I know you didn't mean to die and leave Courtney alone in the world. I know if you'd thought about it, you'd have made sure she had godparents who would have given her a home. But death came before you were ready for it. Though it took her a while, Courtney has finally come to terms with your loss and the anxiety it caused her. She's learned that while it's wise to be prepared for the worst, she shouldn't sit around always expecting it. So if one or both of us dies young, we'll make sure our children will never lack warmth and love and caring. I'm sure you'd want that for them as much as you must have wanted it for Courtney.''

He snapped the locket shut and looked into Courtney's eyes. Tears spilled over and trickled down her cheeks. Tenderly Jeff wiped them away, his lips following the sweep of his thumbs.

''I thought my love for you couldn't be greater,'' she said in a cracked whisper. ''But I've never loved you more than at this moment. Can you understand that?''

''Yes. Because it's the same with me. When I found out our child is growing in your body... God, I can't tell you how much more I cherish you now than when I woke up this morning. And this is only the beginning. Our love will keep on growing, Courtney. It'll get better and better.''

He kissed her then, thoroughly, lovingly, avidly. Sliding down her body, he pressed his lips to her navel. ''This kiss is for both of you,'' he murmured, then ran his hands down her sides and along her thighs. When his fingers slid beneath her panties, she gasped.

"I want to love every inch of you, Court," he rasped, slipping the nylon down her legs.

"Please hurry. I need to feel you next to me."

He made quick work of his remaining clothes and lay down beside her. Together they gave themselves up to the magic touch of fingers, to the moist feel of lips. They stroked and petted until both were weak with pleasure.

And when their moment of fulfillment came, they met it as one.

Courtney stood beside Jeff outside the Herrington mansion. Her stomach was in knots, and she had a death grip on the small bag she clutched in both hands. "You have told them about the baby, haven't you?" she asked as they waited for the massive front door to be opened.

"Not yet. I wanted us to do it together. They were shocked enough to learn that I'm getting married. One thrill at a time."

"I'm nervous, Jeff. Maybe you should have prepared them. What if they think I'm trying to trap you?"

He reached for her hand, lacing her fingers with his. "Not a chance. Especially after my rapid about-face from grouch of the year to the world's most cheerful man. They couldn't ask for better proof of how happy I am."

"Still we have put the cart before the horse, so to speak, and your parents are on the conservative side, aren't they?"

"Stop fretting. I'm sure they know I'm no monk."

Unconvinced, Courtney chewed on her lower lip. "That doesn't mean they won't be angry with me."

"I doubt that." He lifted their locked hands to kiss her fingertips. "After all, you're about to make them grandparents. It's what they've wanted for years."

"When I met them, I wasn't under the impression that I'd made it into their top ten choices for daughter-in-law."

"Relax, sweetheart," Jeff coaxed, realizing that he could measure her nerves by the lightness of her humor. "You're manufacturing trouble again."

"I am not. I'm merely preparing myself for the worst. Weren't you the one who said there's a difference between being ready for a disaster and constantly expecting it?"

Jeff laughed. "I hate a woman with a steel-trap mind."

Just then the door opened, and a poker-faced butler let them in. "Good evening, sir," he greeted, his head inclined in a formal bow.

"Hello, James. You're looking good."

"Not bad for my age, sir."

As they stepped into the entry hall, Jeff explained, "James has been with our family for nearly thirty years." Addressing the older man, he said, "This is Courtney Hughes, my fiancée."

His name was so typical of an old family retainer that it brought a faint smile to Courtney's lips. James welcomed her, and she nodded, wondering if she should offer to shake hands.

Before she could decide, Jeff took her elbow. "Where are my parents?"

"In the library, Mr. Herrington." He folded Courtney's wrap over his arm.

"Good." Jeff was pleased that they'd chosen the cozier quarters over the formal living room.

"Shall I announce you, sir?"

"Thanks, but there's no need to. They're expecting us."

As Jeff guided her down a long hallway, Courtney whispered, "What a contrast to Rudy!"

He chuckled. "James is from the old school. I don't think he's ever called me by my first name. When I was a child, it was 'Master Herrington.'"

"Remind me to make Rudy an honorary uncle. I don't want any little masters or mistresses running around our home. Only kids."

Jeff's heart soared, and he stopped to turn her toward him. "I'm glad you made that plural."

Courtney smiled. "I'm really getting into this mother role. Just think, if it hadn't been for you, I might have gone through life and missed one of its greatest joys."

"You're the one who's a joy." He bent down and kissed her tenderly, ending the embrace far sooner than either would have liked. "We'd better pick this up later. Otherwise I'm going to be in no condition to talk to my parents. Are you ready to see them?"

"Do I have a choice?"

He grinned and gave her bottom a push. "Move, woman. The library's at the end of the hall."

Both Herringtons rose as they entered. Courtney's artist's eye took in the room at a glance—the built-in bookshelves, the mantled fireplace, the walnut furnishings, the overstuffed chairs, the rich Oriental rug. Muted colors set off original paintings by Impressionists Courtney recognized and admired—Monet, Renoir, Pissarro.

To Courtney's surprise, Jeff's mother wore a simple beige skirt and matching tailored blouse, his father casual slacks and an open-necked polo shirt. Somehow she'd been unable to imagine them dressed in anything but formal attire. She felt somewhat out of place in her new two-piece outfit, designed to disguise her expanding waistline.

"Please have a seat, Ms. Hughes," J. E. said, directing her to a wide chair angled beside the fireplace.

"Call me Courtney. Or Court, if you like."

"I suppose we should since you won't be Ms. Hughes for long. Or do you plan to keep your maiden name?"

"No," she replied, gliding a palm across her stomach. "I don't think that's a good idea."

"Good," Mrs. Herrington chimed in as she and her husband took the love seat facing the hearth. "I may be old-fashioned, but I think a woman ought to use her husband's name."

"About the wedding," Jeff began, claiming the arm of Courtney's chair, "we thought—"

"Not so fast," his mother interrupted. "We hardly know Ms.—Courtney. Give us a chance to get acquainted. There's plenty of time to discuss your marriage later."

"I suppose you were astounded about Jeff's getting engaged," Courtney remarked. She didn't know whether her bluntness stemmed from nervousness or a desire to provoke a reaction from his phlegmatic parents. But despite perfect climate control, the atmosphere in the room seemed stifling. Her palms were moist, and she could feel tiny beads of perspiration dotting her hairline.

"We weren't at all surprised to learn he's finally marrying," Grace countered. "But to be honest, we were a bit bewildered when he mentioned your name. I mean we'd seen him with you only once."

"What my wife is trying to say," J. E. interjected, "is that we knew about you, of course, but we thought you and our son were business associates. We had no idea you were seeing each other socially."

Jeff saw the mixture of hurt and uncertainty in Courtney's eyes. "Hey," he said, taking her hand in his, "a grown man doesn't tell his parents everything. Especially the most private things."

His mother smoothed an imaginary wrinkle from her skirt. "Apparently not."

An uncomfortable silence reigned until Jeff's father cleared his throat. "I must say you're quite a talented artist, Courtney. Your illustrations in *Pressed for Time* were first-rate. Weren't they, Grace?"

She gave a perfunctory nod, and Courtney smiled.

"As a businessman, I'm wondering what you intend to do about your agency after you and Jeff marry."

"I wasn't planning to quit working. At least not right away."

Grace's expression was mildly disapproving. "I don't believe a Herrington woman has ever been engaged in gainful employment."

Jeff's fingers grazed the back of Courtney's neck. "Don't you think that's up to Courtney? She's perfectly capable of deciding what she wants to do with her life. And if she chooses to continue with Hughes Designs, that's fine by me."

His mother looked offended. "We weren't trying to tell Courtney what to do, Jeff. But as your wife, she'll have a big house to run, social obligations to meet. I don't see how—"

"Rudy's been looking after me and my house since I moved into it. He can continue to do so. As for social obligations, Courtney isn't into women's clubs, Mother.''

"But the contacts are so important for the Press." She averted her eyes. "Of course, I shouldn't expect Courtney to understand that."

Courtney's spine stiffened. "May I say something here?"

"By all means," J. E. encouraged.

"I know there will have to be some changes in my life when I marry Jeff. In a minute, we'll get to one of the biggest. As for my agency, for some time now I've been thinking of taking on an assistant. I'm not sure I can swing that financially yet, but I thought of a compromise. I have a friend from college, Bill McLean. He's quite creative, and he'd be a real asset to the business. Bill would have joined me from the start, but he was worried that we couldn't attract enough clients to ensure us both a steady income. Since I'm on firm ground now, I think he'd jump at the chance to buy into the business—as a partner."

"If you'd rather not do that," J. E. suggested, "I'm sure Jeff would be glad to pay an employee."

Courtney shook her head. "No. I founded Hughes Designs, and I'll run it on my own. I don't want Jeff's money."

"You could think of it as a good investment for me."

"No, Jeff. We'll keep our business accounts separate."

"That's admirable of you," Grace said, "but hardly necessary."

"Perhaps not monetarily, but my pride's involved here. Aside from that, Bill's been a good friend to me, and I'd like to do something nice for him. The agency would certainly benefit from his expertise, and before long I'm going to need someone else to shoulder part of the workload." She sucked in a breath and let it out slowly. "Particularly when the baby comes."

"I'm pleased you want a family soon, Courtney. I've been looking forward to grandchildren for years."

Jeff hugged Courtney to him and announced, "Isn't it terrific you have only about five more months to wait?"

Grace looked puzzled. "How's that?"

"Courtney and I are expecting a child in March."

If Courtney had felt that the earlier silence in the room was unnerving, she was mistaken. The quiet following Jeff's announcement was so absolute that she was sure she would have heard an ant—if one had dared invade this imposing structure—crawl across the thick Oriental carpet.

"Don't you think congratulations are in order?" Jeff asked.

Grace regarded him through slitted eyes. "I don't know what to think."

"Isn't that like a woman, Dad? She wants grandchildren, but when the time comes, she isn't sure how she feels about being called Grandma."

Grace was not to be swayed by her son's teasing. "My disappointment has nothing to do with the baby."

"I'm glad you're doing the right thing, son," his father put in.

"What kind of comment is that?"

Grace looked as if she'd just found the missing piece to a jigsaw puzzle. "You've gotten Courtney pregnant, so, of course, you must marry her. We wouldn't want our first grandchild to be born illegitimate."

"You're acting as though I'll be serving some sort of sentence. It's no hardship, Mother. I'm crazy about Courtney. I couldn't be happier."

His mother's brisk nod acknowledged Jeff's avowal but at the same time managed to dismiss it as perfunctory. "We must have the wedding as soon as possible. I hope you don't want a big church affair, Courtney. I think that under the circumstances, a small home wedding would be in better taste."

Jeff jumped up, his hands knotted in tight fists. "That's enough! If you're going to take this kind of an attitude, forget it! We'll elope."

"Jeff, don't use that tone with your mother! Apologize at once!"

Grace stretched out a hand. "It's all right, dear."

"No, it isn't. I didn't raise our son to act like some...some—"

"Some what?" Jeff spat out, his face an angry red.

"I don't care how old you are," J. E. shouted, "I won't tolerate a lack of respect."

"Lower your voices," Grace ordered. "James will hear."

"Don't you think it's time you stopped worrying about image, Mother?"

In seconds, parents and son were engaged in a heated argument. Appalled, Courtney jumped to her feet. "Stop it! All of you."

Three pairs of startled eyes snapped to her as if their owners were only then aware that she was in the room. Her tone was quiet but adamant. "I love you, Jeff. I don't expect I'll ever love another man more. But if marrying me is going to come between you and your parents, the wedding is off."

Her gaze settled on his mother and father. "Let me tell you something about family. You said you needed to know me better, Mrs. Herrington, and you're right. I'm not certain how much Jeff's told you, but I grew up in a series of foster homes. One of them was warm and loving, some were okay, and a few were—let me put it this way, I got my share of knocks."

"Courtney, you—"

"Quiet, Jeff, I'm not finished. I don't believe any of you here understand what you've got going for you. Maybe you were an absentee father, Mr. Herrington, and maybe you had your own interests, Mrs. Herrington, but you both cared about Jeff. He has that to hang on to, no matter how resentful he is at being sent away to school or not having kids over to spend the night."

Shock registered on J. E.'s face, pain on Grace's, but Courtney forged ahead. "Since I never had the luxury of a mother and father—at least not for long—I know what a precious thing you've been privileged to share. You may not be aware of it, but together you've forged a strong bond. A friend told me I shouldn't worry about how you two feel because I wouldn't be marrying you, I'd be marrying Jeff. But I don't see it that way. Either we're all in this together, or I'm not in it at all."

She swung around to pick up her bag and found her arm imprisoned by a steely grip. "Courtney, I'm not going to let you go. I love you too much. I want you. I want our baby. I want us to have a real home."

"So do I, Jeff. But not at the cost of alienating you from your parents."

She jerked her arm from his grasp and was across the room when J. E.'s anguished voice halted her. "Young woman, don't you dare walk out that door. That's our grandchild you're carrying."

Pivoting, she saw that Jeff's father was fighting tears. His mother wasn't so successful. She drew a lace hankie from her pocket and dabbed at her eyes. Then slowly, as if she'd aged a hundred years, she turned toward her son. "Why didn't you tell us you felt neglected?"

Jeff couldn't remember ever seeing his mother cry before. He would have preferred to say nothing, but he supposed he owed them an explanation. "As Courtney said, Dad was rarely around when I was a boy."

"I was only trying to keep Herrington Press in good shape," J. E. offered quietly, "so I could pass it on to you."

"I realize that, Dad, but it didn't help much when you missed my Little League games. And you, Mother. Most of the time you were so busy with charities and clubs that you didn't get around to buying me a birthday or Christmas present."

"I simply had trouble deciding because I was afraid what I picked out wouldn't suit you. You were so independent—insisting on doing everything for yourself." She sniffed. "When you were little, you were always filled with too much energy to sit still for long. Even for cuddling. I don't mean to sound self-pitying, but I felt slighted. And a little intimidated."

"Such strong character," J. E. noted proudly, "in one so young. You were a true Herrington. That's why we sent you away to school. We hated to do it. The house seemed like a mausoleum. But we told ourselves we couldn't be selfish. Not when it meant having the best for you."

Jeff's voice came out in a hoarse whisper. "I know, Dad. I know that's what you both wanted, but to a kid it seemed like you were shutting me out."

"I'm sorry, son. If I could turn back the clock, I would. It may be too late for us, but with your child, we'll have a chance to start over and get it right this time."

A tear hung at the corner of Jeff's eye and threatened to topple down his cheek. He looked so forlorn that Courtney thought her heart would break. "God," she said, "it tears me up to see a grown man cry."

He opened his arms, and she ran into them. He held her close, his tears dampening her hair. "How did I ever get so lucky?"

"She's going to make a fine mother, isn't she, Grace?"

"I'll have to be darned good," Courtney jested, "if I'm going to keep this baby from being spoiled."

Grace moved near. "After Jeff was born, I lost four babies. I'd have kept on trying, but the doctor said no." She laid a soft hand on Courtney's shoulder. "Now I have the daughter I always wanted."

Jeff felt a stinging at the back of his throat. "I never knew that. About the miscarriages."

She lifted her shoulders, a weak smile curving her lips. "I didn't want you to be disappointed."

Jeff and Courtney chose to be married in Courtney's church. They decided on a small wedding, limited to family and a few close friends. Mrs. Herrington was proud to be escorted down the aisle by Bill McLean, who, along with Al Schmidt, served as an usher. Frank flew in to stand up with Jeff, and Mary Mitchell served as matron of honor. Dressed in light pink, Jenny and Julie put in sterling performances as flower girls.

For Courtney, the wedding ceremony was one beautiful haze. At Grace's insistence, she borrowed her wedding gown, a ballerina-length silk in pale champagne. Mary gushed that it was the exact color of Courtney's hair. She ordered new satin pumps dyed to match, and Jeff presented her with diamond earrings to go with the spectacular ring on her left hand. Her mother's locket was her something old, and she carried a bouquet of delicate blue flowers, pale yellow roses and baby's breath.

Jeff looked resplendent in a three-piece off-white suit. As she walked down the aisle on the arm of Arthur Granger, Jeff seemed incapable of taking his eyes off her.

The Herringtons hosted a large reception in their home where James and Rudy had their hands full keeping the twins out of trouble. Amelia Meyer showed up and immediately latched onto Bill, who was immensely flattered by her attentions. Courtney's friends and Jeff's seemed to get along fine, and the Herringtons made a special effort to be sure the Grangers felt welcome. Though Mom Granger hadn't been well enough to accompany the other family members, she sent Courtney her love, and Jeff promised that they'd fly to Arizona for a visit after the baby was born.

When the last guest had finally departed, Courtney thanked Jeff's parents for the party, then astonished James and Rudy by seeking them out and giving them both hugs. "You were wonderful to take care of Julie and Jenny. And I know Mary appreciated your help, too."

James blushed. "They are quite a handful, madam."

"An understatement if I've ever heard one," Rudy concurred, rolling his eyes toward the ceiling and making everyone laugh.

Jeff and Courtney spent the night in the same Hyatt suite where they'd conceived their child. Courtney emerged from the bathroom in a filmy emerald peignoir to find Jeff lounging barefoot on the bed—his suit coat and vest discarded, his tie loosened, his shirt collar open.

When Jeff saw her, his hazel eyes darkened with desire. "Courtney," he breathed.

"What do you think?" She twirled about gracefully. "Your mother gave it to me—the day she asked me to call her Grace. You know, I believe your parents are starting to like me."

"Like you? I have a feeling if I'd let you get away, they would've disowned me."

She smiled and waltzed across the room to sit beside him.

Jeff's hands slid provocatively up and down her arms. "And I wouldn't have blamed them."

Ducking down, he began to sprinkle kisses along the slender column of her neck. Courtney tipped her head to give him better access. "Umm-mm, that's nice."

"I'm...glad," he murmured between seductive nips, "you . . . enjoy . . . it."

She sighed. "Don't you think Grace and J. E. will be marvelous grandparents?"

Jeff leaned back on an elbow. "I must be losing my touch. I'm trying to seduce you, and you want to talk about my parents!"

She drew a finger along his jaw. "I'm just trying to tell you that I think we're going to be good friends."

Jeff gave her an adoring smile and brought her hand to his cheek. "You're quite a woman, Mrs. Herrington."

A small frown creased her brow. "That sounds so strange—Mrs. Herrington. Oh, Jeff, I hope I don't disappoint you. I'm not sure how I'll handle being a society wife."

His palm smoothed over her hair and lightly caressed her face. "You're too modest, love."

"No, I'm too blunt. What's more, I still haven't completely conquered my hang-ups. Or my temper." She wrinkled her nose. "No matter how you look at it, I'm no bargain."

"I don't agree." He cupped one breast in his hand and teased the nipple, smiling when it instantly hardened and pricked the pad of his thumb. "Shall I tell you why?"

Courtney's eyes drifted shut on a sigh. "Please. Before I'm too distracted to care."

"Fishing for compliments, are we?" His tongue flicked a path between the valley of her breasts. "Right now, I'd rather stroke something besides your ego."

Her head dropped back, and she lifted her hands to his shoulders for support. "Stalling, are we? You can't think of anything, can you?"

"Actually, the list of your attributes is rather long," he said, scattering kisses over her creamy flesh. "You're bright... beautiful ... witty ... unpredictable... wise ...creative...forthright...caring...and totally lovable. But one of the nicest reasons I consider you a bargain is right here." His hand glided over the gentle swell of her tummy. "When I got you, I got two for the price of one."

Courtney smiled. "What price? I don't recall discussing any payment."

He drew her closer, his mouth hovering above her lips. "I was just coming to that, my love."

* * * * *

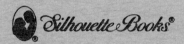

Double your reading pleasure this fall with two Award of Excellence titles written by two of your favorite authors.

Available in September

DUNCAN'S BRIDE
by Linda Howard
Silhouette Intimate Moments #349

Mail-order bride Madelyn Patterson was nothing like what Reese Duncan expected—and everything he needed.

Available in October

THE COWBOY'S LADY
by Debbie Macomber
Silhouette Special Edition #626

The Montana cowboy wanted a little lady at his beck and call—the "lady" in question saw things differently....

These titles have been selected to receive a special laurel—the Award of Excellence. Look for the distinctive emblem on the cover. It lets you know there's something truly wonderful inside!

DUN-1